The North
Water

Also by Ian McGuire

Incredible Bodies

The North Water

Ian McGuire

SCRIBNER

LONDON NEW YORK TORONTO SYDNEY NEW DELHI

First published in Great Britain by Scribner, an imprint of Simon & Schuster UK Ltd, 2016
A CBS COMPANY

SCRIBNER and design are registered trademarks of The Gale Group, Inc.,
used under licence by Simon & Schuster Inc.

1 3 5 7 9 10 8 6 4 2

Simon & Schuster UK Ltd
1st Floor
222 Gray's Inn Road
London WC1X 8HB

www.simonandschuster.co.uk

Simon & Schuster Australia, Sydney
Simon & Schuster India, New Delhi

A CIP catalogue record for this book
is available from the British Library

Hardback ISBN: 978-1-4711-5124-8
Trade paperback ISBN: 978-1-4711-5125-5
eBook ISBN: 978-1-4711-5127-9

This book is a work of fiction. Names, characters, places and
incidents are either a product of the author's imagination or are
used fictitiously. Any resemblance to actual people living or
dead, events or locales is entirely coincidental.

Typeset by M Rules
Printed and bound by CPI Group (UK) Ltd, Croydon CR0 4YY

Simon & Schuster UK Ltd are committed to sourcing paper
that is made from wood grown in sustainable forests and supports the Forest
Stewardship Council, the leading international forest certification organisation.
Our books displaying the FSC logo are printed on FSC certified paper.

To Abigail, Grace and Eve

1

Behold the man.

He shuffles out of Clappison's courtyard onto Sykes Street
and snuffs the complex air—turpentine, fish-meal, mustard,
black lead, the usual grave, morning piss-stink of just-emptied
night jars. He snorts once, rubs his bristled head and readjusts
his crotch. He sniffs his fingers, then slowly sucks each one in
turn, drawing off the last remnants, getting his final money's
worth. At the end of Charterhouse Lane, he turns north onto
Wincolmlee, past the De La Pole Tavern, past the sperm candle
manufactory and the oil-seed mill. Above the warehouse
roofs, he can see the swaying tops of main- and mizzen-masts,
hear the shouts of the stevedores and the thump of mallets
from the cooperage nearby. His shoulder rubs against the
smoothed red brick, a dog runs past, a cart piled high with
rough-cut timber. He breathes in again and runs his tongue

along the haphazard ramparts of his teeth. He senses a fresh need, small but insistent, arising inside him, a new requirement aching to be met. His ship leaves at first light, but before then there is something that must be done. He peers around and for a moment wonders what it is. He notices the pink smell of blood from the pork butcher's, the grimy sway of a woman's skirts. He thinks of flesh, animal, human, then thinks again—it is not that kind of ache, he decides, not yet, it is the milder one, the one less pressing.

He turns round and walks back towards the tavern. The bar is almost empty at this hour in the morning. There is a low fire in the grate and a smell of frying. He delves in his pocket, but all he finds there are breadcrumbs, a jackknife and a halfpenny coin.

'Rum,' he says.

He pushes the single halfpenny across the bar. The barman looks down at the coin, and shakes his head.

'I'm leaving in the morning,' he explains, 'on the *Volunteer*. I'll give you my note of hand.'

The barman snorts.

'Do I look like a fool?' he says.

The man shrugs and thinks a moment.

'Head or tails then. This good knife of mine against a tot of your rum.'

He puts the jackknife on the bar, and the barman picks it up and looks at it carefully. He unfolds the blade and tests it against the ball of his thumb.

'It's a fine knife that one,' the man says. 'Hant never failed me yet.'

The barman takes a shilling from his pocket and shows it. He tosses the coin and slaps it down hard. They both look. The barman nods, picks up the knife and stows it in his waist-coat pocket.

'And now you can fuck off,' he says.

The man's expression doesn't alter. He shows no sign of irritation or surprise. It is as though losing the knife is part of a greater and more complex plan which only he is privy to. After a moment, he bends down, tugs off his sea boots and puts them side by side on top of the bar.

'Toss again,' he says.

The barman rolls his eyes and turns away.

'I don't want your fucking boots,' he says.

'You have my knife,' the man says. 'You can't back away now.'

'I don't want no fucking boots,' the barman says again.

'You can't back away.'

'I'll do whatever the fuck I like,' the barman says.

There's a Shetlander leaning at the other end of the bar watching them. He is wearing a stocking cap and canvas britches caked with filth. His eyes are red and loose and drunken.

'I'll buy ye a drink myself,' he says, 'if ye just shut the fuck up.'

The man looks back at him. He has fought Shetlanders before in Lerwick and in Peterhead. They are not clever fighters, but they are stubborn and hard to finish off. This one has a rusty blubber knife pushed into his belt and a gamy, peevish look about him. After a moment's pause, the man nods.

3

'I'd thank you for that,' he says. 'I've been whoring all night and the whistle's dry.'

The Shetlander nods to the barman, and the barman, with a grand show of reluctance, pours out another drink. The man takes his sea boots off the bar, picks up the drink and walks over to a bench by the fire. After a few minutes, he lies down, pulls his knees up to his chest and falls asleep. When he wakes up again, the Shetlander is sitting at a table in the corner talking to a whore. She is dark-haired and fat and has a mottled face and greenish teeth. The man recognises her, but cannot now recall the name. Betty? he wonders. Hatty? Esther?

The Shetlander calls over to a black boy who is crouching in the doorway, gives him a coin and instructs him to bring back a plate of mussels from the fishmonger's on Bourne Street. The boy is nine or ten years old, slender with large dark eyes and pale brown skin. The man pulls himself upright on the bench and fills his pipe with his last crumbles of tobacco. He lights his pipe and looks about. He has woken up renewed and ready. He can feel his muscles lying loose beneath his skin, his heart tensing and relaxing inside his chest. The Shetlander tries to kiss the woman and is rebuffed with an avaricious squeal. *Hester*, the man remembers. The woman's name is Hester and she has a windowless room on James Square with an iron bedstead, a jug and basin, and an India-rubber bulb for washing out the jism. He stands up and walks over to where the two of them are sitting.

'Buy me one more drink,' he says.

The Shetlander squints at him briefly, then shakes his head and turns back to Hester.

'Just one more drink and that'll be the last you hear of it.'

The Shetlander ignores him, but the man doesn't move. His patience is of the dull and shameless kind. He feels his heart swell then shrink, he smells the usual tavern stench—farts and pipe-smoke and spilled ale. Hester looks up at him and giggles. Her teeth are more grey than green, her tongue is the colour of a pig's liver. The Shetlander takes his blubber knife out of his belt and places it on the table. He stands up.

'I'd sooner cut ye fucking balls off for ye than buy ye another drink,' he says.

The Shetlander is lanky and loose-limbed. His hair and beard are dank with seal grease and he reeks of the forecastle. The man begins to understand now what he must do—to sense the nature of his current urges and the shape of their accomplishment. Hester giggles again. The Shetlander picks up the knife and lays its cold blade against the man's cheekbone.

'I could cut ye fucking nose off too and feed it to the fucking porkers out back.'

He laughs at this idea and Hester laughs with him.

The man looks untroubled. This is not yet the moment he is waiting for. This is only a dull but necessary interlude, a pause. The barman picks up a wooden club and creaks up the hinge of the bar.

'You,' he says, pointing at him, 'are a skiving cunt, and a damned liar, and I want you gone.'

The man looks at the clock on the wall. It is just past noon. He has sixteen hours to do whatever it is he must do. To satisfy himself again. The ache he feels is his body speaking its needs, talking to him—sometimes a whisper, sometimes a mumble, sometimes a shriek. It never goes silent; if it ever goes silent then he will know that he is finally dead, that some other fucker has finally killed him, and that will be that.

He steps suddenly towards the Shetlander to let him know he is not afraid, then steps away again. He turns towards the barman and lifts his chin.

'You can stick that shillelagh up your fucking arse,' he says.

The barman points him to the door. As the man is leaving, the boy arrives with a tin plate of mussels, steaming and fragrant. They look at each other for a moment, and the man feels a new pulse of certainty.

He walks back down Sykes Street. He does not think of the *Volunteer*, now lying at dock, which he has spent the past week labouring to trim and pack, nor of the bloody six-month voyage to come. He thinks only of this present moment— Grotto Square, the Turkish Baths, the auction house, the ropery, the cobbles beneath his feet, the agnostic Yorkshire sky. He is not by nature impatient or fidgety; he will wait when waiting is required. He finds a wall and sits down upon it; when he is hungry, he sucks a stone. The hours pass. People walking by remark him but do not attempt to speak. Soon it will be time. He watches as the shadows lengthen, as it rains briefly then ceases raining, as the clouds shudder across the dampened sky. It is almost dusk when he sees them at last. Hester is singing a ballad, the Shetlander has a grog-bottle in one hand and is conducting her clumsily with the other. He watches them turn into Hodgson's Square. He waits a moment then scuttles round the corner onto Caroline Street. It is not yet night-time, but it is dark enough, he decides. The windows in the Tabernacle are glowing, there is a smell of coaldust and giblets in the air. He reaches Fiche's Alley before them and slides inside. The courtyard is empty except for a line of grimy laundry and the high, ammoniacal scent of horse piss. He stands against a darkened doorway with a half-brick gripped in his fist. When Hester and the Shetlander come into the courtyard, he waits for a moment to be sure, then steps forward and smashes the half-brick hard into the back of the Shetlander's head.

The bone gives way easily. There is a fine spray of blood and a noise like a wet stick snapping. The Shetlander flops sense-lessly forward, and his teeth and nose break against the cobblestones. Before Hester can scream, the man has the blubber knife against her throat.

'I'll slice you open like a fucking codfish,' he promises.

She looks at him wildly, then holds up her mucky hands in surrender.

He empties the Shetlander's pockets, takes his money and tobacco, and throws the rest aside. There is a halo of blood dilating around the Shetlander's face and head, but he is still faintly breathing.

'We need to move that bastard now,' Hester says, 'or I'll be in the shit.'

'So move him,' the man says. He feels lighter than he did a moment before, as if the world has widened round him.

Hester tries to drag the Shetlander around by the arm, but he's too heavy. She skids on the blood and falls over onto the cobbles. She laughs to herself, then begins to moan. The man opens the coalshed door and drags the Shetlander inside by the heels.

'They can find him tomorrow,' he says. 'I'll be long gone by then.'

She stands up, still unsteady from the drink, and tries impossibly to wipe the mud from her skirts. The man turns to leave.

'Give us a shilling or two, will you, darling?' Hester calls out to him. 'For all me trouble.'

It takes him an hour to hunt down the boy. His name is Albert Stubbs and he sleeps in a brick culvert below the north bridge, and lives off bones and peelings and the occasional copper earned by running errands for the drunkards who gather in the shithole taverns by the waterfront, waiting for a ship.

The man offers him food. He shows him the money he stole from the Shetlander.

'Tell me what you want,' he says, 'and I'll buy it for you.'

The boy looks back at him speechlessly, like an animal surprised in its lair. The man notices he has no smell to him at all—amid all this filth he has remained somehow clean, unsullied, as if the natural darkness of his pigment is a protection against sin and not, as some men believe, an expression of it.

'You're a sight to see,' the man tells him.

The boy asks for rum, and the man takes a greasy half-bottle from his pocket and gives it to him. As the boy drinks the rum, his eyes glaze slightly and the fierceness of his reticence declines.

'My name's Henry Drax,' the man explains, as softly as he is able to. 'I'm a harpooner. I ship at dawn on the *Volunteer*.'

The boy nods without interest, as if this is all information he has heard long before. His hair is musty and dull, but his skin is preternaturally clean. It shines in the tarnished moonlight like a piece of polished teak. The boy is shoeless, and the soles of his feet have become blackened and horny from contact with the pavement. Drax feels the urge to touch him now—on the side of the face perhaps or the peak of the shoulder. It would be a signal, he thinks, a way to begin.

'I saw you before in the tavern,' the boy says. 'You had no money then.'

'My situation is altered,' Drax explains.

The boy nods again and drinks more rum. Perhaps he is nearer twelve, Drax thinks, but stunted as they often are. He reaches out and takes the bottle from the boy's lips.

'You should eat something,' he says. 'Come with me.'

They walk together without speaking, up Wincomlee and Sculcoates, past the Whalebone Inn, past the timber yards. They stop in at Fletcher's bakery and Drax waits while the boy wolfs down a meat pie.

When the boy has finished, he wipes his mouth, scours the phlegm from the back of his throat and spits it out into the gutter. He looks suddenly older than before.

'I know a place we can go to,' he says, pointing across the road. 'Just down there, see, on past the boatyard.'

Drax realises immediately that this must be a trap. If he goes into the boatyard with the nigger boy, he will be beaten bloody and stripped down like a cunt. It is a surprise that the boy has misprized him so thoroughly. He feels, first, contempt for the boy's ill-judgement, and then, more pleasantly, like the swell and shudder of a fresh idea, the beginnings of fury.

'I'm the fucker, me,' he tells him softly. 'I'm never the one that's fucked.'

'I know that,' the boy says. 'I understand.'

The other side of the road is in deep shadow. There is a ten-foot wooden gate with peeling green paint, a brick wall and then a snicket floored with rubble. There is no light inside the snicket, and the only sound is the crunch of Drax's boot heels and the boy's intermittent, tubercular wheezing. The yellow moon is lodged like a bolus in the narrowed throat of the sky. After a minute, they are released into a courtyard half-filled with broken casks and rusted hooping.

'It's through there,' the boy says. 'Not far.'

His face betrays a telling eagerness. If Drax had any doubts before, he has none left now.

'Come to me,' he tells the boy.

The boy frowns and indicates again the way he wants them both to go. Drax wonders how many of the boy's companions are waiting for them in the boatyard and what weapons they are planning to use against him. Does he really look, he wonders, like the kind of useless prick who can be robbed by

10

children? Is that the impression he presently gives out to the waiting world?

'Come here,' he says again.

The boy shrugs and walks forward.

'We'll do it now,' Drax says. 'Here and now. I won't wait.'

The boy stops and shakes his head.

'No,' he says, 'the boatyard is better.'

The courtyard's gloom perfects him, Drax thinks, smooths out his prettiness into a sullen kind of beauty. He looks like a pagan idol standing there, a totem carved from ebony, not like a boy, more like the far-fetched ideal of a boy.

'Just what kind of a cunt do you think I am?' Drax asks.

The boy frowns for a moment, then offers him a beguiling and implausible grin. None of this is new, Drax thinks, it has all been done before, and it will all be done over again in other places and at other times. The body has its tedious patterns, its regularities: the feeding, the cleaning, the emptying of the bowels.

The boy touches him quickly on the elbow and indicates again the way he wants them both to go. The boatyard. The trap. Drax hears a seagull squawking above his head, notices the solid smell of bitumen and oil paint, the sidereal sprawl of the Plough. He grabs the nigger boy by the hair and punches him, then punches him again and again—two, three, four times, fast, without hesitation or compunction— until Drax's knuckles are warm and dark with blood, and the boy is slumped, limp and unconscious. He is thin and bony and weighs no more than a terrier. Drax turns him over and pulls down his britches. There is no pleasure in the act and no relief, a fact which only increases its ferocity. He has been cheated of something living, something nameless but also real.

Lead and pewter clouds obscure the fullish moon, there is the clatter of iron-rimmed cartwheels, the infantile whine of a cat in heat. Drax goes swiftly through the motions: one action following the next, passionless and precise, machine-like, but not mechanical. He grasps onto the world like a dog biting into bone—nothing is obscure to him, nothing is separate from his fierce and surly appetites. What the nigger boy used to be has now disappeared. He is gone completely, and something else, something wholly different, has appeared instead. This courtyard has become a place of vile magic, of blood-soaked transmutations, and Henry Drax is its wild, unholy engineer.

2

Brownlee considers himself, after thirty years pacing the quarterdeck, to be a fair judge of the human character, but this new fellow Sumner, this Paddy surgeon fresh from the riotous Punjab, is a complex case indeed. He is short and narrow-featured, his expression is displeasingly quizzical, he has an unfortunate limp, and speaks some barbarously twisted bogland version of the English language; yet nonetheless, despite these obvious and manifold disadvantages, Brownlee senses that he will do. There is something in the young man's very awkwardness and indifference, his capacity and willingness *not* to please, that Brownlee, perhaps because it reminds him of himself at a younger and more carefree stage of life, finds oddly appealing.

'So what's the story with the leg?' Brownlee asks, waggling his own ankle by way of encouragement. They are sitting in the captain's cabin on the *Volunteer*, drinking brandy and reviewing the voyage to come.

'Sepoy musketball,' Sumner explains. 'My shin bone bore the brunt.'

'In Delhi this is? After the siege?'

Sumner nods.

'First day of the assault, near the Cashmere Gate.'

Brownlee rolls his eyes and whistles low in appreciation.

'Did you see Nicholson killed?'

'No, but I saw his body afterwards when he was dead. Up on the ridge.'

'An extraordinary man, Nicholson. A great hero. They do say the niggers worshipped him like a god.'

Sumner shrugs.

'He had a Pashtun bodyguard. Enormous sod named Khan. Slept outside his tent to protect him. The rumour was the two of them were sweethearts.'

Brownlee shakes his head and smiles. He has read all about John Nicholson in *The Times* of London: the way he marched his men through the most savage heat without ever once breaking sweat or asking for water, about the time he sliced a mutinous sepoy clean in two with one blow of his mighty sword. Without men like Nicholson—unyielding, severe, vicious when necessary—Brownlee believes the Empire would have been lost entirely long ago. And without the Empire who would buy the oil, who would buy the whalebone?

'Jealousy,' he says. 'Bitterness only. Nicholson's a great hero, a little bit savage sometimes from what I heard, but what do you expect?'

'I saw him hang a man just for smiling at him, and the poor bugger wasn't even smiling.'

'Lines must be drawn, Sumner,' he says. 'Civilised standards must be maintained. We must meet fire with fire sometimes. The niggers killed women and children after all, raped them, slashed their tiny throats. A thing like that requires righteous vengeance.'

Sumner nods and glances briefly downwards at his black trousers grown grey at the kneepiece and his unpolished ankle boots. Brownlee wonders whether his new surgeon is a cynic or a sentimentalist or (is it even possible?) a little bit of both?

'Oh, there was a good deal of that going on,' Sumner says, turning back to him with a grin. 'A good deal of the righteous vengeance. Yes, indeed.'

'So why did you leave India?' Brownlee asks, shifting about a little on the upholstered bench. 'Why quit the 61st? It wasn't the leg?'

'Not the leg, God no. They loved the leg.'

'Then what?'

'I had a windfall. Six months ago my uncle Donal died suddenly and left me his dairy farm over in Mayo—fifty acres, cows, a creamery. It's worth a thousand guineas at least, more probably, enough, for sure, to buy myself a pretty little house in the shires and a nice respectable practice somewhere quiet but wealthy: Bognor, Hastings, Scarborough possibly. The salt air pleases me, you see, and I do like a promenade.'

Brownlee seriously doubts whether the good widows of Scarborough, Bognor or Hastings would really wish to have their ailments attended to by a shortarse hopalong from beyond the Pale, but he leaves that particular opinion unexpressed.

'So what are you doing sitting here with me,' he asks instead, 'on a Greenland whaling ship? A famous Irish landowner like yourself, I mean?'

Sumner smiles at the sarcasm, scratches his nose, lets it go.

'There are legal complications with the estate. Mysterious cousins have appeared out of the woodwork, counter-claimants.'

Brownlee sighs sympathetically.

'Aint it always the way,' he says.

'I've been told that the case could take a year to be resolved, and until then I have nothing much to do with myself and no money to do it with. I was passing through Liverpool on my way back from the lawyers in Dublin when I ran into your Mr Baxter in the bar of the Adelphi Hotel. We got to talking and when he learned I was an ex-army surgeon in need of gainful employment, he put two and two together and made a four.'

'He's a fierce sharp operator, that Baxter,' Brownlee says, with a twinkle in his eye. 'I don't trust the bastard myself. I do believe he has some portion of Hebrew blood running in his withered veins.'

'I was happy enough with the terms he offered. I'm not expecting the whaling will make me rich, Captain, but it will keep me occupied at least while the cogs of justice turn.'

Brownlee sniffs.

'Oh, we'll make use of you one way or another,' he says. 'There is always work for those that are willing.'

Sumner nods, finishes off his brandy, and places the glass back down on the table with a small clack. The oil lamp depending from the darkwood ceiling remains unlit, but the shadows in the corners of the cabin are deepening and spreading as the light outside begins to fail and the sun slides out of sight behind an iron and redbrick commotion of chimneys and roofs.

'I'm at your service, sir,' Sumner says.

Brownlee wonders for a moment exactly what this means, but then decides it means nothing at all. Baxter is not a man to give secrets away. If he has chosen Sumner for a reason (besides the obvious ones: cheapness and availability) it is probably only that the Irishman is easy-going and pliable and clearly has his mind on other things.

'As a rule, there is not much doctoring to be done on a whaler, I find. When the men get sick, they either get well again on their own or else they turn in on themselves and die—that is my experience at least. The potions don't make a great deal of difference.'

Sumner raises his eyebrows, but appears unconcerned by this casual disparagement of his profession.

'I should examine the medicine chest,' he says, without much enthusiasm. 'There may be some items I need to add or replace before we sail.'

'The chest is stowed in your cabin. There is a chemist's shop on Clifford Street besides the Freemason's Hall. Get whatever you need and tell them to send the bill to Mr Baxter.'

Both men rise from the table. Sumner extends his hand and Brownlee briefly shakes it. Each man for a moment peers at the other one, as if hoping for an answer to some secret question they are too alarmed or wary to ask out loud.

'Baxter won't like that much, I imagine,' Sumner says at last.

'Bugger Baxter,' Brownlee says.

Half an hour later, Sumner sits hunched over on his bunk and tongues his pencil stub. His cabin has the dimensions of an infant's mausoleum and smells, already, before the voyage has even begun, sour and faintly faecal. He peers sceptically into the medicine chest and begins to make his shopping list: *hartshorn*, he writes, *Glauber's salt, Spirit of Squills*. Every now and then he unstoppers one of the bottles and sniffs the dried-up innards. Half the things in there he has never heard of: Tragacanth? Guaiacum? London Spirit? It's no wonder Brownlee thinks the 'potions' don't work, most of this stuff is fucking Shakespearian. Was the previous surgeon some kind of Druid? *Laudanum*, he writes by the eggish light of a blubber lamp, *absinthe, opium pills, mercury*. Will there be much gonorrhoea among a whaling crew? he wonders. Possibly not, since whores in the Arctic Circle are likely to be thin on the ground. Judging by the amount of Epsom salts and castor oil already in the chest, however, constipation will be a sizeable problem. The lancets, he notices, are uniformly ancient, rusty and blunt. He will have to have them sharpened before he begins any bleeding. It is probably a good thing he has brought his own scalpels and a newish bone saw.

After a while, he closes the medicine chest and pushes it back beneath the bunk where it rests beside the battered tin trunk that he has carried with him all the way from India.

Out of habit, automatically, and without looking down, Sumner rattles the trunk's padlock and pats his waistcoat pocket to check he still has the key. Reassured, he stands, leaves the cabin, and makes his way along the narrow companionway and up onto the ship's deck. There is a smell of varnish and wood shavings and pipe-smoke. Barrels of beef and bundles of staves are being loaded into the forehold on ropes, someone is hammering nails into the galley roof, there are several men up in the rigging swinging pots of tar. A lurcher scuffles by then stops abruptly to lick itself. Sumner pauses beside the mizzen-mast and scans the quayside. There is no one there he recognises. The world is enormous, he tells himself, and he is a tiny unmemorable speck within it, easily lost and forgotten. This thought, which would not normally be pleasing to anyone, pleases him now. His plan is to dissolve, to dissipate and only afterwards, some time later, to re-form. He walks down the gangplank and finds his way to the chemist's shop on Clifford Street where he hands over his list. The chemist, who is bald and sallow and missing several teeth, examines the list, then looks up at him.

'That's not right,' he says. 'Not for a whaling voyage. It's too much.'

'Baxter's paying for everything. You can send him the bill directly.'

'Has Baxter seen this list?'

Inside the shop, it is gloomy and the brownish air is sulphurous and thick with liniment. The bald man's finger-ends are stained a glaring chemical orange and his nails are curved and horny; below his rolled-up shirtsleeves, Sumner sees the blue fringes of an old tattoo.

'You think I'd trouble Baxter with shit like that,' Sumner says.

'He'll be troubled when he sees this fucking bill. I know Baxter and he's a tight-fisted cunt.'

'Just fill the order,' Sumner says.

The man shakes his head and rubs his hands across his mottled apron.

'I can't give you all that,' he says, pointing down at the paper on the countertop. 'Or that either. If I do, I won't get paid for it. I'll give you the regular allowances of both and that's all.'

Sumner leans forward. His belly presses up against the burnished countertop.

'I'm just back from the colonies,' he explains, 'from Delhi.'

The bald man shrugs at this intelligence, then sticks his forefinger in his right ear and twists it noisily.

'You know I can sell you a nice piece of birchwood for that limp,' he says. 'Ivory handle, whaletooth, whichever you prefer.'

Without answering him, Sumner steps away from the counter and commences gazing around the shop, as though he suddenly has a good deal of time on his hands and nothing much to fill it with. The sidewalls are crammed with all manner of flasks, bottles and tantali filled with liquids, unguents and powders. Behind the counter is a large yellowing mirror reflecting the hairless verso of the bald man's pate. To one side of the mirror is an array of square wooden drawers, each with a nameplate and a single brass knob in its centre, and to the other is a row of shelves supporting a tableau of stuffed animals arranged in a series of melo-dramatic and martial poses. There is a barn owl poised in the act of devouring a field mouse, a badger at perpetual war with a ferret, a Laocoönian gibbon being strangled by a garter snake.

'Did you do all those yourself?' Sumner asks him.

The man waits a moment, then nods.

'I'm the best taxidermist in town,' he says. 'You can ask anyone.'

'And what's the biggest beast you've ever stuffed? The very biggest, I mean. Tell me the truth now.'

'I've done a walrus,' the bald man says casually. 'I've done a polar bear. They bring them in off the Greenland ships.'

'You've stuffed a polar bear?' Sumner says.

'I have.'

'A fucking *bear*,' Sumner says again, smiling now. 'Now that's something I would like to see.'

'I had him standing up on his hindmost legs,' the bald man says, 'with his vicious claws raking the frigid air like this.' He reaches his orangey hands up into the air and arranges his face into a frozen growl. 'I did it for Firbank, the rich bugger who lives in that big house on Charlotte Street. I believe he still has it in his grand entrance hall, next to his whaletooth hat stand.'

'And would you ever stuff an actual whale?' Sumner asks.

The bald man shakes his head and laughs at the idea.

'The whale can't be stuffed,' he says. 'Apart from the size, which makes it impossible, they putrefy too quick. And besides, what would any sane man want with a stuffed bloody whale anyway?'

Sumner nods and smiles again. The bald man chuckles at the thought.

'I've done lots of pike,' he continues vainly. 'I've done otters aplenty, someone brought me a platypus once.'

'What do you say we change the names?' Sumner says. 'On the bill. Call it absinthe. Call it calomel if you want to.'

'We already have calomel on the list.'

'Absinthe then, let's call it absinthe.'

'We could call it blue vitriol,' the man suggests. 'Some surgeons take a good amount of that stuff.'

'Call it blue vitriol then, and call the other absinthe.'

The man nods once and does a rapid calculation in his head.

'A bottle of absinthe,' he says, 'and three ounces of vitriol will about cover it.' He turns round and starts opening up drawers and picking flasks off the shelves. Sumner leans against the countertop and watches him at his work—weighing, sifting, grinding, stoppering.

'Have you ever shipped out yourself?' Sumner asks him. 'For the whaling?'

The chemist shakes his head without looking up from his work.

'The Greenland trade is a dangerous one,' he says. 'I prefer to stay at home, where it's warm and dry, and the risk of violent death is much reduced.'

'You are a sensible fellow, then.'

'I am cautious, that's all. I've seen a thing or two.'

'You're a fortunate man, I would say,' Sumner answers, gazing round the grimy shop again. 'Fortunate to have so much to lose.'

The man glances up to check if he is being mocked, but Sumner's expression is all sincerity.

'It is not so much,' he says, 'compared to some.'

'It is something.'

The chemist nods, secures the package with a length of twine and pushes it across the counter.

'The *Volunteer* is a good old bark,' he says. 'It knows its way around the icefields.'

'And what of Brownlee? I hear he's unlucky.'

'Baxter trusts him.'

'Indeed,' Sumner says, picking up the package, tucking it under one arm, then leaning down to sign the receipt. 'And what do we think of Mr Baxter?'

'We think he's rich,' the chemist answers, 'and round these parts a man don't generally get rich by being stupid.'

Sumner smiles, and curtly nods farewell.

'Amen to that,' he says.

It has started to rain, and above the residual smell of horse dung and butchery, there is a fresh and clement tang to the air. Instead of returning to the *Volunteer*, Sumner turns to the left and finds a tavern. He asks for rum, and takes his glass into a scruffy side room with a fireless grate and an unpleasing view into the adjoining courtyard. There is no one else sitting in there. He unties the chemist's package, takes out one of the bottles and dispenses half of it into his glass. The dark rum darkens further. Sumner inhales, closes his eyes and downs the concoction in one long gulp.

Perhaps he is free, he thinks, as he sits there and waits for the drug to have its effect. Perhaps that is the best way to understand his present state. After all that has beset him: betrayal, humiliation, poverty, disgrace; the death of his parents from typhus; the death of William Harper from the drink; the many efforts misdirected or abandoned; the many chances lost and plans gone awry. After all of that, all of it, he is still alive at least. The worst has happened—hasn't it?—yet he is still intact, still warm, still breathing. He is nothing now, admittedly (a surgeon on a Yorkshire whaling ship, what kind of reward is that for his long labours?) but to be nothing is also, looked at from a different angle, to be anything at all. Is that not the case? Not lost then, but at liberty? *Free?* And this fear he currently feels, this feeling of perpetual uncertainty, that must be—he decides—just a surprising symptom of his current unbounded state.

Sumner feels a moment of great relief at this conclusion, so clear and sensible, so easily and quickly reached, but then almost immediately, almost before he has a chance to enjoy the new sensation, it strikes him that it is a very empty kind of freedom he is enjoying, it is the freedom of a vagrant or a beast. If he is free, in his current condition, then this wooden table in front of him is also free, and so is this empty glass. And what does *free* even mean? Such words are paper-thin, they crumble and tear under the slightest pressure. Only actions count, he thinks for the ten thousandth time, only events. All the rest is vapour, fog. He takes another drink and licks his lips. It is a grave mistake to think too much, he reminds himself, a grave mistake. Life will not be puzzled out, or blathered into submission, it must be lived through, survived, in whatever fashion a man can manage.

Sumner leans his head back against the whitewashed wall and peers vaguely in the direction of the doorway opposite. He can see the landlord over yonder, behind the bar, hear the clink of pewter and the clatter of a trap-door closing. He feels, rising inside his chest, another warm swell of clarity and ease. It is the body, he thinks, not the mind. It is the blood, the chemistry that counts. In a few more minutes, he is feeling much better about himself and about the world. Captain Brownlee, he thinks, is a fine man, and Baxter is fine also in his way. They are dutiful men, both of them. They believe in act and consequence, capture and reward, in the simple geometry of cause and effect. And who is to say they are wrong? He looks down at his empty glass and wonders about the wisdom of requesting another. Standing shouldn't be a problem, he thinks, but *talking*? His tongue feels flat and foreign, he's not sure, if he tried to speak, what might actually come out—what language exactly? What noises? The landlord, as if sensing his dilemma, glances in his direction and Sumner hails him with the empty glass.

'Right you are,' the landlord says.

Sumner smiles at the simple elegance of this exchange— the need sensed, the satisfaction offered. The landlord enters the side room with a half-full bottle of rum and tops him up. Sumner nods in thanks, and all is well.

It is dark outside now, and the rain has ceased. The courtyard glows yellow with a vague, gaseous light. There are
women's voices in the next room laughing loudly. How long
have I been sitting here? Sumner wonders suddenly. An
hour? Two? He finishes his drink, reties the package, and
stands up. The room seems much smaller than when he first
came in. There is still no fire in the grate, but someone has
placed an oil lamp on a stool near the door. He walks carefully into the next room, peers around for a moment, tips his
hat to the ladies, and regains the street.

The night sky is crammed with stars—the grand zodiacal
sprawl and in between the densely speckled glow of unnameable others. *The starry sky above me and the moral law within.* He
remembers, as he walks, the dissection hall in Belfast, watching that foul old blasphemer Slattery slice happily into a
cadaver. 'No sign of this chap's immortal soul as yet, young
gentlemen,' he would joke, as he delved and tugged, pulling
out intestines like a conjuror pulls flags, 'nor of his exquisite
reasoning faculties, but I'll keep on looking.' He recalls the
jars of sectioned brains, floating helplessly, pointlessly, like
pickled cauliflowers, their spongy hemispheres emptied
entirely of thought or desire. The redundancy of flesh, he
thinks, the helplessness of meat; how can we conjure spirit
from a bone? Yet this street looks lovely despite all that: the
way the dampened bricks glow reddish in the moonlight, the
echoing clack of leather boot heels on stone, the curve and
stretch of broadcloth across a man's back, of flannel across a
woman's hips. The whirl and caw of the gulls, the creak of
cartwheels, laughter, cursing, all of it, the crude harmonics

of the night, coming together, like a primitive symphony. After opium, this is what he likes best: these smells, sounds and visions, the crush and clamour of their temporary beauty. Everywhere a sudden alertness that the ordinary world lacks, a sudden thrust and vigour.

He wanders through squares and alleyways, past courtyard hovels and the houses of the rich. He has no idea which way is north or in what direction the dock now lies, but eventually, somehow, he knows he will sniff his way back there. He has learned to stop thinking at such times and trust his instinct. Why Hull, for instance? Why fucking whaling? It makes no sense, and that is its great genius. The illogic of it, the near-idiocy. Cleverness, he thinks, will get you nowhere, it is only the stupid, the brilliantly stupid, who will inherit the earth. Entering the public square, he encounters a legless and tatterdemalion beggarman whistling 'Nancy Dawson' and knuckling his way along the darkened pavement. The two men pause to talk.

'Which way to the Queen's Dock?' Sumner asks, and the legless beggar points across with his filth-caked fist.

'Over there,' he says. 'Which ship?'

'The *Volunteer*.'

The beggar, whose face is riddled with smallpox scars and whose truncated body halts abruptly just below the groin, shakes his head and giggles wheezily.

'If you chose to ship with Brownlee, you fucked yourself up the arse,' he says. 'Right royally.'

Sumner thinks about this for a moment, then shakes his head.

'Brownlee will do,' he says.

'He will do if you want things fucked up,' the beggar answers. 'He will do if you want to come home fucking penniless or not come home at all. He'll do for all that, I agree with you there. You heard about the *Percival*? You must have heard about the fucking *Percival*?'

The beggar is wearing a grimy and shapeless tam-o'-shanter patchworked from the numerous broken remnants of older and finer headgear.

'I was in India,' Sumner says.

'Ask anyone around here about the *Percival*,' the beggar says. 'Just say the word *Percival* and see what comes back.'

'So tell me then,' Sumner says.

The beggar pauses a moment before beginning, as if to better measure the hilarious breadth of Sumner's naivety.

'Crushed to matchwood by a berg,' he says. 'Three years ago now. Its holds were filled up with blubber at the time and they didn't rescue even one single barrel of it. Not a scrap. Eight men drownded and ten more perished of the cold, and none of those that lived made even sixpunce.'

'Sounds like a misfortune. It could happen to anyone.'

'It happened to Brownlee though, no one else. And a captain that fucking unfortunate doesn't often get another ship.'

'Baxter must trust him.'

'Baxter's fucking deep. That's all I'll say about fucking Baxter. Deep is what Baxter is.'

Sumner shrugs and looks up at the moon.

'What happened to your legs?' he asks.

The beggar looks down and frowns as though surprised to find them gone.

'You ask Captain Brownlee about that one,' he says. 'You tell him Ort Caper sent you. You tell him we was counting up my legs together one fine evening and there seemed to be a couple of 'em missing. See what he says about that one.'

'Why would I ask him that?'

'Because you wouldn't hardly believe the truth of it coming from a man like me, you'd likely write it off as the ravings of a loon, but Brownlee knows the bloody truth of it as well as me. You ask him what happened on the *Percival*. Tell him Ort Caper sends his best regards, see what that does to his digestion.'

Sumner takes a coin from his pocket and drops it into the beggar's outstretched hand.

'Ort Caper's the name,' the beggar shouts after him. 'Ask Brownlee what happened to my fucking legs.'

Further on, he begins to smell the Queen's Dock—its sour, bathetic pong, like meat about to turn. In the gaps between warehouses, between the piled-up planking of timber yards, he can see the tin-cut silhouetted line of whaling ships and sloops. It is past midnight now and the streets are quieter— some muted sounds of drinking from the dockside taverns, the Penny Bank, the Seaman's Molly, now and then the noise of an empty hackney carriage or the grumble of a dustcart. The stars have swivelled, the swollen moon is half hidden behind a bank of nickel-plated cloud; Sumner can see the *Volunteer*, broad-waisted, dark and thick with rigging, a little further down the dock. There is no one walking about the deck, at least no one he can see, so the loading must be complete. They are only waiting for the tide now, and for the steam tug to pull them out into the Humber.

His mind moves to the northern ice fields and the great wonders he will no doubt see there—the unicorn and sea leopard, the walrus and the albatross, the Arctic petrel and the polar bear. He thinks about the great right whales lying bunched in pods like leaden storm clouds beneath the silent sheets of ice. He will make charcoal sketches of them all, he decides, paint watercolour landscapes, keep a journal possibly. And why not? He will have plenty of time on his hands, Brownlee made that plain enough. He will read widely (he has brought his dog-eared Homer), he will practise his disused Greek. Why the fuck not? He will have precious little else to do—doling out purgatives now and then, occasionally certifying the dead, but apart from that it will be a kind of holiday. Baxter implied as much anyway. Implied that the surgeon's job on a whaler was a legal nicety, a requirement to be met, but in practice there was bugger-all to do—hence the risible wages, of course. So yes, he thinks, he will read and write, he will sleep, he will make conversation with the captain when called upon. By and large it will be an easeful, perhaps a mildly tedious, sort of time, but God knows that is what he needs after the madness of India: the filthy heat, the barbarity, the stench. Whatever the Greenland whaling is like, he thinks, it will surely not be anything like that.

3

'The wind's picking up now,' Baxter says. 'I wager you'll make good time to Lerwick.'

Brownlee leans against the wheelhouse and launches a gob of green phlegm over the taffrail and into the broad brown murk of the Humber. To north and south, a scanty shoreline welds the rusted steel of estuary and sky. Ahead, the steam tug chunters flatly onwards, gulls bouncing and water broiling in its wake.

'I truly cannot wait to see what gaggle of shitheads you've got waiting for me in Lerwick,' Brownlee says.

Baxter smiles.

'All good men,' he says. 'All true Shetlanders: hard workers, eager, biddable.'

'You know I aim to fill the main hold when we reach the North Water,' Brownlee says.

'Fill it with what exactly?'

'With blubber.'

Baxter shakes his head.

'You don't need to prove yourself to me, Arthur,' he says. 'I know what you are.'

'I'm a whaling man.'

'You are, indeed, and a damned fine one. The problem we have is not you, Arthur, and it's not me either. The problem we have is history. Thirty years ago any halfwit with a boat and a harpoon could get rich. You remember that. You remember the *Aurora* in twenty-eight? It was back by June— fucking *June*—and with stacks of whalebone as high as my head lashed onto the gunwales. I'm not saying it was easy then, it was never easy, as you know. But it could be done. Now you need—what?—a two hundred-horsepower steam engine, harpoon guns and a lot of luck. And, even then, odds are you'll come back clean as a whistle.'

'I'll fill the hold,' Brownlee insists calmly. 'I'll kick these bastards up the arse and fill the hold, you'll see.'

Baxter steps towards him. He is dressed like a lawyer not a mariner: black calfskin boots, nankeen waistcoat, purple neckerchief, a cutaway coat of navy worsted. His hair is grey and sparse, his cheeks are red and venous, his eyes are rheumy. He has looked mortally sick for years, but he never misses a day at the office. The man is a whited sepulchre, Brownlee thinks, but by Christ, will he talk. Words, words, words—un-fucking-ending, an unstoppable stream of verbiage. He will still be talking his arse off when they put him in the fucking ground.

'We *killed* them all, Arthur,' Baxter goes on. 'It was tremendous while it lasted and magnificently profitable too. We had twenty-five fucking good years. But the world turns, and this is a new chapter. Think of it like that. Not the end of one thing, but the beginning of something better. Besides, no one even wants the whale oil any more—it's all petroleum now, all coal gas, you know that.'

'The petroleum won't last,' Brownlee says. 'That's just a fad. And the whales are still out there—you just need a captain with a nose for it and a crew who can do what's asked.'

Baxter shakes his head and leans in conspiratorially. Brownlee smells pomade, mustard, sealing wax and cloves.

'Don't fuck this up, Arthur,' he says. 'Don't misremember what we're up to here. This is not a question of pride—not your pride and not mine. And this is definitely not about the fucking fish.'

Brownlee turns away without answering. He stares across at the dreary flatness of the Lincolnshire shore. He has never liked the land, he thinks. It is too certain, too solid, too sure of itself.

'Did you get anyone to check the pumps?' Baxter asks him.

'Drax,' he answers.

'Drax is a good fellow. I didn't cut any corners with the harpooners, did I? I trust you noticed that. I got you three of the best. Drax, Jones-the-whale and, *whatshisname*, Otto. Any captain would be happy with those three.'

'They'll do,' he admits, 'they'll all three do, but it don't make up for Cavendish.'

'Cavendish is necessary, Arthur. Cavendish makes sense. We've talked about Cavendish many times already.'

'I heard muttering from the crew.'

'About Cavendish?'

Brownlee nods.

'It's a poor move to make him first mate. They all know him as a worthless cunt.'

'Cavendish is a great turd and a whoremonger, it's true, but he will do whatever he's told to. And when you get to the North Water the very last thing you want is some bastard showing initiative. Anyway, you have your second mate, young Master Black, to help if you get into any difficulties on the way. He has a decent head on him.'

'What do you make of our Paddy surgeon?'

'Sumner?' Baxter shrugs, then chuckles. 'Did you see what I got him for? Two pounds a month, and a shilling a ton. That's a record, near enough. There's something fishy there, of course there is, but I don't believe we need concern ourselves about it. He doesn't want any trouble from us, I'm sure of that.'

'Do you believe the dead uncle?'

'Christ, no. Do you?'

'You think he's been cashiered then?'

'Most probably, but even if he has been, so what? What do they cashier you for over there now? Cheating at bridge? Buggering the bugle boy? I'd say he'll do for us.'

'You know he was at Delhi on the ridge. He saw Nicholson afore he died.'

Baxter raises his eyebrows, nods and looks impressed.

'That Nicholson was a bloody hero,' he says. 'If we had a few more like Nicholson hanging the bastards, and less like that pusillanimous shit Canning giving out pardons left and right, the Empire would be in safer hands.'

Brownlee nods in agreement.

'I heard he could slice a Pandy clean in two with one blow of his sabre,' he says. 'Nicholson, I mean. Like a cucumber.'

'Like a cucumber,' Baxter laughs. 'That would be a sight to see, would it not?'

They are passing Grimsby to starboard and in front of them the fine yellow line of Spurn Point is hoving into view. Baxter checks his pocket watch.

'We've made quick time,' he says. 'All the omens are good.'

Brownlee calls to Cavendish to signal to the steam tug. After a minute or so the tug slows and the line between the vessels slackens. They cast off the line and Brownlee calls for the mainsails to be unfurled. The wind is fresh from the south-west and the glass is steady. Grey clouds clog the eastern horizon. Brownlee glances at Baxter, who is smiling at him.

'A final word before I leave you, Arthur,' he says, nodding downwards.

'Get that fucking rope coiled,' Brownlee calls out to Cavendish, 'and hold her steady, no more sail.'

The two men go down the companionway together and enter the captain's cabin.

'Brandy?' Brownlee asks.

'Since I paid for it,' Baxter says, 'why not?'

They sit down at opposite sides of the table and drink.

'I brought the papers,' Baxter says. 'I thought you might like to see them for yourself.' He pulls two sheets of parchment from his pocket, unfolds them and pushes them across the table. Brownlee looks down for a moment. 'Twelve thousand pounds divided three ways is a considerable heap of money, Arthur,' Baxter goes on. 'You should keep that upmost in your mind. It's a good deal more than you could ever hope to make from killing whales.'

Brownlee nods.

'Campbell better be there,' he says. 'That's all I'm saying. If Campbell isn't there the moment I need him, I'll turn this cunt round and sail her home.'

'He'll be there,' Baxter says. 'Campbell's not as idiotic as he looks. He knows if this one goes well, he's next in line.'

Brownlee shakes his head.

'This is what it comes to,' he says.

'It's the money, Arthur, that's all it is. The money does what it wants to. It doesn't care what we prefer. Block off one passageway and it carves out a new one. I can't control the money, I can't tell it what to do or where to go next—I wish I fucking could but I can't.'

'You better pray there's enough ice up there.'

Baxter finishes off his drink and stands up to leave.

'Oh, there's always ice,' he says, smiling lightly. 'We both know that. And if there's one man alive who has the true knack for finding it, I believe it's you.'

4

They enter Lerwick harbour on the first day of April, 1859. The ashen sky is threatening rain and the low, treeless hills that surround the town are the colour of damp sawdust. Two Peter-head ships, the *Zembla* and the *Mary-Anne*, are already lying safely at anchor, and the *Truelove* from Dundee is expected in the next day. As soon as he has breakfasted, Captain Brownlee goes into the town to visit Samuel Tait, his local shipping agent, and pick out the Shetland portion of the crew. Sumner spends the morning doling out tobacco rations and tending to Thomas Anderson, a deckhand with a painful stricture. In the after-noon he lies on his bunk and falls into a drowse while reading Homer. He is woken by a knock from Cavendish who explains that he is gathering a small party of dedicated seamen for the purposes of testing the achievements of the local distillery.

'Currently the expeditionary party consists of me,'

Cavendish says, 'Drax, who I confess is a fucking heathen with a drink inside him, Black, who is a cool customer and claims only to drink ginger beer or milk, but we shall see about that, and also Jones-the-whale, who is a raging Taff, of course, and therefore a grave fucking mystery to all of us. All in all, it promises to be a most satisfactory evening, I would say.'

They are rowed ashore by Drax and Jones. Cavendish talks all the time, telling them story after story about the vicious knife fights that he has witnessed and the ugly Lerwick women he has fucked.

'By Christ, the ungodly stench of her quim,' he says. 'You would not fucking believe it unless you were standing there.'

Sumner is sitting next to Black in the stern of the rowing boat. Before leaving his cabin, he consumed eight grains of laudanum (just enough, based on previous experience, to make the outing bearable, but not to make him look like a complete fucking fool) and is enjoying the sounds of the water plashing against the blades and the oars creaking in their oarlocks (he is happily ignoring Cavendish). Black enquires whether this is his first visit to Lerwick and Sumner confirms that indeed it is.

'You will find it a backwards sort of place,' Black tells him. 'The land about here is poor and the Shetlanders show no interest in improvement. They're peasants and they have the peasant virtues, I suppose, but nothing else. If you walk about the island a little and see the miserable condition of the farms and buildings, you'll soon know what I mean.'

'And what about the townspeople? Do they make some profit from the whaling trade?'

'A few do, but most are merely corrupted by it. The town as a whole is as filthy and iniquitous as any port—no worse than most perhaps, but certainly no better.'

'And thank fucking God for that,' Cavendish shouts out in response. 'A decent drink and a good wet slice of pussy is what a man requires before he commences the bloody work of whaling, and fortunately those are the only two products that Lerwick excels in.'

'That's quite true,' Black confirms. 'If it's Scottish whisky and cheap sluts you're after, Mr Sumner, you are certainly in the right place.'

'I feel fortunate to have such experienced guides.'

'You *are* fortunate,' Cavendish says. 'We'll show you the ropes, will we not, Drax? We'll show you all the ins and all the outs. You can rest assured about that one.'

Cavendish laughs. Drax, who has not spoken since they left the ship, looks up from his oar and stares at Sumner for a moment as if deciding who he is and what he might be good for.

'In Lerwick,' he says, 'the cheapest whisky is sixpunce a glass and a decent whore will set you back a shilling, or possibly two if your requirements are more specialised. That's about all the knowhow anyone needs.'

'Drax is a man of few words as you can see,' Cavendish says. 'But I like to blabber so we make a fine team.'

'And what about Jones here?' Sumner asks.

'Jones is a Welshman from Pontypool, so no one ever understands a word he's fucking saying.'

Jones turns round and instructs Cavendish to go and fuck himself.

'See what I mean?' Cavendish says. 'Complete fucking gibberish.'

They begin at the Queen's Hotel, then move on to the Commercial, then the Edinburgh Arms. After leaving the Edinburgh Arms, they go over to Mrs Brown's on Charlotte Street and Drax, Cavendish and Jones each pick a girl and go upstairs while Sumner (who can never perform after laudanum and so makes the excuse that he is recovering from a dose of the clap) and Black (who insists with a straight face that he has promised to remain faithful to his fiancée Bertha) stay downstairs drinking porter.

'May I ask you a question, Sumner?' Black says.

Sumner, peering back at him through a thickening haze of intoxication, nods. Black is young and eager but he is also, Sumner believes, more than a little arrogant. He is never openly rude or disdainful, but one senses sometimes a self-belief which is out of scale with his position.

'Yes,' he says, 'you certainly may.'

'What are you doing here?'

'In Lerwick?'

'On the *Volunteer*. What's a man like you doing aboard a Greenland whaling ship?'

'I explained my situation in the wardroom the other evening, I think—my uncle's will, the dairy farm.'

'But then why not find work in a city hospital? Or join another practice for a time. You must know people who could help you. The job of surgeon on a whaling vessel is uncomfortable, dreary and badly paid. It is usually taken by medical students in need of funds, not a man of your age and experience.'

Sumner blows twin tubes of cigar smoke out of his nostrils and blinks.

'Perhaps I am an incurable eccentric,' he says, 'or just a fucking fool. Did you ever think of that?'

Black smiles.

'I doubt either is true,' he says. 'I have seen you reading your Homer.'

Sumner shrugs. He is determined to stay quiet, to say nothing that might suggest the truth of his estate.

'Baxter made me an offer, and I accepted it. Perhaps that was rash of me, but now we have begun I'm looking forward to the experience. I intend to keep a diary, make sketches, read.'

'The voyage may not be as relaxed as you think. You know Brownlee has a great deal to prove—you heard about the *Percival*, I'm sure. He was lucky to get another ship after that. If he fails this time, that will be the end of him. You are the ship's surgeon, of course, but I have seen surgeons made to hunt before. You wouldn't be the first.'

'I'm not afraid to work, if that's what you mean. I'll do my share.'

'Oh, I'm sure you will.'

'And what about you? Why the *Volunteer*?'

'I'm young, I have no family still living, no important friends; I must take risks if I'm to get on. Brownlee is known for being reckless, but if he succeeds he may earn me a good deal of money, and if he fails no blame will attach to me and I'll still have time on my side.'

'You're shrewd enough, for a young man.'

'I don't intend to end up like those others—Drax, Cavendish, Jones. They've all stopped thinking. They no longer know what they're doing, or why they're doing it. But I have a plan. Five years from now, or sooner if I get my share of luck, I'll have my own command.'

'You have a *plan*?' Sumner says. 'And you think that will help you?'

'Oh yes,' he says, with a grin which hovers between the deferential and the supercilious. 'I expect it will.'

Drax comes back down first. He lowers himself into a chair beside Black and lets out a long and noisome fart. The other two men look at him. He winks, then waves to the barmaid for another drink.

'For a shilling I've had worse,' he says.

Two fiddlers start up in the corner and some of the girls begin to dance. A party of deckhands from the *Zembla* arrives and Black walks over to talk to them. Cavendish appears, still buttoning up his britches, but there is no sign of Jones-the-whale.

'Our Mr Black over there is a smug-looking little prick, int he?' Cavendish says.

'He tells me he has a plan.'

'Fuck his fucking plan,' Drax says.

'He wants his own ship,' Cavendish says, 'but he won't get it. He has no fucking idea what's going on here.'

'And what *is* going on here?' Sumner asks.

'Nothing much,' Cavendish says. 'The usual.'

The men from the *Zembla* are dancing with the whores; they are all whooping and stamping their feet on the floorboards. The air is filling with sawdust and peat smoke. There is a warm, fetid odour of tobacco and ashes and stale beer. Drax looks disdainfully across at the dancers and then asks Sumner to buy him another whisky. 'I'll give you my note of hand,' he offers. Sumner waves him away and orders another round.

'You know, I heard all about Delhi,' Cavendish says to him, leaning in.

'And what did you hear?'

'I heard there was money to be made. Loot aplenty. You get anything?'

Sumner shakes his head.

'The Pandys cleaned the city out before we got inside. They took it with them. All that was left when we arrived was stray dogs and broken furniture, the place was ransacked.'

'No gold then?' Drax says. 'No jewels?'

'Would I really be sitting here with you two bastards if I was rich?'

Drax gazes at him for several seconds as if the question is too complex for an immediate reply.

'There's rich and rich,' he says eventually.

'I'm neither one.'

'You saw some famous butchery though, I'd bet,' Cavendish says. 'Some heinous fucking violence.'

'I'm a surgeon,' Sumner says. 'So I'm not impressed by bloodshed.'

'Not *impressed?*' Drax repeats, with a mocking carefulness, as if the word itself is girlish and faintly absurd.

43

'Surprised then, if you like,' Sumner says quickly. 'I'm not surprised by bloodshed. Not any more.'

Drax shakes his head and looks across at Cavendish.

'I'm not too surprised by bloodshed myself. Are you surprised, Mr Cavendish?'

'No, not too often, Mr Drax. I generally find I can take a little bloodshed in my stride.'

After finishing his drink, Drax goes upstairs to look for Jones but can't find him. On his way back to the table, he exchanges words with one of the men from the *Zembla*. As Drax sits down, the man shouts something back at him, but Drax ignores it.

'Not *again*,' Cavendish says.

Drax shrugs.

The fiddlers are playing 'Monymusk'. Sumner watches the grubby, mismatched dancers as they swirl and stamp about. He remembers dancing the polka in Ferozepore in the days before the Mutiny, he remembers the damp heat of the colonel's ballroom and the mingled scent of cheroots and rice powder and rosewater sweat. The tune changes and some of the whores sit down to rest or bend over, hands on knees, to better catch their breath.

Drax licks his lips, gets up from his chair and walks to the other side of the room. He edges between tables until he is standing next to the man he argued with minutes before. He pauses briefly, then leans forwards and whispers some carefully chosen foulness into the man's ear. The man spins round and Drax punches him twice in the face. He raises his fist a third time, but before he can deliver the blow he is dragged backwards and set upon by the other crewmen.

The music stops. There is screaming and cursing and the noise of breaking furniture and smashing glass. Cavendish goes over to help but is immediately knocked to the ground. It is two against six now. Sumner, watching, would prefer to stay neutral—he is a surgeon, not a brawler—but he can count well enough, and he understands his obligations. He puts down his glass of porter and steps across the room.

An hour later, Drax, raw-knuckled, cock-sore and reeking of whisky, rows a diminished party back to the *Volunteer*. Jones and Black are absent, Sumner is coiled in the stern groaning, and Cavendish is lying next to him snoring loudly. The sky above them is moonless and the water around is the colour of ink. If it were not for the whale ship's lanterns and the speckled lights of the shoreline, there would be nothing to see—they would be surrounded by emptiness. Drax leans forwards and then pulls back. He feels the heaviness of the water and then its release.

When they reach the ship, Drax wakes Cavendish from his stupor. Together, they pull Sumner up onto the deck then heft him down to steerage. His cabin door is locked and they have to fish in his waistcoat pockets to find the key. They lay him on the bunk and pull off his boots.

'This unfortunate fellow appears to be in need of a surgeon,' Cavendish says.

Drax pays no attention. He has discovered two keys in Sumner's waistcoat pocket and he is now wondering which lock the second one opens. He looks around the cabin, then notices a padlocked trunk sitting next to the medicine chest underneath the bed. He gets down on his haunches and prods it with his forefinger.

'What are you doing?' Cavendish asks him.

Drax shows him the second key. Cavendish sniffs and wipes a fresh smear of blood from his split lip.

'Probably nothing in there,' he says. 'Just the usual shite.'

Drax pulls the trunk out, opens the padlock with the second key, and starts looking through the contents. He removes a pair of canvas trousers, a balaclava helmet, a cheaply bound copy of the *Iliad*. He finds a slim mahogany case and opens it up.

Cavendish whistles softly.

'Opium pipe,' he says. 'My, my.'

Drax picks the pipe up, looks it over for a moment, sniffs the bowl, then puts it back.

'That's not it,' he says.

'Not what?'

He pulls out a pair of sea boots, a watercolour box, a set of linens, a woollen vest, three flannel shirts, a shaving kit. Sumner shifts onto his side and groans. The two men stop what they are doing and look at him.

'Check the very bottom,' Cavendish says. 'There might be something hidden at the very bottom.'

Drax sticks his hand in and delves about. Cavendish yawns and begins scratching at a mustard stain on the elbow of his coat.

'Anything there?' he asks.

Drax doesn't answer. He puts his other hand deep into the trunk and pulls out a grubby, dog-eared envelope. He removes a document from the envelope and hands it across to Cavendish to read.

'Army discharge papers,' Cavendish says, then, after a moment: 'Sumner's been court-martialled, no pension, out on his ear.'

'For what?'

Cavendish shakes his head.

Drax rattles the envelope, then tips it upside down. A ring falls out. It is gold with two good-sized gemstones.

'Paste,' Cavendish says. 'Must be.'

A small, rectangular looking-glass with bevelled edges is attached by brass corner-pieces to the bulkhead wall above Sumner's head in testament to the vanity of some previous occupant. Drax takes the ring, licks it once, then scrapes it across the surface of the glass. Cavendish watches him, then leans forward and looks hard at the resulting line—long, grey and undulant like a single hair plucked from the scalp of a crone. He licks his index finger and wipes away the dust so as to better gauge the true depth of the scoring. He nods. They look at each other carefully, then they look down at Sumner who is breathing heavily through his nose and appears to be soundly asleep.

'Hindoo loot from Delhi,' Cavendish says. 'The lying bastard. But why not sell it on?'

'Just in case,' Drax explains, as if the answer is obvious. 'He thinks it makes him safer.'

Cavendish laughs and shakes his head in amazement at the folly of such a notion.

'A whaling voyage is full of dangers,' he says. 'A few

unfortunates among us will not get home alive. That's a simple fact.'

Drax nods, and Cavendish continues: 'And if ever a man perishes while on board, of course, it is the appointed task of the first mate to auction off his possessions for the sake of the poor widow. Am I wrong?'

Drax shakes his head.

'You're right,' he says. 'But not yet. Not in Lerwick.'

'Fuck no. Not yet. I don't mean yet.'

Drax puts the ring and the discharge papers back in the envelope. He puts the envelope back into the bottom of the trunk and arranges the rest of the contents over it just as before. He closes the padlock with a click and pushes the trunk back under the bed.

'Don't forget the keys,' Cavendish tells him.

Drax returns the keys to Sumner's waistcoat pocket and the two men step out of the cabin into the companionway. They pause a moment before parting.

'Do you think Brownlee knows?' Cavendish says.

Drax shakes his head.

'No one knows but us,' he says. 'Just thee and me.'

5

They sail north from Lerwick through long days of fog and sleet and bitter wind, days without ease or let-up, when the sea and sky meld together into a damp weft of roiling and impermeable greyness. Sumner stays in his cabin puking incessantly, unable to read or write, wondering what he has done to himself. Twice they are hit by gales from the east. The cables screech, and the ship slumps and pitches amid the seething hillocks of an adamantine sea. On the eleventh day, the weather settles and they encounter sea ice: shallow, disconnected blocks of it, several yards across, rising and falling on the moderated swell. The air is newly cold, but the sky is clearing and they can make out in the far distance the white volcanic nub of Jan Mayen Island. The slop bags are heaved on deck and gunpowder, percussion caps and rifles are given out. The crew begin moulding bullets and sharpening their knives in preparation for the sealing. Two days later, they see the main seal pack for the first time, and at dawn the next day the boats are lowered.

Out on the ice, Drax works alone, moving back and forth, patient and relentless, from one group to the next, shooting and clubbing as he goes. The young ones shriek at him and try to waddle away but are too slow and stupid to escape. The older ones he puts a bullet in. When he has killed a seal, he turns it over, cuts round the hind flippers then slashes it open from the neck to the genitals. He pushes the edge of his knife into the gap between the meat and the blubber and begins to cut and prise away the outer layers. When he is finished, he hooks the severed skin onto a line for dragging and leaves the blood-sodden and meat-streaked krang, like a gruesome afterbirth, on the snow to be pecked at by gulls or eaten by bear cubs. After hours of this, the icepack is as spattered and filthy as a butcher's apron, and each of the five whaleboats is laden with a reeking pile of sealskins. Brownlee signals the men back. Drax hauls his last load, stretches himself, then leans and dips his flensing knife and club in the salt water to rinse off the accumulated gobs of blood and brain matter.

As they are winched on board in dripping bunches, Brownlee counts the sealskins and calculates their value. Four hundred skins will yield up nine tons of oil, he estimates, and each ton at market will bring in, with luck, some forty pounds. They have made a good beginning, but must press on. The seal pack is beginning to divide and scatter, and there is a small flotilla of other whaling ships, Dutch, Norwegian, Scotch and English, gathered at wide intervals along the floe edge, all competing for pieces of the same prize. Before the light fails, he ascends the crow's nest with a telescope and decides on the most promising spot for the next day's hunt. The pack is unusually large this year and the ice, though uneven and thin in places, is still navigable. Fifty tons would be within his grasp if he had a passable crew, and even with the slender bunch of shitwicks he has been given by Baxter, he believes he can net thirty easily, possibly thirty-five. He will send another boat out tomorrow, he decides, a sixth boat. Any cunt who's breathing and can hold a rifle will be out there killing seals.

It is light at four, and they lower the boats again. Sumner is sitting in the sixth boat with Cavendish, the steward, the cabin boy and several of the more persistent malingerers. There is eighteen degrees of frost outside, it is blowing a light breeze and the sea is the colour and consistency of London slush. Sumner, who fears frostbite, is wearing his Ulan cap and a knitted muffler. He is holding his rifle clamped between his knees. After rowing south-east for a half-hour, they see a dark patch of seals off in the middle distance. They anchor the boat to the ice and disembark. Cavendish, whistling 'The Lass of Richmond Hill', leads the way and the rest follow after him in a straggly single file. When they get within sixty yards of the seals, they spread out and commence shooting. They kill three adult seals and club to death six infants, but the rest escape unharmed. Cavendish spits and reloads his rifle, then climbs to the top of a pressure ridge and looks around.

'Over there,' he shouts out to the others, pointing off in different directions, 'over there, and over there.'

The cabin boy stays behind to flense the dead seals, and the rest separate. Sumner walks east. Above the constant creak and whine of moving ice, he can hear the occasional crump of distant gunfire. He shoots two more seals and skins them as best he can. He makes eyelets in the skins with his knife, reeves a rope through the eyelets, ties them together then starts back with the rope over his shoulder.

By noon, he has killed six more seals, and he is a mile from the whaleboat dragging a hundred pounds of ragged sealskin across a succession of broad, loose ice floes. He is groggy with fatigue. His shoulders are raw and aching from the friction of the rope, and the freezing air is savage in his lungs. When he looks up, he sees Cavendish a hundred yards ahead and, further off to the right, another man, darkly clad, walking in the same direction and also pulling skins. He calls out, but the wind whips away his voice and neither one stops or looks about. Sumner presses on, thinking, as he trudges, of the warmth and shelter of his cabin and of the five short-necked bottles of laudanum lined up in the medical chest like soldiers on parade. He takes twenty-one grains now every evening after supper. The others believe he is working on his Greek and mock him for it, but really, while they are playing cribbage or discussing the weather, he is lying on his bunk in a state of unstructured and barely describable bliss. At such times, he can be anywhere and anyone. His mind slides back and forth through the mingled purlieus of time and space—Galway, Lucknow, Belfast, London, Bombay—a minute lasts an hour and a decade flows past in barely an instant. Is the opium a lie, he sometimes wonders, or is it the world around us, the world of blood and anguish, tedium and care, that is a lie? He knows, if he knows nothing else, that they cannot both be true.

Arriving at a yard-wide gap between two floes, Sumner stops a moment. He tosses the end of the rope across to the other side, then takes a step backwards and readies himself to make the short leap. It is snowing now, and the snow fills the air all around and whips against his face and chest. It is better, he has learned from experience, to take off from his bad leg and land on his good one. He takes a short step and then a bigger, quicker one. He bends his knee and pushes upwards, but his standing foot slips sideways on the ice: instead of jumping easily across, he pitches forwards, clown-like and ludicrous—headforemost, arms spinning—into the black and icy waters.

For a long, bewildering moment, he is submerged and sightless. He thrashes himself upright, then flings one arm out and gains purchase on the ice's edge. The ferocious drench of coldness has knocked all the breath from his body; he is gasping for air and the blood is roaring in his ears. He grabs on with the other hand also and tries to heave himself out of the water, but can't. The ice is too slippery, and his arms are too weak from the morning's pulling. The water is up to his neck, and the snow is falling more heavily. He hears the ice around him creak and yawn as it shifts about in the low swell. If the floes move together, he knows he will be crushed between them. If he stays too long in the water, he will lose consciousness and drown.

He retakes his grip and strains to pull himself up a second

time. He dangles in motionless agony for a moment, neither fully in nor out, but both his hands slip off the ice and he crashes backwards. Seawater fills his mouth and nostrils; spitting and harrumphing, he kicks himself afloat. The downwards tug of his sodden clothes seems suddenly gigantic. His belly and groin have already begun to throb from the cold, and his feet and legs are going numb. Where the fuck is Cavendish? he thinks. Cavendish must have seen him fall. He calls out for help, then calls again, but no one appears. He is alone. The rope is within reach, but he knows the skins on the end of it are not heavy enough to bear his weight. He must pull himself up by his own power.

He grabs the edge of the ice for a third time and, kicking harder with both legs, tries to urge himself upwards. He hooks his right elbow up onto the surface, then his left palm. He digs the elbow in and, gasping and groaning with the ungodly effort, he forces himself further up until first his chin and neck, and then a small section of his upper chest, rise above the floe's edge. He presses down again as hard as he can with his left hand, using his elbow as a pivot, and gains an extra inch or two. He believes for a brief moment that the balance is shifting in his favour and he is about to succeed, but as soon as he thinks this, the floe he is pressing on jolts sideways, his right elbow slips away, and his jaw slams down hard onto the sharp angle of the ice. For a brief moment, he gazes up at the white and harrowed sky and then, dazed and helpless, he slumps backwards into the dark water and away.

6

Brownlee dreams he is drinking blood out of an old shoe. It is O'Neill's blood, but O'Neill is dead now from the cold and from drinking seawater. They pass the shoe around and each man, trembling, drinks from it in turn. The blood is warm and stains their lips and teeth like wine. What the fuck, Brownlee thinks, what the fuck. A man has to live, another hour, another minute even. What else is there to do? There are casks of bread floating in the hold, he knows, barrels of beer also, but no one has the strength or cunning to reach them. If they had had more time—but in the darkness it was pandemonium. Twelve feet of water in the hold and in a quarter of an hour they were over with nothing but the starboard bow left showing above the rampant waves. O'Neill is dead but his blood is still warm. The last man licks at the insole, rubs his fingers round the inner heel. The colour is startling. Everything else in the world is grey or black or brown but not the blood. It is a godsend, Brownlee thinks. He says it out loud: *'It is a godsend.'* The men look at him. He turns to the surgeon and gives his instructions. He feels O'Neill's blood in his throat and in his stomach, spreading through him, giving him new life. The surgeon bleeds them all, and then the surgeon bleeds himself. Some men mix their own blood with flour to make a paste, others guzzle it down like drunkards straight from the shoe. It is not a sin, he tells himself, there is no sin left now, there is only the blood and the water and the ice; there is only life and death and the grey-green spaces in between. He will not die, he tells himself, not now, not ever. When he is thirsty, he will drink his own blood; when he is hungry, he will eat his own flesh. He will grow enormous from the feasting, he will expand to fill the empty sky.

7

When Black finds Sumner, he looks dead already. His body is wedged into the narrow crack between two ice floes; his head and shoulders are above the water, but everything else is below. His face is bone white apart from the lips which are a dark, unnatural blue. Is he even breathing? Black leans down to check, but he can't tell—the wind is too loud, and all around the ice is screeching and grating in the swell. Everything about the surgeon appears frozen up and solid. Black takes his sealing rope and secures it around Sumner's chest. He doubts that he can pull him out on his own, but he tries anyway. He yanks him sideways first to dislodge him from the crevice, then, setting his heels in the snow, hauls upwards with all his might. Sumner's stiff and motionless body rises with remarkable ease, as though the sea has decided it doesn't want him after all. Black drops the rope and lunges forward, grabbing the sodden epaulettes of Sumner's greatcoat and pulling the rest of him onto the surface of the ice. He turns him over and slaps him twice across the face. Sumner doesn't respond. Black hits him harder still. One eyelid flickers open.

'Dear God, you're alive,' Black says.

He fires his rifle in the air twice. After ten minutes, Otto arrives with two other men from the search party. The four men take a limb each and carry him back to the ship as fast as they are able. His wet clothes have frozen solid in the arctic air, and it is more like carrying a heavy piece of furniture across the ice than a human being. When they get to the ship, Sumner is lifted aboard with a block-and-tackle and laid out on the deck. Brownlee looks down at him.

'Is the poor cunt even breathing?' he says.

Black nods. Brownlee shakes his head in wonderment.

They carry him down the hatchway into the wardroom and cut off his frozen clothes with shears. Black puts more coal in the stove and tells the cook to boil water. They rub his icy skin with goose fat and wrap him in scalding towels. He doesn't move or speak; he is still alive but comatose. Black remains by his side; the others come in occasionally to stare or offer advice. Around midnight, his eyes flicker briefly open, and they give him brandy which he coughs up along with a smear of dark brown blood. No one expects him to live through the night. At dawn, when they find he is still breathing, they move him out of the wardroom and into his own cabin.

When he comes to, Sumner assumes for a moment that he is back in India, that he is lying in his humid hill-tent on the ridge above Delhi and the sounds of ice blocks crashing against the keel of the *Volunteer* are actually the sounds of heavy ordnance being traded back and forth between the bastions and the pickets. It feels for a moment as if nothing terrible or irrevocable has yet happened to him, as if he has been given, incredibly, a second chance. He closes his eyes and falls asleep again. When he opens them an hour later, he sees Black standing by his bed looking down.

'Can you speak?' Black asks him.

Sumner looks back at him for a moment, then shakes his head. Black helps him up into a sitting position and commences to feed him bouillon from a teacup. The taste and heat of the bouillon is overpowering. After two spoonfuls of it, Sumner closes his mouth and lets the liquid dribble over his chin and down onto his chest.

'By rights you should be dead,' Black tells him. 'You were in that water for three fucking hours. No normal man survives a dunk like that.'

The tip of Sumner's nose and sections of both cheeks just below the eyes are black with frostbite. Sumner doesn't remember the ice or the cold or the ghoulish green water, but he does remember looking up, before whatever happened to him happened, and seeing the sky above him crammed with a billion snowflakes.

'Laudanum,' he says.

He looks hopefully across at Black.

'Are you trying to say something?' Black asks, tipping his head closer in.

'Laudanum,' Sumner says again, 'for the pain.'

Black nods and goes into the medicine chest. He mixes the laudanum with rum and helps him drink it. It burns Sumner's throat, and he thinks for a moment he will vomit it up, but manages not to. He is exhausted by the effort of speaking and doesn't know (since he is definitely not in India) where or who he is. He shudders violently and starts to weep. Black lowers him back down onto the bunk and covers him over with a coarse wool blanket.

In the wardroom that evening, over supper, Black reports that the surgeon is showing signs of improvement.

'Very good,' Brownlee says, 'but there will be no more sixth boat from now on. I don't wish another fucker's death to trouble my conscience.'

'Just bad luck, that's all,' Cavendish says offishly. 'A man slides off the ice in a snow storm, could happen to any of us.'

'Ask me, it worked out well for him,' Drax says. 'The fucker should rightly have been crushed or drowned. After ten minutes in that kind of water, a man's blood gets claggy and his heart gives out, but the surgeon's still alive somehow. He's fucking blessed.'

'*Blessed*?' Black says.

Brownlee holds up his hand.

'Blessed or not,' he says, 'I say there will be no more sixth boat. And while we mariners are busy hunting fish, the surgeon will remain safe in his cabin reading his Homer or pulling on his pizzle or whatever the fuck it is he does in there.'

Cavendish rolls his eyes.

'Easy enough for some bastards,' he says.

Brownlee glares at him.

'The surgeon has his job on this ship, Cavendish, and you have yours. And let that be the fucking end of it.'

Drax and Cavendish meet again at midnight when the watch changes. Cavendish pulls the harpooner to one side and glances around before speaking.

'He may yet die, you know,' he says. 'Have you seen the way he looks?'

'He looks to me like a cunt who's difficult to finish off,' Drax says.

'He's a leathery fucker, that's for sure.'

'You should have popped a ball into him when you had the chance.'

Cavendish shakes his head and waits for one of the Shetlanders to pass them by.

'That would never have flown,' he says. 'Brownlee's fucking sweet on him, and so is Black.'

Drax looks away as he lights his pipe. The sky above them is alive with jiggling stars; a layer of blue-black ice clings to the rigging and coats the deck.

'How much do you think that ring is worth anyway?' Cavendish says. 'I'm thinking twenty guineas, even twenty-five.'

Drax shakes his head and sniffs, as if the very question is beneath him.

'It's not your ring,' he says.

'And it's not Sumner's either. I'd say it belongs to whichever cunt has his hands on it at the time.'

Drax turns back to Cavendish and nods.

'That's about the way it is,' he says.

*

In the darkened cabin, swaddled beneath a thick pile of bearhides and blankets, Sumner, feverish and as weak as a newborn, sleeps, wakes, then sleeps again. As the ship sails north and west through fog and drizzle, under a heavy swell with two feet of ice cladding the hull, and the men chipping it off the deck and gunwales with marlin spikes and mallets, Sumner's opiated mind slips its moorings and drifts backwards, sideways, through fluid dreamscapes as fearsome and as thick with unnameable life as the green Arctic waters which press and crash only twelve wooden inches from his head. He could be anywhere at any time, but his thoughts, like iron rushing to a magnet, return to one place only.

A large yellow building beyond the racquet-court, the astonishing noise and the slaughterhouse stench of meat and excrement, like a scene out of hell. Thirty or more doolies arriving every hour carrying in, three or four at a time, the dead and the wounded. Young men's mangled and exploded corpses tossed into a miasmic outbuilding. The flailing of the wounded and the screams of the dying. Amputated limbs clattering into metal troughs. The incessant sound, as in a workshop or a saw mill, of steel gnawing through bone. The floor wet and sticky with spilled blood, the unstoppable heat, the thud and shake of artillery fire, and the clouds of black flies settling everywhere, on everything, without pause or discrimination—in eyes and ears and mouths, in open wounds. The incredible filth of it all, the howls and the pleading, the blood and shit, and the endless, endless pain.

Sumner works all morning, probing, sawing, suturing, until he is light-headed from the chloroform and nauseous from the generalised butchery. It is far worse than anything he has ever known or imagined. Men who, hours before, he saw boasting and laughing on the ridge are brought to him in pieces. He must do his duty, he tells himself, he must labour diligently. That is all that is possible now, all that any man could do. Like him, the other assistant surgeons— Wilkie and O'Dowd—are drenched with sweat and sunk in blood up to their elbows. As soon as one surgery is over, another one begins. Price, the orderly, checks the doolies as they arrive, discards the already dead and moves the maimed to a place in the queue. Corbyn, the staff surgeon, decides which limbs must be amputated immediately and which might be saved. He was with the Coldstream Guards at Inkerman, a rifle in one hand, a scalpel in the other, two thousand dead in ten hours. He has specks of blood in his moustaches. He chews arrowroot against the stench. This is nothing, he tells the others; this is small fucking beer. They slice and saw and probe for musketballs. They sweat and curse and feel like vomiting from the heat. The wounded men scream constantly for water, but there is never enough to slake their thirst. Their thirst is obscene, their needs are intolerable, but Sumner must bear them anyway, he must continue doing what he does for as long as he is able. He has no time for anger or disgust or fear, no time or energy for anything but the work itself.

By late afternoon, three or four o'clock, the fighting slows and the flow of casualties diminishes at first, then stops completely. Rumour has it that the British troops have stumbled upon a great store of liquor near the Lahore Gate and have drunk themselves into a communal stupor. Whatever the reason, the advance is halted, at least for now, and for the first time in many hours Corbyn and his assistants are able to break from their labours. Baskets of food and carboys of water are brought in, and a number of the wounded are moved back to their regimental hospitals up on the ridge. Sumner, after washing the blood off himself and eating a plate of bread and cold meat, lies down on a charpoy and falls asleep. He is woken by the sounds of fierce argument. A tur-baned man has appeared at the door of the field hospital carrying a wounded child; he is asking for assistance and O'Dowd and Wilkie are loudly refusing.

'Get him out of here,' Wilkie says, 'before I put a ball in him myself.'

O'Dowd picks up a sabre from the corner of the room and makes a show of unsheathing it. The man doesn't move. Corbyn comes over and tells O'Dowd to settle down. He examines the child briefly and shakes his head.

'The wound is too severe,' he says. 'The bone is shattered. He can't live long.'

'You can cut it off,' the man insists.

'You want a son with only one leg?' Wilkie asks.

The man doesn't answer. Corbyn shakes his head again.

'We can't help you,' he says. 'This hospital is for soldiers.'

'British soldiers,' Wilkie says.

The man doesn't move. Blood is dripping from the child's shattered leg onto the newly mopped floor. Clouds of flies are still buzzing around their heads, and every now and then one of the wounded soldiers groans or calls out for help.

'You are not busy,' the man says, looking around. 'You have time now.'

'We can't help you,' Corbyn says again. 'You should go.'

'I am not a sepoy,' the man says. 'My name is Hamid. I am a servant. I work for Farook the money lender.'

'Why are you still in the city? Why didn't you flee with all the others before the assault began?'

'I must protect my master's house and its contents.'

O'Dowd shakes his head and laughs.

'He's a shameless liar,' he says. 'Any man left in this city is a traitor by definition and deserves only hanging.'

'What about the child?' Sumner asks.

The others turn to look at him.

'The child is a casualty of war,' Corbyn says. 'And we are certainly not under orders to assist the offspring of the enemy.'

'I am not your enemy,' the man says.

'So you say.'

The man turns to Sumner hopefully. Sumner sits down again and lights his pipe. The child's blood drips steadily onto the floor.

'I can show you treasure,' the man says. 'If you help me now, I can show you treasure.'

'What treasure?' Wilkie asks. 'How much?'

'Two lakhs,' he says. 'Gold and jewels. See here.'

He lays the child down carefully on a trestle table and removes a small kidskin pouch from his tunic. He offers the pouch to Corbyn, and Corbyn takes and opens it. He tips the coins into his palm, looks at them for a moment, pushes them around with his forefinger, then passes them to Wilkie.

'Many more like that,' the man says. 'Many more.'

'Where is this treasure?' Corbyn asks. 'How far away?'

'Not far. Very close. I can show you now.'

Wilkie passes the coins to O'Dowd, and O'Dowd passes them to Sumner. The coins are warm and faintly greasy to the touch. The edges are unmilled and the surfaces are marked with elegant ribbons of Arabic script.

'You don't really believe him?' Wilkie says.

'How many more like this?' Corbyn asks. 'A hundred? Two hundred?'

'I told you, two thousand,' the man says. 'My master is a famous money lender. I buried them myself before he fled.'

Corbyn walks over to the boy and peels the blood-soaked wrapping from his leg. He peers down and sniffs the gaping wound.

'We could remove it from the hip,' he says. 'But he will probably die anyway.'

'Will you do it now?'

'Not now. When you get back here with all that treasure.'

The man looks unhappy, nods, then leans down and whispers something to the boy.

'You three go with him,' Corbyn says, 'and take Price. Arm yourselves, and if you don't like the way something looks, shoot this bastard and come straight back. I'll stay here with the boy.'

For a moment no one moves. Corbyn looks at them steadily.

'Four equal shares and a tithe each for Price,' he says. 'And what the prize agents don't ever learn about can't hurt them.'

They leave the field hospital and enter the city proper through the smoking wreckage of the Cashmere Gate. They clamber over hillocks of shattered masonry, past piles of smouldering corpses being sniffed at and nibbled by pariah dogs. Above them, tatter-winged vultures flap and complain, mortars fizzle and thump. There is a stench of cordite and scorched flesh, a distant sound of musketry. They wend their way through narrow, blasted streets clogged with broken furniture, eviscerated animals and abandoned weaponry. Sumner imagines behind every barricade and loophole a crouching sepoy ready to shoot. He thinks that the risk they are taking is too great and that the treasure itself is probably a lie, but he knows it would be foolish to refuse a man like Corbyn. The British army is built on influence, and if a man wishes to rise he must be careful who he knows. Corbyn has friends on the Army Medical Board and his brother-in-law is an Inspector of Hospitals. The man himself is boastful and dull to be sure, but to be connected to him by this shared secret, this pile of illegal loot, would not be a bad thing for Sumner at all. It might even, he thinks, be his path out of the 61st Foot and into a more respectable regiment. But only, of course, if the loot is real.

They turn a corner and come across a gun emplacement and a gaggle of drunken infantrymen. One of them is playing the squeezebox, another has his britches down and is evacuating into a wooden bucket; empty brandy bottles are scattered around.

'Who goes there?' one of them shouts.

'Surgeons,' Wilkie says. 'Does any man here require treatment?'

The soldiers look at each other and laugh.

'Cotteslow over there needs his fucking head examined,' one of them says.

'Where are your officers?'

The same man gets to his feet and, squinting, walks unsteadily towards them. He stops a foot or two away and spits. His uniform is ragged and stained with blood and gunsmoke. He smells of vomit, piss and beer.

'All dead,' he says. 'Every single one.'

Wilkie nods slowly and looks off down the street past the gun emplacement.

'And where is the enemy?' he says. 'Is he close by?'

'Oh, he's close enough,' the man says. 'If you look over yonder he may even blow you a wee kiss.'

The other men laugh again. Wilkie ignores them and turns back to confer with the others.

'This is a fucking disgrace,' he says. 'These men should be hanged for dereliction of duty.'

'This is as far as we can get,' O'Dowd says. 'This is the limit of the advance.'

'We are very close now,' Hamid says. 'Two minutes more.'

'Too dangerous,' O'Dowd says.

Wilkie rubs his chin and spits.

'We'll send Price,' he says. 'He can go on ahead and report back. If it looks safe, the rest of us will follow.'

They all turn to Price.

'Not for a fucking tithe,' he says.

'What say we double it?' Wilkie suggests. He looks at the other two and the other two nod in agreement.

Price, who has been squatting, stands up slowly, shoulders his rifle and walks across to Hamid.

'Lead on,' he says.

The others sit down where they are and wait. The drunken soldiers ignore them. Sumner lights his pipe.

'He's an avaricious little shit,' O'Dowd says, 'that Price.'

'If he gets killed, we'll have to make up some tale,' Wilkie says. 'Corbyn won't be happy.'

'Corbyn,' O'Dowd says. 'Always fucking Corbyn.'

'Is it his brother or his brother-in-law?' Sumner asks. 'I can never remember.'

O'Dowd shrugs and shakes his head.

'Brother-in-law,' Wilkie says. 'Sir Barnabas Gordon. I saw him lecture in chemistry at Edinburgh.'

'You'll get nothing out of Corbyn,' O'Dowd says to Sumner, 'don't think you will. He's an ex-Guardsman and his wife's a baroness.'

'After this he'll feel obliged,' Sumner says.

'A man like Corbyn doesn't care to feel obliged. We'll get our share of the loot if the loot exists, but believe me, that will be it.'

Sumner nods at this and thinks for a minute.

'Have you tried him already?'

Wilkie smiles at this, but O'Dowd says nothing.

Ten minutes later, Price comes back and reports that they

have found the house, and the route to it appears safe enough.

'Did you sight the treasure?' O'Dowd asks him.

'He says it is buried in the courtyard inside the house. He showed me where and I started him digging.'

They follow Price through a complication of narrow alleyways, then out onto a wider street where the shops have been ransacked and the houses are shuttered and silent. There is no one else about, but Sumner is sure these buildings must contain people nonetheless—terrified families crouching in the tepid darkness, jihadis and ghazis licking their wounds, making quiet preparation. They hear noises of carousing from nearby and, from further off, the sound of cannon fire. The sun is beginning to set, but the heat is steady and unforgiving. They cross the road, picking their way among the smoking piles of bones, rags and broken furniture, then walk another hundred yards until Price halts in front of an open doorway and nods.

The courtyard is small and square, the whitewashed walls are smeared and grubby, and there are patches of exposed mud brick where the plasterwork has failed. Each wall has two archways let into it, and above the archways runs a ragged wooden balcony. Hamid is squatting down at the centre. He has moved one of the flagstones, and is scraping away at the loose dirt beneath it.

'Help me, please,' he says. 'We must be quick now.'

Price kneels down next to him and begins to dig with his hands.

'I see a box,' he says, after a moment. 'Look, there.'

The others gather round. Price and Hamid tug the box out of the earth, and O'Dowd smashes it open with his rifle butt. The box contains four or five grey canvas sacks.

Wilkie picks up one, looks inside it, and begins to laugh. 'Jesus Christ,' he says.

'Is it treasure?' Price asks.

Wilkie shows the sack to O'Dowd and O'Dowd smiles, then laughs and slaps Wilkie on the back.

Price pulls the other three sacks out of the box and opens them. Two are filled with coins, and the third contains an assortment of bracelets, rings and jewels.

'Oh, fuck me,' Price whispers softly to himself.

'Let me see those darlings,' Wilkie says. Price passes him the smallest bag and Wilkie tips its contents out onto the dusty flagstones. On their knees now, the three assistant surgeons gather round the glistering pile like schoolboys at a game of marbles.

'We prise out all the stones and melt down the gold,' O'Dowd says. 'Keep it simple.'

'We must go back now,' Hamid says again. 'For my son.'

Still gripped by the treasure, they ignore him completely. Sumner leans forward and picks out one of the rings.

'What are these stones?' he says. 'Are they diamonds?' He turns to Hamid. 'Are these diamonds?' he asks, showing him the ring. 'Is this real?'

Hamid doesn't answer.

'He's thinking of that boy,' O'Dowd says.

'The boy's dead,' Wilkie says, not looking up. 'The boy was always fucking dead.'

Sumner looks at Hamid, who still doesn't speak. His eyes are wide with fear.

'What is it?' Sumner asks.

He shakes his head as if the answer is much too complicated, as if the time for explanations has gone and they are occupying, whether they realise it or not, a darker and more consequential phase.

'We go now,' he says. 'Please.'

Hamid takes Price by the sleeve and tries to tug him streetwards. Price snatches his arm away and pulls back a fist.

'Watch yourself now,' he says.

Hamid stands back and raises both his arms above his head, palms facing forwards—it is a gesture of silent refusal but also, Sumner realises, of surrender. But surrender to whom?

There is the crack of a musket from the balcony above them, and the back of Price's head explodes in a brief carnation of blood and bone. Wilkie, swivelling on his heels, points his rifle and shoots wildly upwards but hits nothing, and is then shot twice himself—first through the neck and then high up on the chest. They are being ambushed; the place is alive with sepoys. O'Dowd grabs Sumner by the arm and drags him backwards into the safety and darkness of the house. Wilkie is writhing on the flagstones outside; blood is squirting in crimson pulses from his punctured neck. Sumner pushes open the street door with the toe of his boot and an answering bullet thumps into the doorframe from outside. One of the ambushers vaults over the rickety balcony and dashes towards them screaming. O'Dowd shoots at him but misses. The sepoy's sabre meets O'Dowd's abdomen and emerges, reddened and dripping, halfway up his back. O'Dowd coughs blood, gasps, looks amazed at what has been done to him. As he pushes the sword in still harder, the sepoy's expression is urgent and passionate. His pitch-black eyes bulge wildly; his brown skin is slick with sweat. Sumner is standing two feet away from him, no more; he lifts his rifle to his shoulder and fires. The man's face disappears instantly and is replaced by a shallow, bowl-like concavity filled with meat and gristle, and crazed and shattered fragments of teeth and tongue. Sumner drops his rifle and kicks open the front door. As he steps into the street, a bullet bites him in the calf and another smashes into the wall inches from his head. He staggers, grunts, topples backwards for a second, but then rights himself and commences a lopsided dash for safety. Another bullet whines above his head. He can feel a warm squelch as his left boot fills with blood. From behind him, there is screaming. The street is littered with shattered masonry, potsherds, sackcloth, bones and dust. Shops and kiosks lie empty-shelved on either hand, their sagging shami-anas holed and rotting. He abandons the road and plunges sideways into the crackpot labyrinth of lanes and alleyways.

The high stucco walls are fractured and grease-streaked. There is a smell of sewage, a roar of bluebottles. Sumner limps on, frantic and directionless, until the pain forces him to halt. He crouches in a doorway and prises off his boot. The wound itself is clean enough but the shin bone is broken. He rips a strip of flannel from his shirt-tail and binds the wound as tightly as he can to stop the bleeding. As he does so, a hot wave of nausea and faintness passes over him. He closes his eyes and when he opens them again he sees a black swirl of pigeons wheeling and gathering like airborne spores in the darkening sky. The moon is out already; from all sides there is the constant dreary boom of ordnance. He thinks of Wilkie and O'Dowd and starts to shudder. He takes a long breath in and tells himself to sharpen the fuck up or he will die just like they did. The city will fall tomorrow for sure, he tells himself; when the British troops sober up, they will press forward. If he sits tight and remains alive, they will find him and bring him home.

He gets to his feet and looks about for a place to hide. The door opposite is ajar. He limps across to it, dripping blood as he goes. Behind the door is a room with dusty matting and a broken divan pushed up against one wall. There is an unglazed water jar in one corner, empty, and a tea kettle and glasses scattered over the floor. The single high window looks onto the alleyway and gives little light. On the far wall, an archway concealed by a curtain opens onto another smaller room with a skylight and a cooking stove. There is a wooden cupboard, but the cupboard is empty. The room smells of old ghee, ashes and wood smoke. In one corner of it, a small boy is lying curled on a filthy blanket.

Sumner watches him for a moment, wondering whether he is alive or dead. It is too dark to tell whether he is breathing or not. With difficulty, Sumner leans down and touches the boy's cheek. The touch leaves a faint red fingerprint behind. The boy stirs, moves his hand across his face as though brushing away a fly and then wakes. When he sees Sumner standing there, he is startled and cries out with alarm. Sumner hushes him. The boy stops shouting, but still looks scared and suspicious. Sumner takes a slow step backwards, keeping his eyes on the boy, and lowers himself gradually onto the dirt floor.

'I need water,' he says. 'Look. I am wounded.' He points at his oozing leg. 'Here.'

He reaches into his coat pocket for a coin and realises that he still has the ring. He doesn't remember putting it in his pocket, but here it is. He shows it to the boy, then gestures him to take it.

'I need water,' he says again. '*Pani.*'

The boy looks at the ring without moving. He is around ten or eleven years old—thin-faced, bare-chested and shoeless, wearing a grubby *dhoti* and a canvas vest.

'*Pani,*' he echoes.

'Yes,' Sumner nods. '*Pani,* but tell no one I am here. Tomorrow, when the British soldiers come, I will help you. I will keep you safe.'

After a pause, the boy answers him in Hindustani: a long line of empty, clashing syllables like the bleating of a goat. What is a child doing sleeping in a place like this? Sumner wonders. In an empty room in a city that has become a battleground? Are his family all dead? Is there no one left to protect him? He remembers, twenty years before, lying in the dark in the abandoned cabin after his parents were removed to the typhus hospital in Castlebar. His mother had sworn to him they would come back soon, she had held his two hands tight in hers and solemnly sworn to it, but they never did. It was only William Harper, the surgeon, who happened to recall the missing child, who rode back the next day and found the boy still lying where they had left him. Harper was wearing his green tweed suit that day; his pigskin boots were muddy and wet from the road. He lifted the boy up off the soiled pallet and carried him outside. Sumner remembers, even now, the smells of wool and leather, the damp warmth of the surgeon's steady breathing and his soft easeful curses, like a newfangled form of prayer.

'When the British soldiers get here, I will keep you safe,' Sumner insists again. 'I will protect you. Do you understand?'

The boy stares at him for a moment longer, then nods and leaves the room. Sumner returns the ring to his pocket, closes his eyes, leans his head against the wall and waits. The flesh around his wound is hot and badly swollen. The leg is pulsing with pain, and his thirst is becoming unbearable. He wonders if the boy will betray him now, if the next person he sees will be his murderer. He would be easy enough to kill in his present condition: he has no weapon to defend himself with and little strength left for the struggle even if he had one.

The boy returns with a jug of water. Sumner drinks half of it and uses the remainder to rinse off his wound. Just above the ankle, the shin bone slants backwards at an angle. The foot lolls uselessly below. Compared to the abominations of the field hospital, his case is mild, but the sight fills him with fear nonetheless. He shuffles across to the stove and selects two long sticks of firewood from the pile next to it. He takes his jackknife from his tunic pocket, unlocks the blade, and begins to trim and smooth the wood. The boy watches him impassively. Sumner places one piece of firewood on either side of his leg, then gestures for the blanket that the boy was sleeping on. The boy brings it over to him and he tears it into strips. The boy doesn't move or speak. Sumner leans forward and starts binding the splints with the pieces of dirty blanket. Just tight enough, he tells himself, but not too tight.

Soon he is drenched with sweat and panting. He can feel the sour taste of vomit rising up his throat. The sweat is stinging his eyes and his fingers are trembling. He prods the second strip of blanket underneath his leg and then draws the ends together on top. He tries to tie them in a knot, but the pain is too severe. He gives up, pauses a moment, then tries and fails again. He opens his mouth in a silent scream, then grunts and falls backwards onto the floor. He closes his eyes and waits for his breath to return. His heartbeat is like a heavy door somewhere off in the distance being slammed hard again and again. He waits and, eventually, the shrill pain resolves into a nauseating ache. He rolls over and looks across at the boy.

'You must help me,' he says.

The boy doesn't respond. Small black flies agitate across his lips and eyebrows, but he makes no effort to brush them away. Sumner points down at his leg.

'Tie it for me,' he instructs. 'Tight but not too tight.'

The boy stands up, looks at the wound and says something in Hindustani.

'Tight but not too tight,' Sumner says again.

The boy kneels down, takes hold of the bandage and begins to tie the knot. The bone ends grind together. Sumner cries out. The boy stops, but Sumner impatiently gestures for him to carry on. He finishes the knot and ties the next one and the next one. When the splinting is finished, the boy goes out to the well behind the house, refills the water jug and brings it back. Sumner drinks the water, then falls asleep. When he wakes up the boy is lying next to him. He smells of wet sawdust and is no larger than a dog; his breaths are slow and shallow. In the nearly lightless room, his sprawled body seems like no more than a thickening of the general darkness. Without moving his damaged leg, Sumner reaches out and touches the child as gently as he can manage. He is not sure which part of his body he is touching. The shoulder blade, is it? The thigh? The boy doesn't stir or wake.

'You're a good little fellow,' Sumner whispers to him. 'A good little fellow, that's what you are.'

At first light, the barrage recommences. The explosions are distant to begin with, but then, as the gunners find their range and the British troops gradually advance through the city, street by street, they become closer and louder. The room shakes and a fresh crack jags across the ceiling. They hear the fierce buzz of cannonballs passing overhead, then the dull basso crumble of collapsing walls.

'We sit tight,' Sumner tells the boy. 'We sit tight here and wait.'

The boy nods and scratches himself. He has found a piece of bark to chew on and what looks like the leaves of a turnip. Sumner lights his pipe and silently prays that Tommy Atkins arrives before the house is hit by an artillery shell or overrun by fleeing Pandys. After a while, they hear the rattle of musketry then voices. Someone outside is cursing and yelling commands. There are footsteps overhead and the sound of slamming doors. Sumner feels a sudden and terrifying sense of encroachment and exposure; he feels the urge to crouch down and hide. The boy looks at him expectantly. Sumner grabs onto the stove and pulls himself upright. The pain in his leg is sickening but tolerable. He leans against the boy and together they stumble over to the doorway. There is a boom of cannon fire and then screams. The boy presses himself against Sumner's side. Sumner cracks open the door and peers out. He sees a dead Pandy propped against a wall and, from the gap at the end of the alleyway, the flash of a British uniform. The air is sharp with gunsmoke, full of yellow dust, and loud with the panic and wildness of battle.

'Quick,' he says to the boy, 'quick before they leave us behind.'

They hobble down the alleyway in the direction of the shouting and gunfire, but already the noises are becoming fainter. The battle is moving on. When they reach the thoroughfare, all they see are piles of smashed masonry and scattered, blood-smirched corpses. A British soldier appears from a doorway, carrying a pistol in one hand and a sack of loot in the other. Sumner calls out to him for help. The soldier turns sharply back to look at them. His eyes are wild, and his once-red uniform is befouled with sweat and dirt. Noticing the boy, the soldier stiffens momentarily, then raises his pistol and shoots. The ball hits the boy full in the chest and knocks him backwards. Sumner lowers himself and presses his hands hard against the pulsing wound. The pistol ball has shattered the sternum and passed directly through the heart. Bubbles of blood rise and break on the boy's grey lips, his dark eyes roll back into his head, and in a minute he is dead.

The soldier spits, twitches and begins to reload his pistol. He looks over at Sumner and smiles.

'I have a fucking good eye for the shooting,' he says. 'I always have.'

'You are a fucking imbecile,' Sumner answers.

The soldier laughs and shakes his head.

'I am the one who saved your precious life,' he says. 'Think on that.'

A doolie arrives, and Sumner is lifted onto it. They carry him back through the broken city to the field hospital behind the racquet-court. He is not recognised at first among the hordes of wounded, but when Corbyn sees him, he is quickly moved upstairs and placed in a side room by himself.

He is given food, water and a dose of laudanum, and an adjunct is sent to re-splint and dress his leg. He slips in and out of slumber. He can hear the constant noise of cannon and the intermittent howls of the wounded from the floor below. It is dark before Corbyn comes up to see him. He carries an oil lamp and smokes a cheroot. They shake hands and Corbyn stares down at him for a moment with an expression of sad puzzlement, as though Sumner is a carefully planned experiment that has unexpectedly misfired.

'So the others are all dead?' he asks.

Sumner nods.

'We were caught unawares,' he says.

'You were lucky to survive then.' He lifts the blanket and glances at Sumner's leg.

'The wound is clean and the break isn't so bad. I may need to use a cane for a while, but that's all.'

Corbyn nods and smiles. Sumner watches him expectantly. Soon, he thinks, he will make me an offer, suggest an appropriate reward for my sufferings.

'You must have imagined I was dead also,' Sumner says. 'When no one came back.'

'Indeed,' Corbyn says, 'that was the general assumption.' Then adds, after a pause: 'I am glad, of course, that we were wrong.'

'The treasure was real enough, but there were Pandys hiding in the house.'

'You walked into a trap then. You made a bad mistake.'

'Not a trap,' Sumner says, 'an accident. No one could have guessed they were in there.'

'For a surgeon to leave his post is a serious thing.'

Corbyn's gaze hardens and he watches Sumner carefully. Sumner opens his mouth to speak, then stops himself.

'I trust you understand my meaning,' Corbyn says. 'I am glad you're safe of course, but nonetheless your present situation is not a happy one. There is likely to be a charge.'

'A charge?' Sumner wonders for a confusing moment if this could be part of some larger plan that Corbyn has cooked up in his absence. Some grander strategy for their mutual benefit.

'The circumstances make it unavoidable,' Corbyn goes on. 'The assault was at a crucial stage. To lose three surgeons at such a time . . .' He raises his eyebrows and lazily exhales a tube of grey-brown smoke into the inky darkness.

Sumner feels a sharp tightening across his chest and the beginnings of disorientation, as if the room has started unexpectedly, impossibly, to tilt around him.

'If there is to be any charge,' he says, 'I trust I can rely on your assistance, Mr Corbyn.'

Corbyn frowns and shakes his head dismissively.

'I don't see what assistance I could possibly offer you,' he says lightly. 'The facts of the matter are clear.'

'Your account of yesterday, I mean,' Sumner says. 'The details of what occurred. The boy and so on.'

Corbyn has put the oil lamp down on a side table and is pacing slowly back and forth at the foot of the bed. Before answering, he goes over to the open window and pauses there a while, as if looking out for a dinner guest who is late.

'The general is unlikely to concern himself with the minor details,' Corbyn says. 'When you were needed here, you left the hospital in search of treasure. Three men have died, and you have come back severely wounded. In your absence, your injured comrades, several officers among them, lay untreated and oftentimes in severe agony. That, I fear, is as much as he wants, or is required, to understand.'

'You expect me to hold my tongue then? To take my punishment? I will very likely be dismissed.'

'I'd advise you not to make a bad situation even worse, that's all. To bring my name into this will not serve you well. I can assure you of that.'

There is a pause in which the two men hold each other's gaze. Corbyn's expression is stern, but also calm and self-assured. Beneath the standard military-issue stiffness, there lies a vast and heedless confidence born of wealth and leisure, a sense that the world is malleable, that it will bend to his desires.

Sumner's head has begun to ache. He feels a sour inner swell of anger and self-reproach.

'So you offer me nothing at all for my trouble?'

'I offer you my advice, which is to accept the unfortunate consequences of your own actions. You were unlucky, I agree, but then again you are alive and the others are dead, so perhaps you have something to be grateful for.'

'I still have the treasure,' Sumner tells him.

Corbyn winces and shakes his head.

'No, you are lying about that. You were carrying nothing with you when they brought you in.'

'You checked then,' Sumner says flatly, 'before deciding on this course of action.'

Corbyn's jaw tightens and he looks, for the first time since the conversation began, discomfited.

'Do not provoke me. It will not help your case.'

'I have no case. You know that as well as I do. If I go before the general, my career is over.'

Corbyn shrugs.

'You will be moved up to the regimental hospital later on this evening, and you will receive the official charges in the next day or so. I will see you again at the hearing.'

'Why do you do this to me?' Sumner asks him. 'What's your purpose?'

'My purpose?'

'You are destroying me, and for what?'

Corbyn shakes his head and smiles thinly.

'There is a melancholic strain in the Celtic soul which finds martyrdom appealing, I understand. But in your case, Mr Sumner, the cap hardly fits. I do my duty merely; you would have done much better to do yours.'

With that, he nods a brief goodbye and steps towards the door. Sumner watches him depart, hears the clatter of his boot heels as he descends the wooden stairs and the assonant gabble of his Englishness as he issues another command. As the surgeon lies there, as the truth of his situation settles slowly upon him, he feels the defining elements of his character—eagerness, belief, cussedness; a kind of desperate, unspeakable pride—beginning to slip away. When William Harper died and left him nothing—since everything the man owned had by then been sold or mortgaged or squandered on drink—even then he persisted, his determination didn't flag. He could no longer afford his lectures or lodgings in Belfast, but he recognised the army as another way to rise. It would be much slower and much harder, he knew, but not impossible. He believed he could still do it, *would* still do it somehow. But now, those long-held reserves of resilience and tenacity are wiped out at a stroke. The years of effort, the years of doggedness and patience and guile. Is it possible? And if it is possible, what does it imply? He feels a hot jolt of rage at what Corbyn has done to him and then answering it, just as powerful but broader and more fierce, like a long, grey wave that has been gathering its force and finally reaches the shore, a chilling flood of shame.

8

Three weeks from Jan Mayen Island to Cape Farewell. Clear blue skies above, but the wind is intermittent and changeable, blowing strong and hard from the south on good days, but on others turning blustery and infirm or failing altogether. The crew are kept busy reeving boat falls, splicing whale-lines, overhauling the lances and harpoons. After the success of the sealing, morale is high. Brownlee senses a general optimism among the men, a belief that luck is with them this year and the season will be a good one. The murmurings of discontent he heard in Hull have quieted: Cavendish, although still an irritating prick, is proving competent at his work, and Black, his understudy, is laudably ambitious and shrewd beyond his years. After his near fatal dunking, the surgeon has revived remarkably. He is regaining colour and energy, and his appetite has returned.

Although the blooms of frostbite are raw on his cheeks and the tip of his nose, he can be seen most days pacing the deck for exercise or sketching in his journal. Campbell in the *Hastings* is waiting up the strait ahead of them, somewhere past Disko Island, but the two ships will not meet or attempt to communicate until the moment is right. The underwriters are alive these days to any sign of conspiracy, and a ship so heavily and disproportionately insured as the *Volunteer* is suspicious as it is. His final voyage then. It is not the end he would have wished for, but better this way, surely, than another five years on that coal barge chuntering like a pillock from Middlesbrough to Cleethorpes and back again. None of the others that lived went back to sea after the *Percival*—brains scrambled, limbs missing, twitching and spasming with dread—he was the only one who managed it. The only one sufficiently stubborn or stupid to want to carry on. A man should look forwards and not backwards, that is Baxter's persistent advice to him. What matters is what happens *next*. And although Baxter is without doubt a fucker, a scoundrel and a deep-dyed charlatan, there's some small but solid truth to that, he thinks.

The bergs around the Cape are dense and dangerous as usual. To avoid collisions, it is necessary for the *Volunteer* to run west another hundred miles or so under topsails before steering north-north-east into the middle portion of the Davis Strait. From the foredeck where he sits when it is warm enough, Sumner watches out for birds—curlews, ptarmigans, auks, loons, mallies, eider ducks. Whenever he spots one, he calls to the steersman for an estimate of the latitude and makes a note in his book. If the bird is close enough and a rifle is at hand, he sometimes takes a shot, but more often than not, he misses. His inaccuracy is fast becoming a joke among the crew. Sumner has no interest in natural history; when the voyage is over he will throw the notebook away without looking at it again. He watches for birds like this only to pass the time, to appear busy and to seem normal.

Sometimes, if there are no birds to shoot or write about, he talks with Otto, the German harpooner. Despite his profession, Otto is a deep thinker and has a speculative, mystic bent. He thinks it probable that during the several hours Sumner was missing on the ice, his soul departed his material body and travelled out to the other, higher realms.

'Master Swedenborg describes a Spirit Place,' he explains, 'a broad green valley surrounded by cliffs and mountains, where the dead souls gather before being separated out into the saved and the damned.'

Sumner doesn't wish to disappoint him, but all he remembers is pain and fear, and then a long, dark, unpleasing kind of nullity.

'If there is such a fancy spot somewhere, I never saw sign of it,' he says.

'You may have gone direct up to heaven instead. That is possible too. Heaven is built entirely of light. The buildings, the parks, the people, everything is made of the divine light. There are rainbows everywhere. Multitudes of rainbows.'

'This is Swedenborg again?'

Otto nods.

'You would have met the dead and spoke to them there. Your parents, perhaps. Do you remember that?'

Sumner shakes his head, but Otto is undeterred.

'In heaven they would appear just the same as they did in this life,' he says, 'but their bodies would be made from light instead of flesh.'

'And how can a body be made from light?'

'Because the light is what we truly are, that is our immortal essence. But only when the flesh falls away can the truth shine through.'

'Then what you describe is not a body at all,' he says, 'but a soul.'

'Everything must have its form. The bodies of the dead in heaven are the forms that their particular souls have taken.'

Sumner shakes his head again. Otto is a mountainous, broad-chested Teuton with thick, fleshy features and fists like ham hocks. He can toss a harpoon out fifty yards without a grunt. It is strange to hear him expounding such flimsiness.

'Why would you believe such things?' he asks. 'What good does it do you?'

'The world we see with our eyes is not the whole truth. Dreams and visions are just as real as matter. What we can imagine or think exists as truly as anything we can touch or smell. Where do our thoughts come from, if not from God?'

'They come from our experience,' Sumner says, 'from what we've heard and seen and read, and what's been told to us.'

Otto shakes his head.

'If that were true, then no growth or advancement would be possible. The world would be stagnant and unmoving. We would be doomed to live our lives facing backwards.'

Sumner looks at the distant crenellated line of bergs and land ice, the pale open sky, the dark impatient pitching of the sea. After he came to, he lay in his bunk a full week barely moving or speaking. His body was like a diagram, a sketch that could be rubbed away and begun again, the pain and emptiness like hands moulding and remoulding him, knuckling and stretching out his soul.

'I didn't die in the water,' he says. 'If I had died, I would be new somehow, but there's nothing new about me.'

Short of Disko Island, the ship becomes lodged fast in a floe. They attach ice-anchors to the raft of ice nearest to them and attempt to warp the ship forward using thick lines reefed to the capstans. The capstan bars are double manned, but even so, it is slow and exhausting work. It takes them the whole morning to move a mere thirty feet, and after dinner Brownlee decides, reluctantly, to give it up and wait for the wind to change, and a new lead to open.

Drax and Cavendish take mattocks and descend to retrieve the anchors from the ice. The day is warm and cloudless. The ever present Arctic sun is high and throbbing out a dull, cantankerous kind of furnace heat. The two harpooners, immune to it by now, cast off the warp ropes, hack out the wet ice around the anchors with their mattocks and kick them free. Cavendish hefts the irons up onto his shoulder and begins to whistle the 'Londonderry Air'. Drax, ignoring him, raises his right hand to shield his eyes against the sun and then, after another moment, points off landwards. Cavendish ceases whistling.

'What is it?'

'Bear,' Drax says. 'The next floe over.'

Cavendish shields his eyes and squats down to get a better look.

'I'll get a boat,' he says, 'and a rifle.'

They lower one of the whaleboats onto the ice, and Drax and Cavendish and two others drag it across to the open water. The floe is a quarter-mile wide and hummocky. The bear is pacing at its northerly edge, snapping at the air and sniffing about for seals.

Cavendish through his spyglass spots a trailing cub.

'Mother and child,' he says. 'Look see.'

He hands the glass to Drax.

'That babe's worth twenty pounds alive,' he says. 'We can skin the mother.'

The four men discuss finances for a minute and then, having reached a satisfactory agreement, they pull slowly towards the floe. When they are fifty yards away, they stop rowing and steady the boat. Cavendish, with his knees braced against the bows, lines up his shot.

'I've got a guinea in my locker says I'll put one plumb in her eyeball,' he whispers. 'Who'll match it, now?'

'If you've got a guinea in your locker, then my cock's a cunt,' one of the men retorts.

Cavendish snickers.

'Now, now,' he says. '*Now, now.*'

'Put it in the heart,' Drax says.

'The heart it is,' Cavendish nods, 'and here we go.'

He scowls along the barrel one more time, then shoots. The bullet hits the bear high on the rump. There is a squirt of blood and a roar.

'Fuck,' Cavendish says, looking suspiciously at the rifle. 'The sight must be skewed.'

The bear is circling wildly now, shaking its withers, howling and biting at the air as if fending off an imaginary foe.

'Shoot her again,' Drax says, 'before she runs.'

Before Cavendish can reload, the bear sees them. Instead of running, she pauses a moment, as if thinking what to do, then drops off the ice edge and disappears into the sea. The cub follows her.

The men row forward, scanning the surface, waiting for the two bears to rise. Cavendish has his rifle at the ready, Drax is holding a looped rope to snickle the cub.

'She could have gone back under that ice,' Cavendish says. 'There are cracks and holes aplenty.'

Drax nods.

'It's the babe I want,' he says. 'That babe's worth twenty pounds easy. I know a fellow at the zoo.'

They circle slowly. The wind drops off and the air about them settles. Drax snorts, then spits. Cavendish resists the urge to whistle. Nothing moves, there is silence all around, then, only a yard off the boat's stern, the she-bear's head, like the pale prototype of an archaic undersea god, rises up out of the dark waters. There is a moment of wild commotion, scrambling, shouting, cursing, then Cavendish takes aim and shoots again. The bullet hums past the ear of one of the oarsmen and slaps into the bear's chest. The bear rears up shrieking. Her enormous clawed feet, broad and ragged as tree stumps, crash down on the whaleboat's gunwales, raking and shredding the planks in a frenzied bid for purchase. The boat pitches wildly downwards and seems set to capsize. Cavendish is thrown forwards, dropping his rifle, and one of the oarsmen is tossed overboard.

Drax pushes Cavendish aside and takes an eight-inch boat spade from the side rack. The bear, giving up on the boat, lunges for the thrashing oarsman. She clamps onto his elbow with her teeth and then, with one dismissive shake of her enormous neck, rips away most of his right arm. Drax, standing upright in the still rolling whaleboat, lifts up the boat spade and plunges its chisel edge hard down into the bear's back. He feels the moment of resistance and then the inevitable and irretrievable give as the bear's spine is split asunder by the milled steel edge. He pulls the spade out and brings it down again, and then again, stabbing deeper with each thrust. With the third blow, he pierces the bear's heart and a great purple gout of blood comes steaming to the surface and spreads like India ink across her ragged white coat. The air is filled with a foetid blast of butchery and excrement. Drax feels pleasure at this work, arousal, a craftsman's sense of pride. Death, he believes, is a kind of making, a kind of building up. What was one thing, he thinks, is become something else.

The mutilated oarsman, after some moments of scream-ing, has passed out from his pain and is beginning to sink. The bloody remnants of his lost arm still depend from the dead bear's tusks. Cavendish gets the boathook and drags him back on board. They cut off a length of whale-line and tourniquet his stump.

'That's what I call an almighty fuck-up,' Cavendish says.

'We still have the babe,' Drax says pointing. 'That's twenty pounds right there.'

The bear cub is swimming beside his mother's corpse mewing and nudging the body with his nose.

'A man's lost his fucking arm,' Cavendish says.

Drax takes his looped rope and, using the boathook, slips it over the bear cub's head and pulls it tight. They bore a hole in the dead she-bear's jaw, run a cord through the hole and lash the other end of the cord to the bollard. It is a slow, hard pull back to the ship, and before they get there the oarsman expires from his injuries.

'I've heard of such a thing,' Cavendish says. 'But never seen it happen ere now.'

'If you could shoot straight, he'd still be living,' Drax says.

'I put two solid bullets into her and she still had strength enough to take off a man's arm. What kind of bear is that, I ask you?'

'A bear is a bear,' Drax says.

Cavendish shakes his head and sniffs.

'A bear is a fucking bear,' he echoes, as though the thought had not occurred to him before.

When they get back to the *Volunteer*, they attach the dead

bear to a block-and-tackle and haul her up out of the water until she is suspended over the deck, dangling, shabby and lifeless, from the yardarm, drooling blood. Still down in the water, separated from his parent now, the cub becomes enraged, swimming hither and thither in a fierce, wild-eyed frenzy, snapping at the boathook and pulling back against the rope collar. Drax, on his feet in the whaleboat, calls for an empty blubber cask and, with the help of Cavendish, tugs and prods the bear cub into it. The others toss down a net and haul the cask, filled now with a screaming flailing bear cub, up onto the deck. Brownlee watches from the afterdeck as the cub tries, repeatedly, to escape out of the upright cask and Drax, armed with a stave, prods him down again.

'Lower the mother's body,' Brownlee calls out. 'That's the only way to quiet the beast.'

Flat out on the deck, a hillock of bloodied fur, the she-bear steams like the gargantuan centrepiece of some barely imaginable banquet. Brownlee kicks over the cask, and the cub scurries out, his claws scrabbling and scraping on the wooden deck. There is a moment of panicked swivelling and disorientation (men, laughing, scramble up the rigging to escape) but then he sees his mother's body and rushes to it. He nudges its flank with his nose and starts to helplessly lick the smeared and bloodied fur. Brownlee watches. The cub whimpers, sniffs, then settles himself in the lee of the mother's corpse, flank to flank.

'That cub's worth twenty pounds,' Drax says. 'I know a man at the zoo.'

Brownlee looks at him.

'The blacksmith will rivet you a grille so you can keep him in the cask,' he says. 'More likely than not, he will die before we get home, but if not, every penny he fetches goes to the dead man's people.'

Drax stares back at Brownlee for a moment as if readying himself to disagree, then nods and turns aside.

Later, after the dead oarsman has been stitched up in sailcloth and slid, with gruff and minimal ceremony, over the side, Cavendish skins the she-bear with a hatchet and a flensing knife. The cub, secured now in his cask, watches on, trembling, as Cavendish hacks, cuts and tugs away.

'Can a bear be eaten?' Sumner asks him.

Cavendish shakes his head.

'Bear meat is foul-tasting and the liver is downright poisonous. All that a bear is truly good for is the skin.'

'For ornament then?'

'Some rich man's drawing room. It would have been better for the price if Drax had been less eager with the boat spade, but I suspect the gash can be repaired.'

'And the cub will be sold to the zoological gardens if it lives?'

Cavendish nods.

'A full-grown bear is a sight of fearsome beauty. People will pay a ha'penny a time to see a full-grown bear and think it cheap at that price.'

Sumner crouches down and peers into the darkness of the cask.

'This one might die of heartbreak before we get him home,' he says.

Cavendish shrugs and pauses from his work. He looks back at Sumner and grins. His arms are dyed bright red up to the elbows and his waistcoat and trousers are stippled with gore.

'He will forget the dead one soon enough,' he says. 'Affection is a passing thing. A beast is no different from a person in that regard.'

9

They come to him with wounds and bruises, headaches, ulcers, haemorrhoids, stomach aches and swollen testicles. He gives them poultices and plasters, ointments and balms: Epsom salts, calamine, ipecac. If nothing else works, he bleeds or blisters them, he induces painful vomiting, explosive diarrhoea. They are grateful for these attentions, these signs of care, even when he is causing them discomfort or worse. They believe that he is an educated man and that he must, therefore, know what he is about. They have a kind of faith in him—foolish and primitive perhaps, but real.

To Sumner, the men who come to him are bodies only: legs, arms, torsos, heads. Their flesh forms the front and rear of his concern. Towards the rest of them—their moral characters, their souls—he remains solidly indifferent. It is not his task, he thinks, to educate or move them towards virtue, nor is it his task to judge, soothe or befriend them. He is a medical man, not a priest or a magistrate or a spouse. He will heal their lesions, remedy, where it is possible, their maladies and disease, but beyond that they have no call on him and he, reduced in spirits as he currently is, has no comforts available to give.

One evening, after supper has concluded, Sumner is visited in his cabin by one of the ship's boys. His name is Joseph Hannah. He is thirteen years old, slightly built with dark hair, a broad pale brow and gloomy, sunken eyes. Sumner has noticed him before and remembers his name. He looks, as the ship's boys do, grubby and disarranged, and he appears, as he stands in the doorway, to be suffering from an attack of shyness. He is twisting his cap in his hands and wincing every now and then, as if even the thought of addressing the surgeon is painful.

'Do you wish to speak to me, Joseph Hannah?' Sumner asks him. 'Are you feeling ill?'

The boy nods twice and blinks before responding.

'My stomach is bad,' he confesses.

Sumner, who is seated at the narrow fold-down shelf which serves him as a desk, gets to his feet and beckons the boy forward.

'When did this problem begin?' Sumner asks him.

'Yesterday night.'

'And can you describe the pain to me?'

Joseph frowns and looks perplexed.

'How does it feel?' Sumner asks.

'It hurts me,' he says. 'It hurts me a good deal.'

Sumner nods and scratches the dark nub of frostbitten tissue at the end of his nose.

'Climb onto the bunk,' he says. 'I will examine you there.'

Joseph doesn't move. He looks down at his feet and shudders slightly.

'The examination is a simple one,' Sumner explains. 'I just need to check for the source of the pain.'

'My stomach is bad,' Joseph says, looking up again. 'I need a dose of pepperine.'

Sumner snorts at the boy's presumption and shakes his head.

'I'll decide what it is you need or don't need,' he says. 'Now lie down on the bunk, if you please.'

Joseph reluctantly does as he is asked.

Sumner unbuttons the boy's jacket and shirt, and tugs up his flannel vest. The abdomen, he notes, is not distended and there is no sign of discoloration or swelling.

'Does this hurt?' Sumner asks. 'Or this?'

Joseph shakes his head.

'So where is the pain?' Sumner asks.

'Everywhere.'

Sumner sighs.

'If it is not here or here or here,' he says, prodding the boy's belly impatiently with his fingertips, 'then how can it be everywhere, Joseph?'

Joseph doesn't answer. Sumner sniffs suspiciously.

'Any vomiting?' he asks. 'Any diarrhoea?'

Joseph shakes his head.

There is a dank, faecal odour arising from the boy's scrawny midsection which suggests that he is lying. Sumner wonders if he is touched in the head or merely more stupid than average.

'Do you know what diarrhoea means?' he asks.

'The flux,' Joseph says.

'Remove your trousers, please.'

Joseph gets to his feet, unlaces and removes his boots, then unbuckles his belt and shrugs off his grey worsted trousers. The unpleasant odour increases in strength. Outside the cabin, Black shouts and Brownlee coughs enormously. The boy's knee-length drawers, Sumner immediately notes, are stained and stiffened at the breech with blots of blood and shit.

Piles, for God's sake, Sumner thinks. The boy clearly doesn't know the difference between his stomach and his arsehole.

'Take those off too,' he says, pointing, 'and be sure not to touch anything else with them as you do so.'

Joseph reluctantly pulls off his reeking drawers. His shanks are slight, almost muscleless, there is a faint black arc of hair around the otherwise pale purity of his cock and balls. Sumner instructs him to turn round and put his elbows on the bunk. He would normally be too young to develop piles, but Sumner assumes that the crude shipboard diet of salt junk and biscuits has done for him.

'I will give you some ointment,' he says, 'and a pill. You will feel better soon enough.'

Sumner parts the boy's arse cheeks and glances in for con-firmation. He stares for a few seconds, stands back, then looks again.

'What is this?' he says.

Joseph doesn't move or speak. He is shivering intermit-tently as if the cabin (which is warm) is bitterly cold. After a minute's thought, Sumner steps out into the gangway and calls up to the cook for a bowl of warm water and a rag. When they arrive, he washes between the boy's cheeks and applies a mixture of camphor and lard to his lesions. The sphincter is distorted and torn in places. There are signs of ulceration.

He dries the boy with a towel and gives him a pair of clean undergarments from his own cabinet. He washes his hands with what remains of the water.

'Put your things back on now, Joseph,' he says.

The boy dresses slowly, making sure as he does so not to catch the surgeon's eye. Sumner goes to his medicine cabinet, selects a bottle labelled No. 44 and shakes out a small blue pill.

'Swallow this now,' he says. 'Then come back tomorrow and I will give you another one.'

Joseph scowls at the taste, then swallows it with a gulp. Sumner looks at him carefully—his sunken cheeks, his narrow twiney neck, his hazy and faraway eyes.

'Who did this to you?' he asks.

'No one.'

'Who did this to you, Joseph?' he asks again.

'No one did it to me.'

Sumner nods twice, then scratches his cheekbone hard.

'You may go now,' he says. 'And I'll see you tomorrow for the other blue pill.'

After the boy leaves, Sumner goes back out into the empty mess cabin, opens the iron stove and pushes the stained underwear far back onto the banked and glowing coals. He watches it catch, then closes the stove and returns to his stateroom. He pours a dose of laudanum, but doesn't drink it. Instead, he takes down his copy of the *Iliad* from the shelf above the desk and tries to read. The ship jolts upwards; the timbers grate and whimper. He feels, despite himself, a tightening in his throat and a warm, liquid accumulation in his chest like the beginnings of a sob. He waits a minute longer, then closes the book and goes back out into the mess room. Cavendish is standing by the stove smoking a pipe.

'Where is Brownlee?' Sumner asks him.

Cavendish nods sideways towards the captain's cabin.

'Snoozing, most likely,' he says.

Sumner knocks anyway. After a pause, Brownlee calls for him to enter.

The captain is bent over the logbook, a pen in his hand. His waistcoat is unbuttoned and his grey hair is standing upright. He looks up at Sumner and beckons him inside. Sumner takes a seat and waits while Brownlee scratches out a final few words, then carefully blots his work.

'Little enough to report, I expect,' Sumner says.

Brownlee nods.

'When we reach the North Water, we'll sight more whales,'

he says. 'You can be sure of that. And we'll kill a few of 'em too, if I have anything to say about it.'

'The North Water is the place to be.'

'These days it is. Twenty years ago, the waters about here were full of whales too, but they've all moved north now—away from the harpoon. Who can blame them? The whale is a sagacious creature. They know they are safest where there is most ice, and where it is most perilous for us to follow them. Steam is the future, of course. With a powerful enough steam ship, we could hunt them to the ends of the earth.'

Sumner nods. He has heard Brownlee's theories on whaling already. The captain believes that the further north you sail, the more whales there will be, and he has come to the logical conclusion based on this fact that at the top of the world there must exist a great ice-free ocean, a place not yet penetrated by man where the right whales swim unhindered in numberless multitudes. The captain, Sumner strongly suspects, is something of an optimist.

'Joseph Hannah came to see me today, complaining of a foul stomach.'

'Joseph Hannah, the cabin boy?'

Sumner nods.

'When I examined him, I discovered he had been sodomised.'

Brownlee stiffens briefly at this intelligence, then rubs his nose and frowns.

'He told you this himself?'

'It was evident from the examination.'

'You're sure?'

'The damage was extensive, and there are signs of venereal disease.'

'And who, pray, is responsible for this abomination?'

'The boy will not say. He is frightened, I imagine. He may also be a little simple-minded.'

'Oh, he is stupid enough,' Brownlee says sourly. 'That's for sure. I know his father and his uncle both, and they are fucking imbeciles also.'

Brownlee's frown deepens and he purses his lips.

'And you are sure that this happened on board this ship? That the injuries are recent?'

'Without a doubt. The lesions are quite fresh.'

'The boy is a great fool then,' Brownlee says. 'Why did he not cry out or complain if this was being done to him against his will?'

'Perhaps you could ask him yourself?' Sumner suggests. 'He won't speak to me, but if you order him to name the culprit, it's possible he'll feel obliged to do so.'

Brownlee nods curtly, then opens the cabin door and calls to Cavendish, who is still standing by the stove smoking, to have the boy brought aft from the forecastle.

'What's the little shit done now?' Cavendish asks.

'Just bring him to me,' Brownlee says.

They drink a glass of brandy while they wait. When the boy arrives, he looks pale with terror, and Cavendish is grinning.

'You have nothing to be frightened about, Joseph,' Sumner says. 'The captain wants to ask you a few questions, that's all.'

Brownlee and Sumner are seated next to each other; Joseph Hannah is standing nervously on the other side of the round centre table, and Cavendish is standing behind him.

'Should I stay or leave, Captain?' Cavendish asks.

Brownlee thinks for a moment, then gestures for him to sit.

'You know the habits and personalities of the crewmen better than I do,' he says. 'Your presence may be useful.'

'I certainly know the personality of this little savage,' Cavendish says, cheerfully lowering himself onto the upholstered bench.

'Joseph,' Brownlee says, leaning forward and attempting so far as possible to soften his habitually vigorous tone, 'Mr Sumner, the surgeon, tells me you have sustained an injury. Is that true?'

For a long moment, it seems as if Joseph has either not heard or not understood the question, but then, just as Brownlee is about to repeat it, he nods.

'What injury is this?' Cavendish asks sceptically. 'I have not heard of any injury.'

'Mr Sumner examined Joseph earlier this evening,' Brownlee explains, 'and found evidence, clear evidence, that he has been ill-used by another member of the crew.'

'Ill-used?' Cavendish asks.

'Sodomised,' Brownlee says.

Cavendish raises his eyebrows, but seems otherwise unalarmed. Joseph Hannah's expression does not change at all. His already sunken eyes seem to be receding into his skull, and his breath is coming out in brief but audible pants.

'How did this occur, Joseph?' Brownlee asks him. 'Who is responsible?'

Joseph's bottom lip lolls slick and rubicund. Its sensual obviousness contrasts disconcertingly with the funereal grey of his cheeks and jaw, and the dark, helpless recession of his eyes. He does not reply.

'Who is responsible?' Brownlee asks him again.

'It was an accident,' Joseph whispers in response.

Cavendish smiles at this.

'It is awful dark in that forecastle, Mr Brownlee,' he says. 'Is it not possible the boy merely slipped one night and landed on his arse in an unfortunate fashion?'

Brownlee looks across at Sumner.

'That is meant as a kind of joke, I assume,' the surgeon says.

Cavendish shrugs.

'The place is cramped and cluttered. There is barely an inch of space to move around in. It would be easy enough to trip.'

'It was not an accident,' Sumner insists. 'The idea is ridiculous. Such injuries as I saw could occur in one way only.'

'Did you fall, Joseph,' Brownlee asks, 'or did someone deliberately injure you?'

'I fell,' Joseph says.

'It was not an accident,' Sumner says again. 'That is entirely impossible.'

'Strange, then, that the boy thinks it was,' Cavendish points out.

'Because he's scared.'

Brownlee pushes himself back from the table, gazes at the other two men for a moment and then at the boy.

'Who are you scared of, Joseph?' he asks.

Sumner is surprised by the stupidity of the question.

'The boy is scared of everyone,' he says. 'How would he not be?'

Brownlee sighs at this, shakes his head, and looks down at the rectangle of polished walnut framed by his outstretched hands.

'I am a patient sort of fellow,' he says. 'But my patience surely has its limits. If you have been mistreated, Joseph, then the man who has mistreated you will be punished for it. But you must tell me the whole truth now. Do you understand?'

Joseph nods.

'Who did this to you?'

'No one.'

'We can protect you,' Sumner says quickly. 'If you do not tell us who is responsible, it may happen again.'

Joseph's chin is touching his breast, and he is staring fervently down at the floor.

'Do you have anything to say to me, Joseph?' Brownlee asks. 'I will not ask you again.'

Joseph shakes his head.

'It is being in the captain's cabin which has made him lose his tongue,' Cavendish says. 'That's all. When I found him in the forecastle, he was laughing and making merry with his friends. Any injury he may have suffered, if he has suffered any injury at all, has had no great effect on his character, I can tell you that.'

'This boy has been grievously assaulted,' Sumner says, 'and the man responsible is aboard this ship.'

'If the boy will not identify his attacker and if he insists, indeed, that he has not been attacked at all, but only suffered some kind of accident, then nothing further can be done,' Brownlee says.

'We can seek witnesses.'

Cavendish snorts at this.

'We are on a whaling ship,' he says.

'You may go now, Joseph,' Brownlee tells him. 'If I wish to speak to you again, I will send for you.'

The boy leaves the cabin. Cavendish yawns, stretches and then gets to his feet and follows after.

'I will instruct the men to keep their quarters tidier in future,' he says, looking back facetiously at Sumner, 'to avoid any more such accidents.'

'We will move the lad out of the forecastle,' Brownlee assures Sumner when Cavendish is gone. 'He can bed down in steerage for a while. It's a displeasing business, but if he refuses to point the finger, then the matter must be dropped now.'

'What if Cavendish himself is the culprit?' Sumner says. 'That would explain the boy's silence.'

'Cavendish has a good many faults,' Brownlee says, 'but he is certainly not a sodomite.'

'He seemed amused by the situation.'

'He is a prick and a brute, but so are half the men on this

bark. If you are seeking persons of gentleness and refinement, Sumner, the Greenland whaling trade is not the place to look for them.'

'I will speak to the other cabin boys,' Sumner suggests. 'I will find out what they know about Cavendish and Joseph Hannah and then I will come back to you with my findings.'

'No, you will not,' Brownlee answers firmly. 'Unless the boy changes his tune, the matter will be dropped now. We are here to kill whales, not root out sin.'

'A crime has been committed.'

Brownlee shakes his head. He is becoming irritated by the surgeon's unwarranted persistence.

'One boy has a sore arse. That is all. It is unfortunate, I agree, but he will recover soon enough.'

'His injuries were more severe than that. The rectum was distended, there were signs . . .'

Brownlee stands up, making no effort now to hide his impatience.

'Whatever particular injuries he may have, it is your job, as surgeon, to treat them, Mr Sumner,' he says. 'And I trust you have the skills and necessaries to do so successfully.'

Sumner looks back at the captain—his heavy brow and fierce grey eyes, his crumpled nose and stubbled, leaden jowls—and decides, after no more than a moment's hesitation, to accede. The boy will live after all. He is right about that.

'If I lack for anything, I will let you know,' he says.

Back in the cabin, he swallows the laudanum and lies back down on his bunk. He is weary from the effort of arguing and soured by his sense of failure. Why would the boy not help himself? What power could the culprit have over him? The questions grab and trouble Sumner, but then, after a minute or two, the opium begins to take effect, and he feels himself sliding back into a soft, warm, familiar state of carelessness. What does it matter, he thinks, if he is surrounded by savages, by moral baboons? The world will continue on as it wants to anyway, as it always has, with or without his approval. The anger and disgust he felt for Cavendish minutes before are like smudges on the far horizon now—ideas, suggestions only, nothing more important or noticeable than that. I will get to everything in its own good time, he thinks vaguely, there's no need to rush or hurry.

Sometime later, there is a knock on his cabin door. It is Drax the harpooner complaining of a gash on his right hand. Sumner, blinking, invites him to come in. Drax, squat and broad-shouldered, his beard dense and reddish, seems to fill the small space almost completely. Sumner, feeling still a little light-headed and imprecise from the laudanum, examines his wound, then wipes it clean with a piece of lint and applies a dressing.

'It's not serious,' Sumner assures him. 'Keep that dressing on for a day or so. It will heal quickly after that.'

'Oh, I've had worse,' Drax says. 'Much worse than this.'

Drax's barnyard scent, dense and almost edible, dominates the room. He is like a beast at rest in its stall, Sumner thinks. A force of nature temporarily contained and pacified.

'I hear one of the cabin boys was hurt.'

Sumner has finished rolling up the remaining bandage and

is returning the scissors and the lint to the medicine chest. The edges of his vision are faintly blurred and his lips and cheeks feel chill and numb.

'Who told you that?'

'Cavendish did. He said you had your suspicions.'

'They're more than that.'

Drax looks down at his strapped hand, then brings it up to his nose to sniff.

'Joseph Hannah is a well-known liar. You shouldn't believe what he tells you.'

'He hasn't told me anything yet. He won't speak to me. That's the problem. He's too scared.'

'He's feeble-minded, that one.'

'How well do you know the boy?'

'I know his father Frederick Hannah,' Drax says, 'and I know his brother Henry also.'

'Captain Brownlee has decided the matter is closed anyway. Unless the boy changes his mind, nothing more will be done.'

'So that's the end of it?'

'Probably.'

Drax peers at him carefully.

'Why did you choose to become a surgeon, Mr Sumner?' he asks. 'An Irish fellow like yourself. I'm curious.'

'Because I wished to advance. To rise from my humble origins.'

'You wished to advance, but now here you are on a Yorkshire whaler fretting over cabin boys. I wonder what has happened to all those grand ambitions?'

Sumner closes the medicine chest and locks it. He puts the key in his pocket, and glances at himself quickly in the wall mirror. He looks a good deal older than his twenty-seven years. His brow is scored, and his eyes are rimmed and baggy.

'I have simplified them, Mr Drax,' he says.

Drax grunts with amusement. His lips stretch out into a pantomime version of a grin.

'I do believe I've done the same,' he says. 'I do believe I have.'

10

They cross into the North Water by the last week of June and near dawn the following day, Black strikes their first whale. Sumner, woken from his slumbers by the sounds of shouting and boot heels pounding the deck, follows the progress of the hunt from high up in the crow's nest. He sees the first iron go in, and the wounded whale descend. Twenty minutes later, he sees it rise again, closer to ship but nearly a mile from where it first went down. Black's harpoon, he can see through the spyglass, is still dangling from its broad flank and blood is sluicing brightly from its leadish skin.

Otto's boat is closest to it now. The oarsmen ship their oars and the steersman sculls them steadily forward. Otto crouches in the bows with the harpoon's wooden shaft gripped tightly in his fists. With a giant horse-like snort, audible from Sumner's perch in the crow's nest, the whale exhales a V-shaped flume of greyish vapour. The boat and crew are temporarily obscured, but when they reappear, Otto is up on his feet and the harpoon is poised above his head—its barb pointing downwards and the shaft forming a black hypotenuse against the sullen sky. The whale's back looks from Sumner's eyrie like a sunken island, a grainy volcanic hump of rock peeping from the waves. Otto hurls the iron with all his strength, it sinks in deep, up to the foreganger, and the whale instantly convulses. Its body bends and spasms, the eight-foot flukes of its enormous tail break from the water then crash back down. Otto's boat is tossed wildly about and the oarsmen are thrown from their seats. The whale descends again but only for a minute. When it rises, the other boats are gathered round ready: Cavendish is there, Black, Drax. Two more harpoons are sunk deep into the whale's black flank, and then they begin with the lances. The whale is still alive, but Sumner can see that it is damaged now beyond repair. The four harpooners pierce and probe. The whale, still hopelessly resisting, blows out a plume of hot vapour mixed with blood and mucus. All around it, the smashed and blood-stained waters boil and foam.

Drax, far below in the hectic midst of the killing, bears down hard on the butt of his lance and whispers out a string of gross endearments.

'Give me one last groan,' he says. 'That's it, my darling. One last shudder to help me find the true place. That's it, my sweetheart. One more inch and then we're done.'

He leans in harder, presses, seeking out the vital organs.

The lance slides in another foot. A moment later, with a final roar, the whale shoots out a plume of pure heart's blood high into the air and then tilts over lifeless onto its side with its great fin raised like a flag of surrender. The men, empurpled, reeking, drenched in the fish's steaming, expectorated gore, stand up in their flimsy boats and cheer their triumph. Brownlee on the quarterdeck wafts his billycock hat in circles above his head. The men on the deck roar and caper. Sumner, watching it all from above, feels a brief thrill of victory also, a sense of sudden, shared advantage, of obstacles overcome and progress made.

They bore two holes in the tail and secure the dead whale to the bow of Cavendish's boat. They lash the fins together, retrieve and coil the whale-lines, and then begin to tow the corpse back to the ship. As they row, they sing. Sumner, descended to the deck, hears their voices coming across the water, tuneful, gruff, carried by the cool damp wind. 'Randy Dandy O', 'Leave Her, Johnny'. Three dozen men in unison. He feels again, and almost against his will this time, that he is part of something larger and more powerful than himself, a joint endeavour. Turning away, he notices Joseph Hannah standing by the forehatch talking happily with the other cabin boys. They are re-enacting the recent kill, they are throwing imaginary harpoons, plying imaginary lances. One is Drax, one is Otto, one is Cavendish.

'How are you, Joseph?' he asks him.

The boy looks back at him blankly, as if they have not met before.

'I'm well, sir,' he answers. 'Thankee.'

'You must come to my cabin again tonight for your pill,' he reminds him.

The boy nods glumly.

What has the boy told his friends about his injuries? Sumner wonders. Has he made up some story or do they know the truth? It strikes him that he should question the other boys also. He should examine them too. What if they have suffered in the same way? What if the secret is not Joseph's alone but is something they share between them?

'You two,' he says, pointing to the other boys. 'After supper you come to my cabin with Joseph. I want to ask you some questions.'

'I am on the watch, sir,' one of them says.

'Then tell the watch commander that the surgeon, Mr Sumner, has asked to speak to you. He will understand.'

The boy nods. All three of them, he can see, wish he would now leave them alone. The game is still vivid in their minds, and his is the voice of dullness and authority.

'Go back to your pleasures now,' he tells them. 'I will see the three of you after supper.'

The whale's right fin is lashed onto the larboard gunwale with its head facing sternwards. Its dead eye, not much larger than a cow's, peers blindly upwards at the shuffling clouds. Strong lines are secured to the nose-end and rump, and its belly is heaved a foot or so out of the water by means of a block attached to the mainmast and a rope hooked onto the whale's neck area and brought to tension through the windlass. Brownlee, after measuring the corpse's length with a knotted line, estimates it will yield up ten tons of oil and half a ton or more of whalebone—a value of close to nine hundred pounds at market, if prices hold firm.

'We may yet be rich, Mr Sumner,' he says, with a wink.

After resting and taking a drink, Otto and Black strap iron crampons to their sea boots for grip and climb down onto the whale's belly. They carve out strips of blubber with long-handled knives and chisel off the baleen and the jaws. They cut off the tail and the fins, and then remove the nose and rump tackles, and allow the dilapidated purple carcass that remains to sink under its own weight or be eaten by sharks. The flensing takes four hours in all and is accompanied throughout by the stench of grease and blood, and the endless cawing of fulmars and other carrion birds. When it is over, when the blocks of blubber are stowed in the flens-gut, the deck is scoured a dull white, and the knives and spades are rinsed clean and put away, Brownlee orders an extra ration of rum for each sailor. There are cheers from the forecastle at the news and, only a little later, the sound of a Scottish fiddle and the thump and cry of men dancing jigs.

Neither Joseph Hannah nor his friends appear, as they were bidden, at Sumner's cabin after supper. Sumner wonders whether to search them out in the forecastle, but then decides against it. There is nothing that can't wait until the morning and, in truth, Joseph's simpleton wretchedness is beginning to gall him. The boy is a hopeless case, he thinks: feeble-minded, a congenital liar according to Drax, prone no doubt to hereditary disease (both mental and corporeal) of every kind. Evidence suggests he is the victim of a crime, but he will not name his abuser, will not even admit that he has been abused—perhaps he has forgotten who it was, perhaps it was too dark to see or perhaps he does not think of it as a crime at all, but as something else instead? Sumner tries to imagine inhabiting the mind of a boy like that, tries to grasp what it would feel like to see the world through Joseph Hannah's sunken, shifting squirrel eyes, but the effort seems both absurd and faintly terrifying—like a nightmare of being transformed into a cloud or a tree. He shudders briefly at the thought of such Ovidian transformations, then, with relief, reopens the *Iliad* and reaches into his coat pocket for the small brass key that commands the medicine chest.

The next day, two more whales are killed and flensed. Sumner, since he is otherwise unoccupied, is given a pick-haak and a long leather apron. Once the strips of blubber have been hauled on board ship and cut up into foot-square blocks, it is the surgeon's newly appointed task to take the blocks from the foredeck to the hold and pitch them down to the men working below, who will store them in the flens-gut until the time comes for making off. It is dirty and exhausting work. Each block of blubber weighs twenty pounds or more, and the ship's deck is soon slick with blood and grease. He slips over several times, almost topples into the hold on one occasion but is saved by Otto, and ends the day bruised and aching, and yet with a sense of rare satisfaction: the crude, physical pleasure of a task accomplished, of the body tested and proved. He sleeps for once without the aid of laudanum and in the morning, despite the ungodly stiffness in his shoulders, neck and arms, breakfasts well on barley porridge and salt fish.

'We will make a whaleman of you yet, Mr Sumner,' Cavendish jokes, as they sit in the mess cabin smoking their pipes and warming their feet by the stove. 'Some surgeons would be too dainty for the pick-haak, but you took to it nicely, I'd say.'

'Flensing is a good deal like cutting turf,' Sumner says, 'and I did plenty of that when I was a boy.'

'That's it then,' Cavendish says. 'It's in your blood.'

'The whaling's in my blood, you think?'

'The working,' Cavendish says, with a smile. 'The Irishman is a labourer at heart; that's his true calling.'

Sumner spits into the stove, and listens to it fizzle. He knows enough of Cavendish by now not to take his taunts to heart, and his mood is too light this morning to be seriously baited.

'And what is the Englishman's true calling, I wonder, Mr Cavendish?' he answers. 'To grow fat off the labours of others, perhaps?'

'There are them that are born to toil, and them that are born to grow rich,' Cavendish says.

'I see. And which one are you?'

The mate leans back complacently in his chair and flares his pinkish lower lip.

'Oh, I'd say my time is coming, Mr Sumner,' he says. 'I'd say it's coming pretty soon.'

It is a quiet morning. No more whales are sighted and the hours before noon are spent cleaning the decks, reeving lines and restocking the whaleboats. Sumner, who has not seen or spoken to Joseph Hannah since the time he saw him horsing with his friends near the forehatch, decides to seek the boy out. He notices one of the other cabin boys on deck and asks for Joseph's whereabouts.

'We were told he was to bed down in the tween decks from now on,' the boy says. 'I haven't seen him since yesterday.'

Sumner ventures into the fore-tween decks, where he finds a grubby wool blanket nestled between a sail chest and a pile of bundled staves but no other sign of the boy. He climbs back up and looks about. After checking that Joseph is not hidden from sight behind the spare boats, the windlass or the deck house, he peers down into the forecastle. Some of the men are on their bunks asleep, others are seated on sea chests smoking, reading or carving wood.

'I am looking for Joseph Hannah,' he calls. 'Is the boy down there?'

The seated men turn to look at him. They shake their heads.

'We hant seen him,' one answers. 'We thought he were staying aft with you, Mr Sumner.'

'With me?'

'In officers' quarters. On account of his illness.'

'And who told you that?'

The man shrugs.

'That's all what I heard,' he says.

Sumner, touched now with the beginnings of impatience, returns to his cabin and retrieves a candle with the intention of exploring the holds (although why the boy would be concealing himself anywhere in the holds is beyond him). He sees

Black emerging from the captain's cabin carrying the brass sextant.

'I'm looking for Joseph Hannah,' Sumner says to him. 'Have you seen the boy about?'

'The one with the sore arse?' Black says. 'No, I can't say I have.'

Sumner shakes his head and sighs.

'The *Volunteer* is not such a large vessel. I'm surprised a boy can so easily go missing.'

'There are a thousand nooks and crannies on a ship like this one,' Black says. 'He's probably off pulling his pizzle somewhere. Why do you need him?'

Sumner hesitates, aware that his concern with the health of Hannah's fundament has already become something of a joke among the officers.

'I have a task for him,' Sumner says.

Black nods.

'Well, he'll emerge by and by, you can be sure of that. The boy is an awful malingerer, but he'll not miss his rations when they're served.'

'Perhaps you're right,' Sumner says, looking at the candle for a moment, then dropping it into his jacket pocket. 'Why should I trouble to search for someone who doesn't want to be found?'

'There are other cabin boys,' Black agrees. 'Ask one of those.'

Later that afternoon, since there are still no signs of whales and the weather is calm enough, Brownlee orders the men to commence the making off. They reduce the sails and begin to break out the main hold. Eight or ten casks, previously filled with water for ballast, are brought up onto the deck, thereby exposing the lowest stratum of casks, the ground tier, which will be first to be filled with the minced-up blubber. The men on deck make ready the equipment (speck trough, lull, chopping blocks and knives) needed to separate blubber from muscle and skin, and to cut it into pieces small enough to be squeezed through the bunghole of a cask. Sumner keeps an eye out for Joseph Hannah, assuming he will appear soon enough, roused by all this commotion from whatever hiding place he has found.

'Where's that little shit Hannah disappeared to?' Cavendish shouts out. 'I need some knives taken down for sharpening.'

'He's missing,' Sumner says. 'I was looking about for him this morning.'

'He's a shiftless little cunt, that one,' Cavendish says. 'I'll show him the true meaning of a sore arse when I discover him.'

The casks on deck are emptied of water one by one, by means of an iron hand pump. Otto takes charge of this operation, inserting the pump's end into the bunghole, draining off each cask and then mopping it dry. The ballast water, which sloshes across the deck and out through the fore-channels, gives off a noxious, sulphurated reek caused by long contact with the rotting residues of blubber left in the casks from previous voyages. Other men climb the rigging to escape this eye-watering miasma or tie scarves across their noses as they work, but Otto, putty-faced, thick-shouldered, slow and deliberate in all his actions, seems immune to the repellent stench. After emptying four casks, he discovers the fifth one has been damaged. The head has been partly stove in and most of the water appears to have leaked out already. He calls over the cooper and asks if it can be repaired. The cooper leans down, pulls out a piece of the broken cask head and examines it.

'It aint rotted away,' he says (he has his hand against his nostrils as he speaks). 'No reason for this to crack on its own.'

'But it's cracked all right,' Otto says.

The cooper nods.

'Best break it up and start again,' he says.

He tosses the splintered wood aside, then peers indifferently and without expectation back into the half-empty barrel. He sees curled up inside it, part submerged in the remnants of the ballast water, like some monstrous fungal knottage bred and nurtured in the fetid petri of the hold, the torn, dead and naked body of Joseph Hannah, cabin boy.

11

They carry Hannah's body down to the mess cabin and lay it out on the table for Sumner to examine. The room is crowded but silent. Sumner, who can feel the heat of the other men's breathing and sense the dour intensity of their concentration, wonders what they expect him to do exactly. Bring the boy back to life? The fact that he is a surgeon makes no difference any more. He is as helpless and useless as they are. Trembling, he takes hold of Joseph Hannah's hairless chin and moves it gently upwards to better note the dark chain of bruises around his neck.

'Strangled,' Brownlee says. 'It's a fucking outrage.'

There is a murmur of assent from the other men in the room. Sumner, feeling a degree of reluctance and shame, turns the boy over onto his side and pulls apart his pale buttocks. Some of the spectators lean in to look.

'The same or worse?' Brownlee asks.

'Worse.'

'Fuck.'

Sumner glances up at Cavendish, who has looked away and is whispering something to Drax. He turns the boy over again and presses down on his ribs to count the fractures. He opens the child's mouth, and notes that two of his teeth are missing.

'When did this happen?' Brownlee barks. 'And how in God's name is it possible that no one noticed?'

'I last saw the boy the day before yesterday,' Sumner says. 'Just before the first flensing.'

There is a garbled rush of other voices as the rest of the men in the room recall their last encounters with the dead boy. Brownlee shouts them down.

'Not all together,' he says. 'By Christ.'

The captain is pale and furious; his agitation is profound. He has never even heard of a murder occurring on a whaleship before—there are fights between crewmen, of course, plenty of those, stabbings even, on some rare occasions, but not an outright murder and not of a *child*. It is an appalling thing, he thinks, repellent, sickening. And that it should happen now, on his final voyage, as if the *Percival* was not enough to darken his reputation for ever. He looks around at the twenty or thirty crewmen packed into the mess cabin—grubby and bearded all of them, their faces burned and blackened by the Arctic sun, their blunt hands clasped in front of them as though at prayer or pushed deep into pockets. This is Jacob Baxter's doing, he tells himself, that unrighteous bastard, he chose this idiot crew, he set this whole unnatural scheme in motion, he is responsible for the calamitous consequences, not I.

'Whoever is guilty will be taken back to England in chains and hanged,' Brownlee says, scanning the vacant twitching faces. 'I promise you that.'

'Hanging's too good for a fucker such as that,' one man says. 'He should have his balls cut off first. He should have a red hot poker rammed up his arse.'

'He should be whipped,' someone else suggests, 'whipped down to the fucking bone.'

'Whoever he is, whatever he is, he will be punished according to the extent of the law,' Brownlee says. 'Where is the sailmaker?'

The sailmaker, an aged, lugubrious man with vague blue eyes, steps forward, his greasy beaver cap clutched in his hands.

'Stitch the boy into his shroud now,' Brownlee tells him. 'We'll bury him betimes.' The sailmaker nods and sniffs. 'And the rest of you men get back to your duties.'

'Will we continue with the making off now, Captain?' Cavendish asks.

'Indeed we will. This atrocity is no excuse for idleness.'

The men nod meekly. One of them, a boat-steerer named Roberts, raises his hand to speak.

'I saw the boy down in the forecastle after the first whale was flensed,' he says. 'He was listening to the fiddler and watching the men dance their jigs.'

'That's true,' another man says. 'I saw him there too.'

127

'Did anyone see Joseph Hannah later?' Brownlee asks. 'Did anyone see him yesterday? Speak up.'

'He was sleeping in the tween decks,' someone says. 'That's what we all believed.'

'Someone here knows what happened to him,' Brownlee says. 'The ship is not so large that a boy can be killed without making some noise or leaving some trace.'

No one answers. Brownlee shakes his head.

'I will find the man who did this and see the bastard hanged,' he says. 'That is a certainty. That is something you may all rely on.'

He turns to the surgeon.

'I would speak to you in my cabin now, Sumner.'

Once inside the cabin, the captain seats himself, removes his hat and commences rubbing his face with the heels of his hands. When he has finished rubbing, his face is bright red and both his eyes are bloodshot and watery.

'Whether he acted out of pure evil or from a fear of being exposed for his perversions, I don't know,' Brownlee says. 'But whosoever sodomised the boy killed him also. That is plain enough.'

'I agree.'

'And do you suspect Cavendish still?'

Sumner hesitates, then shakes his head. He knows the first mate is an oaf, but he is less sure that he could be a murderer.

'It might be anyone,' he admits. 'If Hannah was sleeping in the tween decks the night before last, then almost any man on the ship could have gone in there, strangled him and lowered the body down into the hold without too much risk of being noticed.'

Brownlee scowls.

'I moved him from the forecastle to keep him away from difficulty, but I succeeded in abetting his murder.'

'He was a wretched and ill-starred child, all-in-all,' Sumner says.

'Fuck, yes.'

Brownlee nods and pours them both a glass of brandy. Sumner feels humiliated, weakened, by this new outrage, as if the boy's cruel death is a part of his own profound and lengthier diminishment. His right hand shakes as he drinks the brandy. Outside the room, the sailmaker whistles 'The Bonnie Boat' as he sews the dead boy into his canvas coffin.

'There are thirty-eight men and boys left aboard this ship,' Brownlee says. 'If we take away the two of us and the two remaining cabin boys, that leaves thirty-four. After the making off is finished, I will speak to all of them singly if necessary, I will find out what they know, what they have seen and heard, and what they suspect. A man does not develop such foul proclivities overnight. There will have been signs and rumours, and the forecastle is a hive of gossip.'

'The man, whoever he is, is likely insane,' Sumner says. 'There's no other explanation. He must be afflicted with some disease or corruption of the brain.'

Brownlee grinds his jaw one way then the other, and pours himself another brandy before replying. When he speaks, his voice is low and taut.

'What kind of a crew has that Jew bastard Baxter afflicted me with?' he says. 'Incompetents and savages. The filth and shite of the dockyards. I am a whaling man, but this is not whaling, Mr Sumner. This is not whaling, I can assure you of that.'

The making off continues for the rest of the day. When it is done and the blubber casks are safely stowed away, they bury Joseph Hannah at sea. Brownlee grumbles some suitable verses from the Bible over the body, Black leads the men in a rough-hewn hymn, and the canvas shroud, weighted with shot, is tossed over the stern and swallowed by the flintish swell.

Sumner has no appetite for dinner. Instead of eating with the others, he goes up to walk on the deck, smoke a pipe and take some air. The bear cub is growling and whimpering in his wooden cage, chewing on his paw and scratching himself constantly. His coat is dull and matted now, he smells of excrement and fish oil, and looks as lank and scrawny as a greyhound. Sumner gets a handful of ship's biscuit from the galley, balances the pieces on the blade of a flensing knife and tips them through the metal grate. They are gobbled up instantly. The bear cub growls, licks his muzzle and glares back at him. Sumner puts a cup of water down on the deck a foot or so in front of the cask and then prods it forward with the toe of his boot until it is close enough for the bear cub's long pink tongue to reach. He stands and watches him drink. Otto, who is commander of the watch, walks over and joins him.

'Why go to the trouble of catching and caging a bear if you plan only to let it starve?' Sumner asks him.

'If the bear's sold, all the money goes to the dead man's widow,' Otto says. 'But the dead man's widow isn't here to feed him, and Drax and Cavendish feel under no obligation. We could set him free, of course, but the mother's dead and he's too young to survive on his own.'

Sumner nods, picks up the empty water cup, refills it, puts it back down and prods it forward with his toe. The bear drinks for a while longer, then stops drinking and retreats into the rear of the cask.

'What's your opinion of the recent events?' Sumner asks. 'What would your Master Swedenborg say of this atrocity?'

Otto looks solemn for a moment. He strokes his broad black beard and nods several times before answering.

'He would tell us that great evil is the absence of good and that sin is a kind of forgetfulness. We drift away from the Lord because the Lord allows us to do so. That is our freedom but also our punishment.'

'And do you believe him?'

'What else should I believe?'

Sumner shrugs.

'That sin is remembering,' he offers. 'That good is the absence of evil.'

'Some men believe that, of course, but if it were true, then the world would be chaos and the world is not chaos. Look around, Sumner. The confusion and stupidity are ours. We misunderstand ourselves, we are very vain and very stupid. We build a great bonfire to warm ourselves and then complain that the flames are too hot and fierce, that we are blinded by the smoke.'

'Why kill a child though?' Sumner asks. 'What sense can be made of that?'

'The most important questions are the ones we can't hope to answer with words. Words are like toys: they amuse and educate us for a time, but when we come to manhood, we should give them up.'

Sumner shakes his head.

'The words are all we have,' he says. 'If we give them up, we are no better than the beasts.'

Otto smiles at Sumner's wrong-headedness.

'Then you must find out the explanations on your own,' he says. 'If that's what you truly think.'

Sumner bends down and looks at the orphaned bear. He is crouched at the back of the cask panting and licking at a puddle of his own urine.

'I would rather *not* think,' he says. 'It would be pleasanter and easier, I'm sure. But it seems I cannot help myself.'

Shortly after the burial, Cavendish requests to speak to Brownlee in his cabin.

'I've been asking questions,' he says. 'I've been squeezing and grinding the bastards, and they've given up a name.'

'What name?'

'McKendrick.'

'Samuel McKendrick, the carpenter?'

'The same. They say he has been seen ashore in public houses canoodling with the Molly men. And this last whaling season when he shipped aboard the *John o' Gaunt*, it is well known he was sharing his berth with a boat-steerer, man name of Nesbet.'

'And this was in plain sight?'

'It's dark in the forecastle, as you know, Mr Brownlee, but let's say noises were heard at night. Noises of a certain unmistakable kind, I mean.'

'Bring Samuel McKendrick to me,' Brownlee says. 'And find Sumner also. I want the surgeon to hear whatever it is he has to say.'

McKendrick is a slight fellow, pale of skin and unrobust. His beard is wispy and yellowish; he has a slender nose, a narrow almost lipless mouth and large ears tinged red by the cold.

'How well did you know Joseph Hannah?' Brownlee asks him.

'I doesn't know him hardly at all.'

'You must have seen him in the forecastle though.'

'I seen him, yes, but I doesn't know him. He's just a cabin boy.'

'And are you not fond of the cabin boys?'

'Not especially.'

'Are you married, McKendrick? Do you have a wife waiting for you at home?'

'No, sir, I int and I don't.'

'But you have a sweetheart there, I suppose?'

McKendrick shakes his head.

'Perhaps you don't like women much, is that it?'

'No, it's not that, sir,' McKendrick says. 'It's more that I have not found a woman that's quite suitable for me as yet.'

Cavendish snorts at this. Brownlee turns, glares at him briefly, then continues his questioning.

'I have heard you prefer the company of men. That is what I've been told. Is that true?'

McKendrick's expression doesn't change. He seems neither scared nor agitated nor especially surprised by this accusation of unnaturalness.

'It int true, sir, no,' he says. 'I am as red-blooded as the next man over.'

'Joseph Hannah was sodomised before he was killed. I suppose you know that already.'

'That is what all the fellows in the forecastle are saying, sir, yes.'

'Did you kill him, McKendrick?'

McKendrick frowns as though this question makes no sense.

'*Did* you?'

'No, that int me, sir,' he says placidly. 'I int the one you seek.'

'He is a plausible fucking liar,' Cavendish says. 'But I have half a dozen men who will testify to his well-known reputation as a buggerer of young boys.'

Brownlee looks at the carpenter who seems, for the first time since the questioning began, less than comfortable.

'It will not go well for you if you are found to be lying, McKendrick,' he says. 'I warn you now. I will be severe.'

McKendrick nods once, then scans the cabin ceiling before replying. His eyes are grey and fidgety, and there is something like a smile playing about his narrow lips.

'It hant ever been boys,' he says. 'The boys int to my taste.'

Cavendish snorts derisively.

'You really expect us to believe you are so very particular about whose arse you lay siege to. From what I hear, after a pint or two of whisky, you would fuck your own granddad.'

'It int a matter of laying siege to anything,' McKendrick says.

'You are a fucking disgrace,' Brownlee says, jabbing his forefinger in McKendrick's face. 'And whether you are a murderer or not, I should have you whipped.'

'I int a murderer.'

'You are a proven liar though,' Brownlee says. 'We have established that beyond a doubt already. And if you lie about one thing, why will you not lie about anything else?'

'I int a bloody murderer,' McKendrick says again.

'If you allow me to examine him briefly, Mr Brownlee,' Sumner says, 'there may be indications one way or the other.'

Brownlee looks quizzical.

'What indications would those be?' he says.

'The boy had a slew of sores around his arse, if you remember. If the sores are venereal, which is likely, the culprit may have them too. There may also be some soreness or abrasion on the culprit's penis. A child's fundament is quite narrow, after all.'

'Oh, fuck me,' Cavendish says.

'Very well,' Brownlee says. 'McKendrick, remove your clothes.'

McKendrick doesn't move.

'Do it now,' Brownlee says, 'or I swear we'll do it for you.'

Reluctantly, slowly, McKendrick undresses in front of them. His legs and arms look strong but scrawny; between his dark red nipples there is a small, whiskery patch of light brown hair. For such a slight and colourless man, he possesses, Sumner notices, as he begins his examination, an unusually large and gaudy set of genitalia. The balls are heavy, dark and pendulous; the yard, although not abnormally long, is as thick as a dog's snout, and its end piece as broad and shiny as a kidney.

'No visible chancres,' Sumner reports. 'No signs of soreness or abrasion either.'

'Perhaps he used a gob of lard to ease his entrance,' Cavendish says. 'By any chance, did you check Hannah's arsehole for signs of lubrication?'

'I did, and there were no residues to speak of.'

Cavendish smiles.

'Precious little gets past you, Mr Sumner,' he says. 'I swear to God.'

'No fresh cuts or scratches on the arms or neck as might be caused by a struggle either,' Sumner says. 'You may put your clothes back on now, McKendrick.'

McKendrick does as he is told. Brownlee watches silently as he dresses himself and, when he is finished, instructs him to wait outside in the mess cabin until they call him back in.

'There is your murderer, right there,' Cavendish says. 'Whether his cock is chafed or not, he's the guilty one, I tell you.'

'It's possible, but we have no convincing proof,' Sumner says.

'He's a self-confessed sodomite. What further proof do you need?'

'A confession,' Brownlee says. 'But if he won't confess, I'm minded to put him in irons anyway and let the magistrates deal with him when we get back to port.'

'What if he's not the one?' Sumner says. 'Are you content to have the actual murderer walking free around the ship?'

'If it's not McKendrick, then who the fuck could it be?' Cavendish asks. 'Exactly how many sodomites do you think we have crammed aboard this vessel?'

'I would be surer of his guilt if someone had seen the two of them together,' Sumner says.

'Put McKendrick in irons for now, Cavendish,' Brownlee says. 'Then let the rest of the crew know we wish to speak to anyone who has seen him talking to Hannah or paying the boy any sort of attentions. Sumner is most likely right. If he is guilty, there will be a witness.'

12

In the wardroom, Drax listens as the others talk. They are
talking about the boy again even though the boy is dead and
gone. This afternoon they wrapped his body up in canvas and
dropped it over the ship's stern; he watched it sinking under
the water. The boy is nothing now. He is not even an idea or
a thought, he is nothing, but they are talking about him still.
On and on they go. On and on. What is the fucking point of
that? Drax chews his boiled beef, drinks deeply from his mug
of tea. The beef is salty-sour, but the tea is sweet. He has a bite
mark on his forearm a half-inch deep. He can feel it throb
and itch. It would have been quicker and easier, he knows, to
cut the boy's throat, but a knife was not to hand. He doesn't
plan these things. He only acts, and each action remains separate and complete in itself: the fucking, the killing, the
shitting, the eating. They could come in any order at all. No

one is prior or superior to the rest. Drax lifts his dinner plate up in front of his face like a looking glass, and licks it clean of gravy.

He listens.

'It's McKendrick,' Cavendish says. 'For sure it is, I know a murderer when I see one, but Brownlee thinks he needs more proof.'

Drax knows McKendrick. He is a feeble, girlish, blood-shy fellow who could not kill someone if you put a pistol in his hand, pointed it for him and offered to pull the trigger yourself.

'Why McKendrick?' he asks.

'Because he's an infamous sodomite. You can see him in the dockyard taprooms every night, buying arse and giggling with the other pansies.'

Drax nods. McKendrick will be his stand-in then, he thinks, his scapegoat. He will dangle from the rope end while Drax stands and watches and applauds.

'What kind of proof does Brownlee look for?' he asks.

'He wants a witness. Someone who has seen the two of them together.'

Drax rubs the crumbs from his beard, grumbles out a fart, and then reaches into his pocket for his pouch of negro-head tobacco.

'I've seen them together,' he says.

The others look at him.

'When?' Sumner says.

'I seen them standing by the deckhouse late one night. McKendrick mooning over the boy, cooing and billing, paddling his neck, trying to give him little kisses. The boy didn't appear to like it much. 'Bout a week ago that was.'

Cavendish claps his hands together and laughs.

'That should do it,' he says.

'Why didn't you mention this before?' Sumner asks. 'You were there when the captain asked us all what we had seen.'

'Must have slipped my mind,' Drax says. 'My wits are not quite so sharply tuned as yours are, Mr Sumner, I suppose. I'm the forgetful type, see.'

Sumner looks at him, and Drax looks back. He feels easy and qualmless. He knows the surgeon's kind too well—he will quibble and ask questions all day long, but he will never dare to act. He is a talker and not a doer.

They go along to Brownlee's cabin and Drax tells the captain what he saw. Brownlee has McKendrick brought up from the hold in irons, and instructs Drax to repeat what he has said word for word in front of the prisoner.

'I saw him laying hands on the dead boy,' he says calmly. 'Trying to kiss and cuddle with him. By the deckhouse, this was.'

'And why did you not tell me this before now?'

'I didn't think of it before, but when McKendrick's name was mentioned as the murderer, then it all came back.'

'That is a fucking lie,' McKendrick says. 'I never once touched the boy.'

'I saw what I saw,' Drax says. 'And no man can tell me I didn't.'

He finds the lying comes easy enough, of course. Words are just noises in a certain order and he can use them any way he wishes. Pigs grunt, ducks quack and men tell lies: that is how it generally goes.

'And you will swear to this?' Brownlee asks him. 'In a court of law?'

'On the Holy Bible,' Drax says. 'Yes, I will.'

'I will enter your account in the ship's log then and have you set your mark on it,' Brownlee says. 'It is best to have a written record.'

McKendrick's previous calmness has dissolved now. His face, pale and narrow, is badged with redness, and he is shaking with rage.

'There is not a word of truth in it,' he says. 'Not a word of truth. He is spewing out lies.'

'I have no reason to lie,' Drax says. 'Why would I trouble myself with that?'

Brownlee looks to Cavendish.

'Is there bad feeling between these two men?' he asks. 'Any reason to consider the story may be false or malicious?'

'None that I have heard of,' Cavendish says.

'Have you two shipped together afore?' Brownlee asks them. Drax shakes his head.

'I barely know the carpenter,' he says. 'But I saw what I saw by the deckhouse. And I am telling it as it was.'

'But I know who you are, Henry Drax,' McKendrick says fiercely back. 'I know where you have been and what you have done there.'

Drax sniffs and shakes his head.

'You don't know nothing about me,' he says.

Brownlee looks to McKendrick.

'If you have some accusation to make, you should make it now,' he says. 'If not, I would advise you to close your trap and keep it closed until the magistrate asks you to open it again.'

'I never touched that boy. Boys are not my taste, and whatsoever I done with my fellow men I never had no accusations or complaints concerning that. This man here, the one who is lying about me, who seems set to get me hanged by the neck, has done much worse and more unnatural crimes than I ever done.'

'You'll dig yourself into a deeper hole with such blabbing,' Cavendish warns him.

'A man can't get much deeper than fucking dead,' McKendrick says.

'What crimes are you speaking of?' Sumner says.

'Ask him what he done in the Marquesas,' McKendrick says, looking straight at Drax. 'Ask him what he et when he was out there.'

'Do you understand him?' Brownlee says. 'What is he talking about now?'

'I have passed some time with the South Sea niggers,' Drax explains, 'that's all it is. I have some tattoos they gave me on my back, and a fund of good and profitable stories to show for it, nothing more.'

'What ship were you on?' Brownlee asks him.

'The *Dolly*, out of New Bedford.'

'Would you take the word of a cannibal against that of an honest and God-fearing white man?' McKendrick shouts. 'Will any magistrate in their right mind?'

Drax laughs at this.

'I'm no fucking cannibal,' he says. 'Don't pay no heed to his bollocks.'

Brownlee shakes his head and sniffs.

'I have rarely heard such desperate nonsense,' he says. 'Take this shameless piece of shite below and chain him to the mainmast before I lose my fucking temper.'

When McKendrick is gone, Brownlee enters Drax's account of what he saw into the ship's log and has him certify it with his mark.

'You will be expected to testify in the court, no doubt, when McKendrick comes to trial,' Brownlee says. 'And the log will be shown as evidence also. McKendrick's lawyer, if he can afford one, will attempt to blacken your name, I 'spect. That is what such vultures generally do. But you will stand up to him, I'm sure.'

'I don't like to be accused or talked at in that way,' Drax admits. 'That don't please me any.'

'The word of a lone sodomite will carry no great weight, you can be sure of that. You must stand your ground, that's all.'

Drax nods.

'I'm an honest man,' he says. 'I tell only what I saw.'

'Then you have nothing to fear.'

13

The news of McKendrick's guilt spreads instantly through
the ship. Those few who considered themselves friends of the
carpenter find it hard to believe he is a murderer, but their
doubts are quickly overpowered by the breadth and weight
of the more generally held certainty that he must be one.
After his second interview with Brownlee, he is kept chained
in the forehold, eats alone, and shits and pisses into a bucket,
which is emptied daily by a cabin boy. After a week or so of
this, his identity as a criminal and a pervert is so secure in the
minds of the crew it is hard to believe he was ever truly one
of them. They remember him as separate and strange, and
assume that whatever seemed usual about him was only a
clever way of covering up those deeper deviancies. Occasionally, one or two men venture into the hold to taunt him or
ask him questions about his crime. When they do so, they

find him oddly unrepentant, sour, baffled, belligerent, as if he doesn't yet (not even now) realise the truth of what it is he has done.

Brownlee wants nothing more than to get back to the appointed business of slaughtering whales, but for the next several days they are beset by foul weather—drenching rain and thick fog—which conceals their prey and makes the fishing impossible. Domed and circled by the clamminess and murk, they grind mutely southwards through a loose patchwork of pancake ice and slurry. When the weather finally opens up, they have passed Jones Sound and Cape Horsburgh to the west, and are in sight of the entrance to Pond's Bay. Brownlee is all eagerness to proceed, but the sea ice is abnormally dense for the season and they are forced to delay a while longer. The *Hastings* moors alongside them, and so do the *Polynia*, the *Intrepid* and the *Northerner*. Since there is no work to be done while they are waiting for the wind to change, the captains move freely between the five ships, dining in each other's cabins and passing time in conversation, argument and reminiscence. Brownlee tells his old stories often and easily: the coal barge, the *Percival*, everything before. He is not ashamed of what he has been or done: a man makes his mistakes, he tells them, a man suffers as he must suffer, but the readiness is all.

'So are you ready?' Campbell asks him lightly. They are sitting alone in Brownlee's cabin. The plates and dishes have been cleared away, and the others have already returned to their ships. Campbell is a shrewd and knowing fellow, friendly to a degree, but also secretive and superior at times. There is a hint of mockery in his question, Brownlee thinks, a definite suggestion that his part in Baxter's machinations is the finer one.

'I hear that if all goes well, you will be next,' Brownlee says. 'Baxter told me that himself.'

'Baxter thinks the whaling trade is finished,' Campbell says. 'He wants to settle up now, buy himself a modest manufactory.'

'Aye, but he's wrong about that. These seas are still crammed full of fishes.'

Campbell shrugs. He has an upturned nose, broad cheeks and long side-whiskers; his narrow lips are poised in a semi-permanent pout giving Brownlee the uncomfortable impression that, even when he appears silent and absorbed in his own thoughts, he is always just about to talk.

'If I was a gambling man, Baxter is one horse I'd like to put a little of my money on. He doesn't fall at many fences; he jumps 'em pretty clean, I'd say.'

'He's a shrewd fucker, I'll give you that.'

'So *are* you ready?'

'We've got time enough to kill a few more whales. No need to rush on, is there?'

'The whales is small change in this game,' Campbell reminds him. 'And you may not get too many good chances to sink her nicely and make it look just as it should. It's the way it looks that matters most, remember. We can't make it any too obvious or the underwriters will start up with their querying, and that's what none of us wants. You least of all.'

'There's a deal of ice about this year. It won't be so hard to manage.'

147

'Sooner is better than after. If we leave it too long, I risk getting trapped myself, then where the fuck would we be?'

'Give me a week in Pond's Bay,' Brownlee says. 'A week more only, and then we can look about for the right spot to get well nipped.'

'A week will do it, and then I say we head back northward,' Campbell says, 'up to Lancaster Sound or thereabouts. No one will follow us up there. You find yourself a snug little lead near some hefty land ice and wait for the wind to blow the floes back in on you. And from what I've seen of your crew, those fuckers won't be doing too much to help.'

'I'm minded to leave that carpenter where he is.'

'Accidents do happen,' Campbell agrees. 'And a man like him aint so likely to be missed.'

'It's a fucking outrage,' Brownlee says. 'Did you ever even hear of such a thing? A little girl is one thing. A little girl I halfway understand. But not a fucking cabin boy, good God, no. It's evil times we live in, I tell you, Campbell, evil and unnatural.'

Campbell nods.

'I'd venture the Good Lord don't spend much time up here in the North Water,' he says, with a smile. 'It's most probable he don't like the chill.'

When the ice opens up, they enter the bay, but the whaling is poor. There are scarcely any sightings, and on the few occasions the boats are lowered, the whales quickly disappear below the ice and there are no strikes. Brownlee begins to wonder

148

whether Baxter might be right after all—perhaps they *have* killed too many whales. He finds it hard to believe that the vast and teeming oceans could be emptied out so quick, that such enormous beasts could prove so fucking fragile, but if the whales are still about, they are certainly learning to hide themselves well. After a week of these dispiriting failures, he accepts the inevitable, signals as agreed to Campbell and announces to the men that they are leaving Pond's Bay and turning north to seek for better luck elsewhere.

Even with the aid of laudanum, Sumner cannot sleep for more than an hour or two consecutively. Joseph Hannah's death has aggravated and incited him in ways he doesn't understand. He would like to forget it now. He would like to rest, as the others appear to rest, in the certainty of McKendrick's guilt and eventual and inevitable punishment, but he finds himself signally unable to do so. He is troubled by memories of the boy's dead body laid out on the varnished tabletop where every night they eat their dinner still, and of McKendrick standing naked—ashamed, passive, gazed upon—in the captain's cabin. The two bodies should match, he thinks, should fit together like twin pieces of a puzzle, but whichever way he twists and turns them in his mind, he can't make a whole.

Late one night, about a fortnight after the carpenter's arrest, as the ship moves north past looneries and icebergs, Sumner descends into the forehold. McKendrick in his slop suit is lying in the small space that has been cleared for him amid the various boxes and bundles and casks. His legs have been chained together, one either side of the mast, but his hands are both free. There are some fragments of biscuit on a tin plate, and a cup of water and a lighted candle by his side. Sumner can smell the high tang of the slop bucket. The surgeon hesitates for a moment, then leans down and shakes him by the shoulder. McKendrick unfurls himself slowly, sits up with his back against a packing case and gazes indifferently at his latest guest.

'How's your health?' Sumner asks him. 'Do you require anything from me?'

McKendrick shakes his head.

'I'm hale and hearty enough, considering,' he says. 'I 'spect I will live until they choose to hang me.'

'If it comes to a trial, you know you will have a better chance to make your case. Nothing is decided yet.'

'A man like myself finds few friends in an English court of law, Mr Sumner. I'm an honest fellow, but my life will not stand for too much peering into.'

'You're not the only one who feels that way, I'd say.'

'We're all sinners, right enough, but some sins are punished harder than others. I int a murderer and never was one, but I'm many other things, and it's the other things they would wish to hang me for.'

'If you're not the murderer, then someone else on this ship is. If Drax is lying, as you claim he is, it's possible he either killed the boy himself or knows the man who did and is seeking to protect him. Have you thought of that?'

McKendrick shrugs. After two weeks in the hold, his skin has taken on a greyish tinge, and his blue eyes have turned murky and recessed. He scratches at his ear, and a piece of skin flakes off and flutters to the floor.

'I thought of it all right, but what good will it do me to accuse another man if I have no proof and no witnesses of my own?'

Sumner takes a pewter flask from his pocket, passes it over to McKendrick, then takes it back and has a sip himself.

'I am running short on baccy,' McKendrick says, after a moment. 'If you could spare a pinch, I'd be much obliged to you.'

Sumner passes him his tobacco pouch. McKendrick takes the pouch with his right hand after jamming the pipe between the middle two fingers of the left. With the pipe secured in this peculiar fashion, he fills the bowl and damps it down with his right thumb.

'What's the trouble with your hand?' Sumner asks him.

'It's only the thumb,' he says. 'Got crushed by a cock-eyed fellow with a lump hammer a year or two back and haven't been able to move it even a quarter-inch one way or the other since then. Makes some difficulties for a man in my trade, but I've learned to make the adjustment.'

'Show me.'

McKendrick leans forward and holds out his left hand. The fingers are normal, but the joint of the thumb is badly misshapen and the thumb itself appears stiff and lifeless.

'So you cannot grip with this hand at all?'

'Only with the four fingers. 'Tis lucky it was my left one, I suppose.'

'Try to grip my wrist,' Sumner tells him, 'like this.'

He rolls up his sleeve and holds out his bare arm. McKendrick grips it.

'Squeeze as hard as you can.'

'I'm squeezing now.'

Sumner feels the pressure of the four fingers digging into his armflesh, but from the thumb, nothing at all.

'Is that the best you can do?' he says. 'Don't hold back.'

'I aint holding anything back,' he insists. 'Man hit my thumb bone with a fucking great lump hammer two years ago aboard the *Whitby*, I tell you, when we were in dock repairing a hatch cover. Smashed it near to pieces. And I have plenty of witnesses to *that* occurrence—including the captain himself—who will happily swear on the Bible to his foolishness.'

Sumner tells him to let go, then tugs his shirtsleeve back down.

'Why didn't you tell me about your injured hand when I examined you before?'

'You weren't asking after my hand, if I recall.'

'If you can't grip any better than that, how could you have strangled the boy? You saw the bruises on his neck.'

McKendrick pauses and then looks suddenly wary, as if the surgeon's implications are too large and too hopeful to be easily absorbed.

'I saw them right enough,' he says. 'He had a string of bruises all around his neck just so.'

'And there were two large bruises at the front. Do you remember those? One almost on top of the other. I thought at the time they must have been caused by the two thumbs pressing hard down on the gorge.'

'You remember them?'

'I remember them clearly,' Sumner says. 'Two large bruises, one on top of the other one, like two smudges of ink.'

'But I don't have two good thumbs no more,' McKendrick says slowly. 'So how did I make them bruises?'

'That's right,' Sumner says. 'I need to talk to the captain now. It looks like the fellow with the lump hammer may have saved your neck.'

14

Brownlee listens to the surgeon's arguments, hoping keenly as he does so that they are wrong. He has no desire to release McKendrick. The carpenter is a convincing culprit, and if he is released (which is the end Sumner seems, for some mystifying reason of his own, to seek) there is no one else aboard the ship who can take his place without a deal of trouble and complication.

'A scrawny cunt like Hannah can be strangled with one hand easy enough, I'd say,' Brownlee argues, 'thumb or no thumb. McKendrick isn't tall, but he's plenty strong enough for that.'

'Not with the bruises patterned as they were on Hannah's neck, though. The twin thumb marks were as clear as day.'

'I don't remember thumb marks. I remember a good many bruises, but there is no way on earth of knowing which particular fingers caused which particular marks.'

'Before the burial, I made sketches of Hannah's injuries,' Sumner says. 'I thought a court might want to see them if it comes to a trial. Look here.' He puts a leatherbound sketch-book on the table in front of the captain and opens it to the relevant pages. 'Do you see what I mean now? Two large oval bruises one above the other one, there and there.'

He points. Brownlee looks, then rubs his nose and scowls. He is irritated by the surgeon's conscientiousness. What business does he have making ink sketches of a boy's dead body?

'The boy was sewn up in his shroud already. How could you have sketched him?'

'I asked the sailmaker to loosen the stitches, then had them tightened again while the making off was going on. It was easy enough to do.'

Brownlee turns the pages of the sketchbook and winces. There is a detailed rendering of the boy's damaged and ulcerated rectum, and a labelled diagram of his broken ribs.

'These pretty pictures of yours prove bugger-all,' he says. 'McKendrick was seen making advances to the boy, and he is a known and notorious sodomite. Those are the solid facts of the matter. Anything else is guesswork and fancy.'

'The thumb of McKendrick's left hand is damaged beyond repair,' Sumner says. 'It is physically impossible for him to have committed this crime.'

'And you are free to express that opinion to the magistrate as soon as we return to England. Perhaps he'll be more convinced by it than I am, but in the meantime, while we are at sea and I'm the captain, McKendrick stays where he is.'

'As soon as we land back in England, the real killer will

leave the ship and disappear from sight, you do realise that? He will never be caught.'

'Should I arrest the entire fucking crew on suspicion of murder? Is that what you recommend?'

'If it's not McKendrick who killed the boy, it's most likely Henry Drax. He's lying about the carpenter to save himself.'

'You have been reading too many penny dreadfuls, Mr Sumner, I swear to it.'

'Let me at least examine Drax as I did McKendrick. If he's a murderer then it's still not too late for the signs to be apparent.'

Brownlee shifts sideways in his chair, tugs down on his stubbled earlobe and sighs. Although the surgeon is certainly annoying, there is something admirable in his persistence. He is a dogged little fucker, all in all.

'Very well,' he says. 'If you must. Although if Drax objects to being poked and prodded, I'm not so inclined to press the issue.'

When Drax is called for, he makes no objection. He drops his britches in front of them and stands there grinning. The captain's cabin fills with a stink of stale urine and potted meat.

'At your pleasure, Mr Sumner,' Drax says, giving the surgeon a coquettish wink.

Sumner, breathing only through his mouth, bends and examines, with the aid of a magnifying glass, the dangling parabola of Drax's glans.

'Pull back the foreskin, please,' Sumner says.

Drax does as he is asked. Sumner nods.

'You have the crabs,' he tells him.

'Aye, I usually do have them. But that int a hanging offence now, is it, Mr Sumner?'

Brownlee chuckles. Sumner shakes his head and then stands up.

'No visible chancres,' he says. 'Show me both your hands now.'

Drax holds them out. Sumner looks at the palms, then turns them over. They are as black and rough as lumps of pig iron.

'The cut on your hand has healed, I see.'

'That wont anything,' he says. 'Just a scratch.'

'And you have full use of all your digits, I suppose.'

'Of my *what*?'

'Fingers and thumbs.'

'I do indeed, thanks God.'

'Take off your pea coat and roll up your sleeves.'

'Do you doubt me, Mr Sumner?' Drax asks, as he tugs his arms out of the jacket and starts to unbutton his shirtfront. 'Do you doubt me when I tell what I saw by the deckhouse?'

'McKendrick denies it. You know he does.'

'But McKendrick is a sodomite and what is the word of a sodomite worth in a court of law? Not too much, I'd say.'

'I have good reason to believe him.'

Drax nods at this and continues to undress. He takes his shirt off and his flannels. His chest is dark-pelted, broad and stoutly muscled; his belly is proudly bulbous, and both his arms are coated in a chequerworked swirl of blue tattoos.

'If you believe the word of that cunt McKendrick, then you must fancy I'm a liar.'

'I don't know what you are.'

'I'm an honourable man, Mr Sumner,' Drax says, pressing down gradually on the word *honourable* as if honour itself is a complex and esoteric notion, but one he is proud to have mastered. 'That's what I am. I do my duty and I have no cause to feel any shame because of it.'

'What do you intend by that, Drax?' Brownlee asks him. 'We're all honourable men here, I think, or honourable enough at least for the requirements of our calling which is a dirty enough kind of business, as you know.'

'I think the surgeon gets my drift,' Drax says. (He is standing fully naked now—thick-limbed, fistic, unashamed. His face is burned brown and his hands are black from toil, but the rest of his skin—where it is visible beneath the mats of dark hair and the panoply of crude tattooing—is a pure pinkish white like the skin of a babe.) 'Him and me are old pals, after all. I helped him search his way back to his cabin after that famous night in Lerwick. You likely won't remember, Mr Sumner, since you were fast asleep at the time, but me and Cavendish had a good look around before we left to make sure your necessaries was safe and sound just as they should be. Nothing disturbed or out of place.'

Sumner, staring at Drax, instantly understands. They have rooted through his sea chest, read the discharge papers, seen the looted ring.

Brownlee is looking at him curiously.

'Do *you* know what the fuck he's talking about?' he says.

Sumner shakes his head. He casts his eye unthinkingly over Drax's arms and torso, breathing carefully as he does so, pushing back against the inner uproar.

'Do you doubt my knowledge or competency as a surgeon?' he says (sounding preposterous even to himself). 'I have served an apprenticeship and have certificates from the Queen's College of Belfast.'

Drax smiles at this, then laughs. His yellowy cock thickens and twitches noticeably upwards.

'You have your little scrap of paper, Mr Sumner, and I have mine. Now, which one of those two little scraps of paper weighs the most, I wonder, in an English court of law? I never did learn my letters, so I'm not the one to say, but a good lawyer would likely have an opinion, I suppose.'

'I have my evidence,' Sumner says. 'It is not a matter of my opinion or my reputation. Who I am, or who I have been, is not the question.'

'And what evidence do you hold against *me*?' Drax asks more fiercely. 'Tell me that.'

'We are not accusing you of any crime,' Brownlee says. 'That's not why we are here. McKendrick is still down in the hold in chains, remember. Sumner is merely curious about some details of the outrage, that is all.'

Drax ignores Brownlee and continues staring at Sumner.

'What evidence do you hold against *me*?' he says again. 'Because if you have none, then it's thee against me, I'd say. My solemn word, sworn on the Bible, against yours.'

Sumner steps backwards and digs his hands into his pockets.

'You are lying about McKendrick,' he says. 'I know very well you are.'

Drax turns to Brownlee and taps his finger to his ear.

'Is the ship's surgeon a little hard of hearing, Captain?' he says. 'I keep asking him the same fucking question and he don't seem to notice it at all.'

Brownlee scowls, then licks his lips. He is beginning to regret agreeing to Sumner's request. Drax may be something of a savage, but that is no good reason to accuse him of child murder. It is hardly surprising he has taken the hump.

'What evidence do we hold against Drax in this matter, Sumner? Tell us now, please.'

Sumner looks down at the floor between his feet for a moment and then up at the cabin's pitched glass skylight.

'I have no evidence against Henry Drax,' he confesses flatly. 'None at all.'

'Then let's call an end to this nonsense,' Brownlee says. 'Get your fucking clothes back on and get to work.'

Drax gazes dismissively at Sumner for a long moment, then reaches down and lifts his britches from the cabin floor. Each of his movements is considered and powerful, his body, stinking and rotund as it is, clagged and filthy in its folds and creases, possesses a ghastly voluptuousness nonetheless. Sumner looks on without watching. He is thinking of the medicine chest and the delicious pleasures it contains. He is thinking of the Achaeans and the Trojans and the meddlings of Athena and Ares. McKendrick will hang for sure, Sumner realises. This crime requires a villain and he has been appointed to the post. He will dangle and kick at the end of a rope. There is no way out now, no Hera to pluck him from the scaffold.

Drax bends and then straightens, prods his legs into the

161

holes of his britches and pulls them up his thighs. His broad back and pungent arse are patched with fur; his socked feet are blockish and simian. Brownlee looks on impatiently. The outrage is behind him now, and his mind is on other things. McKendrick will swing for what he did, and that is that. What matters now is the sinking of the ship, which is a tricky business to get right. She needs to go down slow enough to ensure that all the cargo can be saved, but not so slow that any last gasp repairs are possible. And there is no way of being sure beforehand how the ice will behave and how close or far away Campbell will be able to plausibly manoeuvre the *Hastings*. The underwriters are alive these days to various kinds of trickery; if they sense a conspiracy, they will descend on the crew in port and commence offering them rewards for useful information. If it is not done right, he could end up in a cell in Hull gaol rather than enjoying his retirement strolling on the strands of Bridlington.

'What's that gash on your arm?' he says to Drax. 'Have you cut yourself again? Sumner will give you a plaster for that if you ask him sweetly, I'm sure.'

'It's nothing,' Drax says. 'A scratch with a harpoon, that's all.'

'Looks worse than nothing to me,' Brownlee says.

Drax shakes his head and picks his pea coat off the table.

'Let me see it,' Sumner says.

'It's nothing,' Drax says again.

'It's your good right arm and I can see from here it's swollen and weeping,' Brownlee says. 'If you can't hurl a harpoon or pull an oar, you'll be no earthly fucking use to me. Show it to the surgeon now.'

Drax hesitates a moment, then holds out his arm.

The wound, high on the forearm near the elbow, half hidden by hair and ink, is narrow but deep, and the site around it is severely swollen. The skin, when Sumner touches it, is tense and hot. An areola of green pus has gathered around and below the scabbing. And the scabbing itself is sticky and raw.

'The purulence needs to be lanced and the remnants drawn out with a poultice,' Sumner says. 'Why didn't you come to me before now?'

'It don't trouble me,' Drax says. ''Tis just a nick.'

Sumner goes to his cabin and returns with a lancet, which he heats for a minute over the candle flame. He takes a piece of lint padding and presses it against the wound, then makes a brief incision with the lancet. A green-pink mixture of blood and pus spills out and soaks into the padding. Sumner presses harder and the wound exudes yet more of the foul liquid. Drax stands immobile and silent. The red and swollen skin has flattened out, but there remains a strange and singular lump.

'There's something lodged inside there,' Sumner says. 'Look here.'

Brownlee approaches and peers over the surgeon's shoulder.

'Might be a splinter of wood,' he says, 'or possibly a piece of bone.'

'You say you did this with a harpoon?' Sumner asks.

'That's right,' Drax says.

Sumner presses at the small lump with his fingertip. It slides for a moment beneath the skin and then emerges white and blood-covered from the wound's opening.

'What the fuck is that?' Brownlee says.

Sumner catches the object in the soiled padding and rubs it clean. He looks at it only once and knows immediately. He glances quickly at Drax, then shows the object to Brownlee. It is a child's tooth, pale and grain-like, broken off at the root.

Drax snatches his arm away. He looks at the tooth, still in Sumner's hand, and then at Brownlee.

'That thing int mine,' he says.

'It was in your arm.'

'It int mine.'

'It's evidence,' Sumner says. 'That's what it is. And it's all the evidence we need to see you hanged.'

'They won't hang me,' Drax says. 'I'll see you both in hell afore that happens.'

Brownlee steps to the cabin door, opens it and calls out for the first mate. The three men eye each other carefully. Drax is still only half-dressed, his chest is bare and he has his shirt and pea coat clutched in his left hand.

'I won't be chained neither,' he says. 'Not by cunts like you two.'

Brownlee shouts again for Cavendish. Drax glances around the cabin for any usable weapon. There's a brass sextant lying on the table to his right and, in a pinewood rack on the wall beside him, a spyglass and a heavy whalebone walking stick tipped with an ebony pommel. He doesn't move or reach for them yet. He calmly waits his moment.

164

They hear the clatter and curse of Cavendish descending from the deck and making his way through steerage. When he steps into the cabin and the others turn towards him, Drax grabs the whalebone off the rack and swings it directly into Brownlee's forehead striking him just above the left eye socket and breaking the skull. He pulls it back to swing again, but Cavendish grabs hold of his arm. The two men struggle mutely for a moment. When Drax drops the whalebone, Cavendish reaches down for it and the harpooner grabs him by the hair and brings his knee up hard into his face. Cavendish drops sideways onto the rag carpet, groaning and drooling blood. Sumner, watching on, has yet to move. He is still holding the lancet in one hand and the dead child's tooth in the other.

'What's the point of this?' he says. 'You can't escape from here.'

'I'll take my chances in a whaleboat,' Drax says. 'I won't go back to England to be hanged.'

He picks the whalebone off the floor and hefts it for a moment. The ebony pommel is slick with Brownlee's blood.

'And I'll be taking that tooth off you afore I leave,' he says.

Sumner shakes his head, then steps forward and puts the tooth and the lancet down on the tabletop between them. He glances upwards through the skylight but no one is there. Why is Black not on the quarterdeck as usual? he wonders. Where is Otto?

'You can't kill us all,' he says.

'I 'spect I can kill enough of you though. Now turn about.' He waves with the whalebone to indicate his meaning.

After a moment's pause, Sumner does as he is told. While Drax quickly dresses himself, the surgeon stands staring at the dark wood panelling of the cabin wall. On the top of the skull, he wonders, or off to one side? One blow or two? If he calls out now, it is possible that someone might hear him. But he doesn't call out. He closes his eyes and holds his breath. He waits for the fatal blow to fall.

There is a sudden quick commotion outside. A loud rattle of voices. And then, as the cabin door flies open, the unreal roar of a shotgun blast. Dust and fragments of the ceiling cascade around Sumner's head. He swivels about and sees Black standing in the doorway aiming the second barrel directly at Drax's chest.

'Give the stick to Sumner now,' Black tells him.

Drax doesn't move. His mouth is hanging open and his tongue and teeth are wetly visible.

'I can kill you now,' Black says, 'or I can shoot your bollocks off and let you bleed out for a while. Whichever you prefer.'

After a pause, Drax nods, smiles faintly, then hands the stick to Sumner. Black steps into the cabin and looks down at Brownlee and Cavendish, unconscious and bleeding on the floor.

'What the fuck have you been doing here?' he says.

Drax shrugs and looks down at the tooth lying on the table where the surgeon left it.

'That tooth int none of mine,' he says. 'The surgeon dug it out my arm, but how it got there is the gravest kind of mystery.'

15

For four days and nights, Brownlee lies insensible on his cot, open-eyed but barely breathing. The left side of his face is blackened and misshapen. His eye is swelled shut. Unknown liquids ooze out of his ear; high on his forehead where the skin is split apart, the bone is palely visible. Sumner thinks it unlikely that he will live and, if he does live, impossible that his mind will ever fully recover. He knows from experience that the human brain cannot tolerate such contusions. Once the skull is breached, the situation is almost hopeless, the vulnerability is too immense. He has seen such injuries on the battlefield, from sabre and shrapnel, rifle butts and the hooves of horses—unconsciousness is followed by catatonia, occasionally they shout out like lunatics or weep like children, something inside them (their soul? their character?) has been scrambled, reversed. They have lost their bearings. It is generally better, he thinks, if they die, rather than go on inhabiting the twilit half-world of the mad.

Cavendish has a badly broken nose and has lost several of his front teeth, but is otherwise unaltered. After a brief period on his back, sipping bouillon soup from a serving spoon and taking opium against the pain, he rises and resumes his duties. On a gloomy morning with clouds clagging the horizon and the scent of rain hovering in the air, he gathers the men on the foredeck and explains that he is taking command of the *Volunteer* until Brownlee recovers. Henry Drax, he assures them, will certainly hang back in England for his murderous and mutinous acts, but for now he is firmly chained in the hold, rendered incapable of mischief, and he will play no further part in the voyage.

'You may ask yourself how such a fiend came to move among us, but I have no good answer to that,' he says. 'He bamboozled me as much as he did any man. I've known some deviant and malignant fuckers in my time, but none, I confess, a patch on Henry Drax. If the good Mr Black here had chose to put that other shotgun barrel in his chest when he had the opportunity, I for one would not be mourning over much, but, as it is, he is caged below like the beast he is and will not see the daylight till we land again in Hull.'

Among the crew, the sense of amazement as to what occurred in Brownlee's cabin is soon replaced by a general certainty that the voyage itself is cursed. They remember the gruesome stories of the *Percival*, of men dying, going mad, drinking their own blood for sustenance, and ask themselves why they were ever foolish or ill-advised enough to sign on for a ship commanded by a man so notable for his fearsome ill-luck. Even though the ship is less than a quarter full of blubber, they would like nothing better now than to turn round and sail directly home. They fear that worse is yet to come, and they would rather reach home with empty pockets but still breathing than end up sunk for ever below the Baffin ice.

According to Black and Otto, who do not try to keep their opinions to themselves, it is too late in the season to be in these waters—the majority of whales have swum further south by now, and the further north they stray as the summer recedes, the greater the risk of ice. It was Brownlee's own particular idiosyncrasy, they say, to set them on this northerly course in the first place, but now he is no longer in command, the most sensible action is to return to Pond's Bay with the rest of the fleet. Cavendish, however, takes no account of either the superstitions of the crew or the suggestions of the other officers. They continue moving northwards in the company of the *Hastings*. Twice they see whales in the distance and lower for them, but without success. When they reach the entrance to Lancaster Sound, Cavendish lowers a boat and has himself rowed across to the *Hastings* to confer with Campbell. On his return, he announces over dinner in the mess that they will enter the Sound as soon as a suitable passage opens up in the ice.

Black stops his eating and stares at him.

'No man has ever caught a whale this far north in August,' he says. 'Read the records if you doubt me. We're wasting our time here at best, and if we enter the Sound, we're putting ourselves at risk also.'

'A man don't profit unless he takes a little risk from time to time,' Cavendish says lightly. 'You should show more boldness, Mr Black.'

'It is foolishness, not boldness to enter Lancaster Sound this late in the season,' Black says. 'Why Brownlee took us north again I can't say, but I know if he were here, even he would not consider taking us into the Sound.'

'What Brownlee would or wouldn't do is moot, I'd say, since he can't speak or even raise his hand to wipe his arse. And since I'm the one in command now, not you or him'— he nods at Otto—'I guess what I say goes.'

'This voyage is marked with enough calamity already. Do you really want to add yet more to the total?'

'Let me tell you something about myself,' Cavendish says, leaning in a little and lowering his voice. 'Unlike some per-haps, I don't come whaling for the fresh air or the fine sea views, I don't even come for the pleasing company of men like you and Otto here. I come whaling to get my money, and I will get my money any way I can. If your opinions came in gold with the Queen's head stamped upon 'em, I might pay them a little mind, but since they don't, you won't be too offended, I hope, if I take no fucking notice of them at all.'

When Brownlee dies two days later, they dress him in his velvet morning coat, stitch him into a stiff canvas shroud and carry the body on a pine plank to the stern rail. Drizzle is falling, the sea is the colour of boot polish and the sky is

wadded with cloud. The crew sing 'Rock Of Ages' and 'Nearer
My God To Thee', and Cavendish leads them all in an off-
kilter version of the Lord's Prayer. The voices of the mourners
as they sing and pray are low and reluctant. Although they
mistrusted Brownlee by the end, believing him unlucky, the
nature of his death is a blow to the general confidence. That
Drax, who they thought was reliable, even admirable, is actually a murderer and a sodomite, and McKendrick, who they
thought was a murderer and a sodomite, is actually an innocent victim of Drax's godless machinations, has created
among the men of the forecastle feelings of perplexity and
self-doubt. Such unlikely reversals make them uneasy and
fitful. Their world is hard and raw enough, they think, without the added burden of moral convolution.

As the men disperse, Otto appears by Sumner's side. He
touches the surgeon's elbow and leads him forward until
they are standing by the bowsprit looking out at the dark sea,
the low grey cloud and, in the middle distance, separated
from the *Volunteer* by several loose floes of ice, the *Hastings*.
Otto's expression is sombre and gravid. Sumner senses he has
news to impart.

'Cavendish will kill us all,' the harpooner whispers. 'I've
seen it pass.'

'You're allowing Brownlee's death to depress your spirits,'
Sumner says. 'Give Cavendish a little time, and if we see no
whales in the Sound, we'll be in Pond's Bay again before you
know it.'

'*You* will survive, but you will be the only one. The rest of
us will drown or starve or perish of the cold.'

'Nonsense. Why would you say such things? How can you possibly know?'

'A dream,' he says. 'Last night.'

Sumner shakes his head.

'Dreams are just a way to clear the mind; they're a form of purging. What you dream is whatever's left over and can't be used. A dream is nothing but a mental shite-pile, a rag-and-bone shop of ideas. There is no truth in them, no prophecy.'

'You will be killed by a bear—when the rest of us are already dead,' Otto says. 'Eaten, swallowed up somehow.'

'After what's happened here, your fears are understandable,' Sumner says. 'But don't confuse them with our destiny. All that's behind us now. We're safe.'

'Drax is still alive and breathing.'

'He is down in the hold chained to the mainmast, bound hand and foot. He cannot escape. Set your mind at rest.'

'The corporal body is just one way of moving through the world. It's the spirit which truly lives.'

'You think a man like Henry Drax has any spirit worthy of the name?'

Otto nods. He looks, as he usually does, serious, eager and faintly surprised by the nature of the world around him.

'I've encountered his spirit,' he says. 'Met with it in other realms. Sometimes it takes the form of a dark angel, sometimes a Barbary ape.'

'You're a good fellow, Otto, but what you are saying is folly,' Sumner tells him. 'We're not in danger any more. Set your mind at ease and forget the fucking dream.'

*

During the night they enter Lancaster Sound. There is open water stretching to the south of them, but to the north, a granular and monotone landscape of ice boulders and melt pools, sculpted smooth by wind in places, but elsewhere cragged, roughened and heaved upright into sharp-edged moguls by the alternations of the seasons and the dynamisms of temperature and tide. Sumner rises early and, as has become his habit, gathers a bucket of rinds, crusts and scourings from the galley. He takes a large metal spoon and, crouching by the bear cub's cask, prods a portion of the cold and grease-bound mass between the grillework. The bear sniffs, gobbles, then bites down fiercely on the empty spoon. Sumner, after twisting the spoon free, feeds him another portion. When the bear has emptied the bucket, Sumner refills it with fresh water and allows him to drink. He then heaves the cask upright, detaches the metal grille and, with a careful quickness born of practice and several previous near calamities, slips a loop of rope around the bear's neck and pulls it taut. He lowers the cask and allows the bear to dash forwards and across the deck, his black claws scarifying the wooden planking. Sumner secures the end of the leash to a nearby cleat and swills out the cask with seawater, chasing the accumulated bear shit out through the forechannels with a broom.

The bear, high-rumped and grimy-yellow at his haunches, growls then settles himself against the lip of a hatchway. He is watched at a distance by the ship's dog, Katie, a bow-hipped Airedale. Every day for weeks now, dog and bear have rehearsed a similar pantomime of wariness and curiosity, closeness and retreat. The men enjoy this daily spectacle. They egg them on, shout encouragements, jab them forward with boots and boathooks. The Airedale is smaller but much lighter on her feet. She dashes forwards, stiffens a moment, then wheels away again yelping with excitement. Probing and grandly tentative, the bear swaggers after her, his wedge-shaped head, tipped with blackness like a burnt match, gauging the air. The dog is all eagerness and fear, all trembling alertness; the bear, stolid, earth-bound, heavy-limbed, feet like frying pans, moves as though the air itself is a barrier that must be slowly pushed through. They close to within a foot of each other, nose to nose, black eyes locked in ancient and wordless convocation. 'I'll have thruppence on the bear,' someone hollers. The cook, leaning on the lintel of the galley door, amused, tosses a chunk of bacon between them. Bear and dog together lunge for it, collide. The Airedale, bunched up and squealing, spins across the deck like a top. The bear gobbles the bacon and looks about for more. Men laugh. Sumner, who has been leaning on the mainmast, straightens, unwraps the leash from its cleat and prods the bear back towards the freshened cask with the bristle end of the broom. The bear, realising what is happening, refuses for a moment, bares his teeth and then accedes. Sumner pulls the cask upright, refastens the grille and lays it back down on the deck.

All day the wind blows steadily from the south. The sky above is pale blue, but on the far horizon, dark clouds are racked in slender lines above the mountain tops. In the late afternoon, they spy a whale a mile off the port bow and lower two boats. The boats pull quickly away and the *Volunteer* follows after them. Cavendish watches proceedings from the quarterdeck. He is wearing Brownlee's snuff-coloured greatcoat and carrying his long brass spyglass. Now and then, he calls out a command. Sumner can see that he is taking a childish pleasure in his new authority. When the boats reach the whale, they realise that it is dead already and has begun to bloat. They signal for the ship to come closer and then tow it across. Black is commanding the first boat, and he and Cavendish have a shouted conversation about the state of the carcass. Despite the signs of rot and depredation, they decide that there is sufficient blubber left to make it worth their while to flense it.

They attach the decomposing body of the whale to the ship's gunwales where it dangles like a vast and wholly rotten vegetable. Its tar black skin is flaccid and intermittently abscessed; pale and cankerous growths mottle its fins and tail. The men who are cutting in wear dampened neckerchiefs across their faces and puff strong tobacco against the miasma. The blocks of blubber they slice and peel away are miscoloured and gelatinous—much more brown than pink. Swung up onto the deck, they drip not blood, as usual, but some foul straw-coloured coagulation like the unspeakable rectal oozings of a human corpse. Cavendish strides about shouting instructions and generalised encouragement. Above him sea birds gather, wheeling and cacophonous, in the noisome air, while below in the grease-stained water, drawn in by the mixed aromas of blood and decay, Greenland sharks gnaw and tug at the whale's loose kiltings.

'Give them sharks a knock or two on the bonce,' Cavendish shouts down to Jones-the-whale. 'Don't want them swallowing our profits now, do we?'

Jones nods, takes a fresh blubber spade from the malemauk boat, waits for one of the sharks to come close enough and then stabs at it, opening up a foot-long gash in its side. A loose-knit garland of entrails, pink, red and purple, slurps immediately from the wound. The injured shark thrashes for a moment, then bends backwards and starts urgently gobbling its own insides.

'Christ, those sharks are fucking beasts,' Cavendish says.

Jones finally kills it with a second spade-blow to the brain, then kills another one the same quick way. The two grey-green bodies, blunt and archaic, pumping out cloudy trails of blood, are further savaged before they sink by the attentions of a third and smaller animal who leaves them as gnawed and ragged as apple cores, then slips away before Black can dispatch him also.

When the flensing is half completed, they sever the whale's enormous lower lip and raise it onto the deck, exposing one side of the headbone. Otto, like a woodsman attacking a fallen oak, sets to the bone with an axe and a handspike. It is almost two feet thick and elegantly beaded at the extremities like a skirting board. When both sides of the bone are severed, they attach the bone-geer, crack off the upper jaw in one complete piece and manoeuvre it carefully with block-and-tackle so it hangs tent-like above the deck with the black strips of baleen drooping from it like the bristles of a gigantic moustache. The baleen is then detached

176

from the jaw with spades and separated into smaller sections for stowing. What remains of the upper jawbone is stowed in the hold.

'By Christmas, the bones of this dead and gruesome stinker will be nestling in the delicately perfumed corsets of some as yet unfucked lovely dancing the Gay Gordons in a ballroom on the Strand. That's a thought to fairly make your head spin, is it not, Mr Black?' Cavendish says.

'Behind every piece of sweet-smelling female loveliness lies a world of stench and doggery,' Black agrees. 'He's a lucky man who can forget that's true or pretend it isn't.'

After another hour, the job is all but done, and the bloated and filthy smelling krang is cut free. They watch it drift away among a shrieking cloud of gulls and petrels. Balanced on the rim of the western horizon, the narrow Arctic sun glows and fades like a breathed-on ember.

Sumner sleeps easily that night and in the morning rises again to feed the bear. When the slops bucket is empty, he lassoes a rope about the bear's neck and secures the rope end while he rinses out the cask. Although the wind is freshening and the deck has been washed clean, there is a lingering smell of decay from yesterday's flensing. Instead of settling down as usual, the bear paces back and forth and sniffs the air. When the dog approaches him, he wheels away, and when she nudges him gently, he growls. The dog wanders off a while, lingers at the galley door and then returns. She wags her tail and steps closer. They stand for a moment watching each other, then the bear pulls back, stiffens, raises his right front paw and in one fluid downward movement rakes his fossil claws along the dog's shoulder-blade, ripping open the sinew and muscle to the bone and dislocating the shoulder joint. A watching crewman whoops and cheers. The dog screams abominably and skitters sideways spraying out blood onto the deck. The bear lunges forward, but Sumner grabs the rope leash and pulls it back. The Airedale is squealing and blood is pumping out from the open wound. The black-smith, watching on from his forge, selects a heavy hammer from the rack, walks over to where the dog is lying, trem-bling and pissing herself in a pool of blood, and strikes her once, hard, between the ears. The squealing stops.

'You want I should kill the bear too?' the blacksmith asks. 'I'll do it happily enough.'

Sumner shakes his head.

'It's not my bear to kill,' he says.

The blacksmith shrugs.

'You're the one as feeds it every day, so I'd say it's yours as much as anyone's.'

Sumner looks down at the bear still straining at the rope's end, still gasping and growling and scratching at the deck in a primitive and implacable fury.

'We'll let the vicious fucker be,' he says.

16

About midday, the wind veers suddenly from south to north, and the loose pack of drift ice which clogs the middle of the Sound, and which previously posed no danger, begins to move gradually towards them. Cavendish moors the ship to the edge of the southerly land floe and orders the men to cut out an ice dock for protection and be quick about it. Equipment is brought up from the hold—ice saws, gunpowder, ropes and poles—and the men leap over the gunwales and down onto the ice. Their dark silhouettes move urgently across the unmarked surface of the floe. Black paces off the dock's required length and breadth, then drives boarding pikes into the ice to mark the angles and midpoints of each side. The men are divided into two teams to make the first long cuts. They erect wooden tripods with pulleys at the apex. They reeve ropes through each of the pulleys and attach a fourteen-foot steel ice saw to each end. Eight men are attached to each rope to deliver the upward cutting stroke, and another four take hold of wooden handles on the saw end to drive it down again. The ice is six feet thick and the dock's sides are two hundred feet in length. Once the two sides are cut, they cut across the end, and then cut again from one corner to the midpoint of the right-hand side. From there, they cut another diagonal line in the opposite direction from the midpoint to the ice's edge. After two hours' labour, a final horizontal cut across the middle of the dock leaves the floe divided into four separate triangles, each one several tons in weight. The men are sweating and gasping from their work. Their heads steam like puddings on a plate.

From the quarterdeck, Cavendish watches the pack advance towards him. As it continues to approach, blown on by the wind, the breaches in it heal and what was previously a loose agglomeration of separate floes and fragments becomes a seamless field of solid-seeming ice moving imperceptibly but unstoppably down upon them. In the middle distance, enormous blue-white icebergs loom like broken and carious monuments. The thinner ice around their bases rumples and tears like paper. He checks the *Hastings'* position with Brownlee's brass telescope, sniffs, then lights his pipe and spits across the rail.

Out on the ice, Black pushes charges of gunpowder down into the nearest diagonal cut and lights the fuse. After a few seconds' pause, there is a dull thud, a high plume of water and then a broader cascade of shattered ice. The large triangular blocks divide and break apart, and the men in teams drag the several fragments out of the dock with grappling hooks. When the dock is entirely cleared of ice, they warp the ship into it—tugging the bows in first, then swinging the stern round to straighten. They moor her to the floe with ice anchors then climb back on board, wet and exhausted. Handfuls of coal are thrown into the cabin stoves and a round of grog is served. Sumner, who has assisted with the cutting and feels knocked up and wretched from the effort, eats his tea in the mess, then takes a dose of laudanum and settles in his cabin to rest. Although he drops into sleep easily enough, he is woken intermittently by the great percussions of the ice field, the thunderous explosion of one floe meeting another one. He thinks of artillery, of the fifteen pounders thumping on the ridge, the sickening overhead roar of shell and cannonball, then stuffs his ears with cotton wool and reminds himself that their ship is safe enough and that the dock they have made for it is strong and secure.

In the early hours of the morning, with the wind still gusting hard from the north and the sky a luminant, unstarred smear of mauve and purple, one large corner of the ice dock fractures under the pressure of the pack and the broken-off segment is driven hard onto the *Volunteer's* stern post, propelling the ship forwards and sideways. The bows are driven into the other end of the ice dock and, with an enormous wail of strained and splitting wood, the ship is viciously squeezed between the land ice and the moving pack. The timbers screech, the vessel spasms upwards. Sumner, torn from his tranquil dreams, hears Cavendish and Otto hollering down the hatchway. As he scrambles to get into his sea boots, he feels the ship shudder and dislocate, the boards beneath his feet begin to tremble and separate, his books and medicines cascade down from the shelves, the door lintel shatters. On deck there is uproar. Cavendish is loudly ordering the evacuation of the ship. The whaleboats are being lowered onto the ice, men are frantically gathering their possessions and hauling provisions and equipment up from the holds. Chests, bags and mattresses are pitched over the bulwarks; provision casks are rolled down the gangway onto the floe, seized upon and rolled away. A sail is spread on the ice, and the bedding and mattresses are thrown onto it. The whaleboats are filled with food, fuel, rifles, ammunition, then covered with tarpaulins and dragged a safe distance from the groaning ship. Cavendish bellows commands and imprecations, and every now and then joins in—kicking a cask across the deck or tossing a sack of coal out onto the ice. Sumner runs back and forth from the ship to the floe then back again, hauling and carrying, taking what is given to him and leaving it wherever he is told. His head is in a ferment. He understands from snatched conversations with Black and Otto that their situation is perilous: when the ice-dock fractured, the ship was most likely stoved-in fore or aft and it is only the upward pressure of the ice that is presently stopping her from sinking completely.

Cavendish raises the inverted ensign as a signal of distress, then orders the blacksmith down into the forehold to release Drax from his chains. They strip the captain's cabin, the bread locker, the line room and the galley, and make ready to cut the rigging when necessary. Drax emerges from below decks bare-headed, shirtless, wearing a filthy pea coat, ruined brogans, and smelling strongly of piss. His ankles are free, but his wrists are still crudely manacled. He looks scornfully about him and smiles.

'I'd say there's no need for such girlish fucking panicking,' he says to Cavendish. 'There int but two foot of water down in that hold.'

Cavendish tells him curtly to go and fuck himself, then turns away to continue supervising the unloading.

'I was down there when she was nipped,' Drax continues, undeterred. 'I saw it with my own eyes. She bent a good deal all right, but she didn't break. This ice'll ease off in a little while and you can send McKendrick down there with his caulking iron; he'll fix her up nicely.'

Cavendish, after pausing for thought, sends the blacksmith back onto the ice, leaving Drax and himself alone on the half-deck.

'You'll keep your fucking mouth shut now,' Cavendish tells him, 'or I'll put you back where you were and let you take your chances.'

'She int sinking, Michael,' Drax tells him calmly. 'You may dearly wish she was, but she int. I can promise you that.'

Three weeks in the chill and darkness of the forehold have had no noticeable effect. Back on deck, Drax looks intact, unweakened, as if the imprisonment was merely a necessary interlude, and now the story proper has resumed. Below their feet, the deck shakes and the ship groans and crackles under the rasping pressure of the ice.

'Listen to her squeal now,' Cavendish says, 'creaking and wailing like a sixpunny whore. You honestly think she can stand much more of that if she int stoved in already?'

'She's a good strong ship, doubled and fortified: ice knees, ice plates, stanchions and the rest. She's old but she int weak. I'd say she could stand a good deal of squeezing still.'

The sun, which never fully set, is beginning to rise again. The ship's distended shadow spills across the larboard ice. To north and south, the purple tips of distant mountains gleam. Cavendish takes his hat off, scratches his head and looks over at the men still working on the floe. They are building tents from spars, poles and stun-sail booms. They are kindling fires on iron cressets.

'If she don't sink now, I can always sink her later.'

Drax nods.

'True,' he says. 'But that wont look half so good. You built a fucking *ice dock*.'

Cavendish smiles.

'It was a rare stroke of luck the way it broke like that. Don't happen too often, does it?'

'No, it don't. And it appears you're good and safe here on the fast ice too. Campbell can warp back easy if a lead opens up. With a bit of luck, you won't need to walk more than a mile or two to get to him. And the rest of them think she's stoved in already, I expect. They won't be making any trouble.'

Cavendish nods.

'She won't survive this one,' he says. 'She can't.'

'She will if you let her, but if you knocked a plank or two

out of her arse, she surely wouldn't. Give me ten minutes down there with an axe, that's all. Why fuck about?'

Cavendish sneers.

'You kill Brownlee with a walking stick and you honestly think I'm going to gift you a fucking axe?'

'If you don't believe me, go look down there for yourself,' he says. 'See if I'm lying.'

Cavendish licks his lips and paces round the deck a while. The wind has slackened off, but the dawn air is stiff and cold around them. Out on the floe, men are shouting and the ship beneath is keeping up its ghoulish groans.

'Why kill the boy?' Cavendish says to him. 'Why kill Joseph Hannah? What's the benefit in that?'

'A man don't always think on the benefits.'

'So what does he think on?'

Drax shrugs.

'I do as I must. Int a great deal of cogitation involved.'

Cavendish shakes his head, curses abominably and peers up at the paling sky above. After some moments of silence, he walks to the gunwale and calls down to a cabin boy to bring him a lantern and an axe. The two men descend to the tween decks and then, with Drax leading the way, down into the forehold. The air is dank and frigid, the lantern's yellow light illuminates a stanchion, the hold beams, the ribbed surface of the stacked casks.

'Dry as a fucking bone,' Drax says.

'Raise some of them casks up over there,' Cavendish tells him. 'I can hear water leaking in, I swear it.'

'Nowt but a dribble,' Drax says. He squats and heaves up a

cask and then another one. The two men lean in and peer downwards at the dark curving of the hull. Water is spraying through a breach where the timbers have separated and the caulking has dropped away, but there is no sign of serious damage.

'*Fuck*,' Cavendish whispers. 'Fuck. How can that be?'

'Like I told it,' Drax says. 'She bent a good deal, but she didn't ever break.'

Cavendish puts down the lantern and the axe, and the two of them together begin moving away more casks until they are standing on the bottom-most tier and most of the timbers on the starboard bow are exposed.

'She won't sink unless you make her do it, Michael,' Drax says. 'That's how it is.'

Cavendish shakes his head and reaches for the axe.

'Nothing's fucking simple in this world,' he says.

Drax steps back to give him room to swing. Cavendish pauses and turns to look at him.

'This don't put me under any obligation,' he says. 'I can't free you now. Not after Brownlee. A cabin boy is one thing, a cabin boy is plenty bad enough, but not the fucking captain.'

'And I int asking for it,' Drax says. 'I wouldn't presume.'

'Then what?'

Drax shrugs, sniffs and gathers himself.

'If the time ever comes,' he says slowly, 'all I ask is you don't hinder me, don't stand athwart. Allow events to take their natural course.'

Cavendish nods.

'I turn the blind eye,' he says. 'That's what you're asking.'

'The time may never come. I may hang in England for what I done and rightly so.'

'But if it ever does come.'

'Aye, if it ever does.'

'And what about my fucking nose?' Cavendish says, pointing.

Drax smiles.

'You were never no Adonis, Michael,' he says. 'I 'spect some would call that an improvement.'

'You have some fair-sized fucking balls, to say that to a man hefting an axe.'

'Like a fine big pair of tatties,' Drax confirms lightly, 'and I'll even let you stroke 'em if you like.'

For a moment, they hold each other's gaze, and then Cavendish turns away in disgust, swings the axe and lets its ground steel edge bite down hard into the ship's already dampened timbers, eight, nine, ten times until the doubled planking creaks, swells and begins to splinter inwards.

17

Within two hours, the ship has pitched forward so far that its bowsprit is lying flat against the ice and the foremast has snapped clean in two. Cavendish sends Black aboard with a team of men to salvage the booms, spars and rigging, and cut down the other masts before they break off also. De-masted and with only its stern poking above the piled-up ice around it, the ship appears rumpish and ludicrous, an emasculated mockery of what it was, and Sumner wonders how he could ever have believed such a fragile conglomeration of wood, nails and rope could protect or keep him safe.

The *Hastings*, their means of escape, is four miles to the east, moored to the edge of the land floe. Cavendish fills a small canvas knapsack with biscuits, tobacco and rum, shoulders it and sets off walking across the ice. He comes back several hours later looking drained and footsore, but well satisfied, and announces that they have been offered refuge and hospitality by Captain Campbell and should begin transferring men and supplies without delay. They will work in three gangs of twelve, he explains, using the whaleboats as sledges. The first two gangs, one led by Black and the other by Jones-the-whale, will leave immediately, while the third will stay by the wreck until they return.

Sumner spends the afternoon asleep on a mattress in one of the jury-rigged tents covered over with rugs and a blanket. When he wakes, he sees that Drax is sitting close by, guarded by the blacksmith, with his wrists manacled together and each leg chained to a triple sheave block. Sumner has not seen Drax since the murderous assault in Brownlee's cabin and is surprised by the immediacy and force of his revulsion.

'Don't be afeared, doctor,' Drax calls to him. 'I int about to do anything too desperate with these wooden baubles dangling off me.'

Sumner pushes back the rugs and blanket, gets to his feet and walks over.

'How's your arm?' he asks him.

'And which arm would that be?'

'The right one, the one that had Joseph Hannah's tooth embedded in it.'

Drax dismisses the question with a shake of the head.

'Just a nick,' he says. 'I'm a quick healer. But, you know, how that tooth got in there is still beyond me. I can't explain it at all.'

'So you have no remorse for your actions? No guilt for what you've done?'

Drax's mouth lolls half open, he wrinkles up his nose and sniffs.

'Did you think I was going to murder you down in the cabin?' he asks. 'Split open your skull like I did Brownlee. Is that what you were thinking?'

'What else were you intending?'

'Oh, I don't intend too much. I'm a doer not a thinker, me. I follow my inclination.'

'You have no conscience then?'

'One thing happens, then another comes after it. Why is the first thing more important than the second? Why is the second more important than the third? Tell me that.'

'Because each action is separate and distinct, some are good and some are evil.'

Drax sniffs again and scratches himself.

'Them's just words. If they hang me, they will hang me 'cause they can and 'cause they wish to do it. They will be following their own inclination as I follow mine.'

'You recognise no authority at all then, no right or wrong beyond yourself?'

Drax shrugs and bares his upper teeth in something like a grin.

'Men like you ask such questions to satisfy themselves,' he says. 'To make them feel cleverer or cleaner than the rest. But they int.'

'You truly believe we are all like you? How is that possible? Am I a murderer like you are? Is that what you accuse me of?'

'I seen enough killing to suspect I int the only one to do it. I'm a man like any other, give or take.'

Sumner shakes his head.

'No,' he says. 'That I won't accept.'

'You please yourself, as I please myself. You accept what suits you and you reject what don't. The law is just a name they give to what a certain kind of men prefer.'

Sumner feels a pain growing behind his eyeballs, a sour sickness curdling in his stomach. Talking to Drax is like shouting into the blackness and expecting the blackness to answer back in kind.

'There is no reasoning with a man like you,' he says.

Drax shrugs again and looks away. Outside the tent the men are playing a comical game of cricket on the snow using staves for bats and a ball made of sealskin and sawdust.

'Why do you keep that gold ring?' he asks. 'Why not sell it on?'

'I keep it for remembrance.'

Drax nods and rolls his tongue around his mouth before answering.

'A man who is scared of hisself int much of a man in my book.'

'You think I'm scared? Why would I be scared?'

'Because of whatever happened over there. Whatever it was you did or didn't do. You say you keep it for remembrance, but that int it at all. It can't be.'

Sumner steps forward and Drax rises to confront him.

'Whoa there now,' the blacksmith says. 'Sit the fuck down and shut the fuck up. Show some respect to Mr Sumner.'

'You don't know me at all,' Sumner tells him. 'You have no idea who I am.'

Drax sits back down and smiles at him.

'There int too terribly much to know,' he says. 'You int as complicated as you think. But what little there is to know, I'd say I know it well enough.'

Sumner leaves the tent and walks across to one of the whaleboats to check his medicines and sea chest have been safely stowed for the next day's journey across the ice. He unfixes the tarpaulin and scans the casks, boxes and rolled-up bedding squeezed inside. Even after shifting things about and peering into the gaps, he can't see what he is looking for. He replaces the tarpaulin and is about to go over to the other boat to check there when Cavendish calls to him. He is standing by a pile of rigging and the two severed masts. The bear, asleep in his cask, is lying next to him.

'You need to shoot that fucking bear,' he says, pointing down. 'If you do it now you'll have time enough to skin him before we leave in the morrow.'

'Why not take him with us? There'll be room enough on the *Hastings*, surely.'

Cavendish shakes his head.

'Too many mouths to feed already,' he says. 'And I int about to ask the men to drag that fucker four miles across the ice. They have enough to haul as it is. Here.' He gives him a rifle. 'I'd gladly do it myself except I hear you've grown fond of the beast.'

Sumner takes the rifle and crouches down to look into the cask.

'I won't shoot him when he's sleeping like that. I'll take him over yonder and let him wander about a little first.'

'Do it howsoever you like,' Cavendish says. 'Just so long as he's gone by morning.'

Sumner attaches a rope to the metal grille and, with Otto's assistance, begins to move the cask. When he estimates they are far enough from the edge of the makeshift camp, they stop, and Sumner unhooks the latch, kicks the grille open and retreats. The bear ambles out onto the ice. He is almost twice as large now as when they caught him. He has grown plump from Sumner's regular morning feedings, and his previously grubby fur is bright and clean. They watch him ambling about, heavy-pawed, phlegmatic, sniffing the cask, then nudging it twice with his snout.

'He can't survive on his own even if we let him go,' Sumner says to Otto. 'I've spoiled him with feeding. He wouldn't know how to hunt.'

'Better to shoot him now,' Otto agrees. 'I know a furrier in Hull, will give you a fair price for the skin.'

Sumner loads the rifle and takes his aim. The bear stops moving and turns sideways, exposing his broad flank as if offering himself to Sumner as the easiest possible target.

'Just behind the ear is quickest,' Otto says.

Sumner nods, tightens his grip on the stock and lines up the shot. The bear turns calmly to look at him. His thick white neck, his garnet eye. Sumner wonders for a moment what the bear must be thinking and immediately wishes he hadn't. He lowers the rifle and hands it to Otto. Otto nods.

'An animal has no soul,' he says. 'But some love is possible nonetheless. Not the highest form of love, but still love.'

'Just fucking shoot him,' Sumner says.

Otto checks the rifle, then lowers onto one knee to set himself. Before he can take aim, however, the bear, as if sensing something important has altered, stiffens suddenly then wheels heavily round and starts running, his broad columnar legs thudding against the ice and his claws kicking up brief clods of loose snow. Otto fires quickly at his retreating hindquarters but misses, and by the time he reloads the bear has disappeared behind a pressure ridge. The two men chase after him, but they cannot match the bear's speed across the ice. They get to the top of the ridge and fire off another hopeful shot, but the distance is already too large and the bear is moving too rapidly. They stand where they are, with the wreck behind them and the snow-clad cordillera ahead, and watch his galloping, rhythmical whiteness fade gradually into the broader and more static whiteness of the floe.

That night the wind veers from north to west and a violent storm blows up. One of the makeshift tents is ripped from its moorings, the framework of spars and booms that holds it up collapses, and the men inside, scoured by frigid blasts of wind and snow, are forced to chase the loose and cartwheeling canvas out across the ice. Eventually, when it snags on a hummock, they wrestle it down and drag it, writhing and flapping, back to the camp. The gale makes repairs impossible, so instead they secure what they can with ropes and ice anchors and seek shelter in the second tent. Sumner, who cannot sleep because he has no laudanum, helps them drag inside what remains of their dampened bedding and make space on the floor. The noise outside is enormous. The ice is moving again and Sumner can hear, below the shrill descant of the wind and the rattling and straining of the canvas, an occasional vast concussion as the pack roves and breaches.

Otto and Cavendish venture out to check the safety of the whaleboats and come back shivering and wreathed in snow. The men wrap themselves in blankets and cluster round the feeble heat of a small iron stove up on bricks in the middle of the tent. Sumner, on the fringes, curls up on himself, pulls his cap down over his eyes, and attempts to sleep but can't. He is sure now that the medicine chest containing his supply of opium has been transferred to the *Hastings* already, that it was included in error, along with his sea chest, in the supplies carried by the first party. One night without opium, he thinks, is easy enough, but if this storm persists and they are forced to stay on the ice a second night, he will begin to sicken. He curses himself for not paying closer attention to his necessaries, and he curses Jones for not being more careful about what was packed in the boats. He closes his eyes and tries to imagine he is elsewhere, not Delhi this time but Belfast, sitting in Kennedy's drinking whisky, rowing on the Lagan or in the dissecting rooms with Sweeney and Mulcaire, smoking cheap shag and gabbing about the girls. He falls, after a while, into a murky restless kind of drowse, not fully asleep but not awake either. The rest of the men coagulate into a dark and snoring heap beside him, the collective warmth of their pressed-together bodies clinging to them briefly, then dissipating upwards in the chill and swirling air.

After a few more hours, the storm appears to have steadied itself, to have reached an equilibrium which may presage its end, when, with a fearsome crash, the floe itself, the very surface they are sleeping on, jolts upwards. One pole of the tent collapses, and the iron stove topples over, sending red-hot coals spilling out and setting blankets and pea coats alight. Sumner, bewildered, chest tight with alarm, pulls on his boots and dashes outside into the gloom. Through a stuttering veil of snow, he sees at the floe edge a bluish iceberg, immense, chimneyed, wind-gouged, sliding eastwards like an albinistic butte unmoored from the desert floor. The berg is moving at a brisk walking pace and as it moves, its nearest edge grinds against the floe and spits up house-sized rafts of ice, like swarf from the jaws of a lathe. The floe shudders beneath Sumner's feet; twenty yards away a jagged crack appears, and he wonders for a moment if the entire plateau might crumble under the strain and everything, tents, whaleboats, men, be pitched into the sea. No one now remains in the second tent. The men who were inside it are either standing transfixed like Sumner or are busy pushing and dragging the whaleboats further away from the edge in a desperate effort to keep them safe. Sumner feels, as he watches, that he is seeing something he shouldn't rightly see, that he is being made an unwilling party to a horrifying but elemental truth-telling.

As quickly as the chaos began, however, it ceases. The berg loses contact with the edge of the ice, and the shuddering cacophony of impact gives way to the remnant howling of the wind and the oaths and curses of the men. Sumner notices for the first time that snow is pelting against the left side of his face and gathering in his beard. He feels for a moment wrapped up, cocooned, made strangely private by the fierceness of the weather, as if the world beyond, the real world, is separate and forgettable, and he alone inside the whirl of snow exists. Someone tugs his arm and points him backwards. He sees that the second tent is now ablaze. Mattresses, rugs and sea chests are burning fiercely; what remains of the canvas is whipping about in the high wind and flaming like a tar barrel. The rump of the crew stare aghast, their helpless faces brightened by the high dancing flames. Cavendish, after kicking at the embers and bewailing his ill-luck, yells for them to take refuge in the remaining whaleboats. Working rapidly but without method, they empty out the two boats, pack themselves inside like cargo, then pull the tarpaulins taut across the top. The resultant spaces are fetid and coffin-like. The air inside is sparse and pungent, and there is no light at all. Sumner is lying on bare, cold timbers, and the men arrayed around him are talking loudly and bitterly about the incompetence of Cavendish, the astonishing ill-luck of Brownlee, and their desire, above all and despite everything, to get home alive. Exhausted but sleepless, his muscles and inner organs beginning to itch and agitate with the unmet need for opium, he tries again to forget where he is, to imagine he is somewhere better, happier, but he can't succeed.

In the morning, the storm has abated. The day is cool and damp with grey cloud overhead and flat bands of fog concealing the floe edge and lying like layered quartz across the dark faces of the distant mountains behind. They pull back the snow-laden tarpaulins and climb out of the whaleboats.

198

The burnt and blackened fragments of the second tent and most of what it contained are strewn untidily across the ice in front of them. Some of the spars, half sunk in pools of meltwater, are still smouldering. While the cook boils water and cobbles together a rough version of breakfast, the men pick and poke through the lukewarm embers for anything still usable and worth preserving. Cavendish strolls among them, whistling and making ribald jokes. He carries an enamelled mug of steaming beef tea in his left hand. Every now and then, he bends down like a gentleman fossil hunter to pick up a still-warm knife blade or a solitary boot heel. For a man who has just seen his ship crushed, and narrowly survived an iceberg and then a fire in the night, he appears, Sumner thinks, unusually good-humoured and carefree.

After eating, they repack the whaleboats, then raise up the one surviving tent, weigh down its edges with provision casks and settle inside with playing cards and pipe tobacco to wait for Black, Jones and the others to return from the *Hastings*. After an hour or so, as the fog lifts, Cavendish goes outside with his telescope to check for signs of the returning party. After a while, he calls out for Otto and, after a while longer, Otto calls out for Sumner.

Cavendish hands Sumner the telescope and points east without speaking. Sumner extends the telescope and looks through it. He is expecting to see, off in the distance, Black, Jones and the rest of the crew tugging the four empty whaleboats across the ice towards them, but in fact he sees nothing at all. He lowers the telescope, squints into the distant emptiness, then raises the telescope to his eye and looks again.

'So where are they?'

Cavendish shakes his head, curses and starts angrily rubbing the nape of his neck. His previous calmness and good humour has disappeared. He is pale-faced and tight-lipped. His eyes are wide open and he is breathing hard through his nose.

'The *Hastings* is gone,' Otto says.

'Gone where?'

'Most likely, she ventured out into the pack last night to escape from the bergs,' Cavendish says sharply. 'That's all there is to it. She will find her way back to the floe edge soon enough. Campbell knows just where we are. All we need to do is wait for him here. Show a bit of faith and a bit of fucking patience.'

Sumner looks through the telescope again, sees, again, nothing but sky and ice, then looks at Otto.

'Why would a ship unmoor in the midst of a storm?' he asks. 'Wouldn't she be safer remaining where she was?'

'If a berg is bearing down, the captain does what's needed to save the ship,' Otto says.

'Exactly,' Cavendish says. 'Whatever you have to do, you do it.'

'How long might we have to wait here?'

'That all depends,' Cavendish says. 'If she finds open water, it could be today. If not . . .'

He shrugs.

'I don't have my medicine chest,' Sumner says. 'It was taken across already.'

'Is any man here sick?'

'Not yet, no.'

'Then I'd say that's about the least part of our fucking worries.'

Sumner remembers watching the iceberg through the grey veil of flailing snow: many-storeyed and immaculate, moving smoothly and unstoppably forward with the frictionless non-movement of a planet.

'The *Hastings* could be sunk,' he realises. 'Is that what you mean?'

'She int sunk,' Cavendish tells him.

'Are there other ships that can rescue us?'

Otto shakes his head.

'Not near enough. It's too late in the season and we're too far north. Most of the fleet have left Pond's Bay by now.'

'She int sunk,' Cavendish repeats. 'She's somewhere out there in the Sound, that's all. If we wait here, she'll come back right enough.'

'We should go out with the whaleboats to search,' Otto says. 'It was a fierce wind last night, she could have been blown miles off to the east. She could be stoved in, nipped, rudderless, anything at all.'

Cavendish frowns, then nods reluctantly, as if eager to think of a better, easier solution but utterly unable to do so.

'We'll find her soon enough when we go out there,' he says quickly, snapping shut the brass telescope and shoving it into his greatcoat pocket. 'She won't be far off, I'd say.'

'What if we don't find her?' Sumner asks. 'What then?'

Cavendish pauses and looks at Otto, who stays silent. Cavendish tugs his ear lobe and answers in a ludicrous music hall brogue.

'Den I hope you brought your swimming togs along widje, Paddy,' he says. ''Cause it's an awful long focking way to anywhere else from hereabouts.'

They spend the rest of the day out in the whaleboats, rowing first east along the edge of the land ice, then turning north towards the centre of the Sound. The storm has broken up the pack, and they move without difficulty through the irregular fragments of drift and brash ice, steering around them when necessary or poking them aside with the blades of their long oars. Otto commands one boat and Cavendish the other. Sumner, who has been promoted to steersman, imagines every moment that they will sight the *Hastings* on the horizon—like a single dark stitch against the coarse, grey blanket of the sky—and that the fear that is aching inside him, that he is struggling to contain, will dissolve like mist. He senses among the crewmen an anxiety edged with bitterness and anger. They are searching for someone to blame for this perilous string of misfortunes, and Cavendish, whose promotion to the captaincy is unearned and tainted with unnaturalness and violence, is the most deserving and obvious candidate.

They return to the ramshackle and burnt-over camp, weary, bone-chilled and low in spirits, having pulled hard all day and seen no sign of the *Hastings* nor found any indication of her possible fate. The cook builds a fire from barrel staves and sawn-up sections of the mizzen-mast and fashions a sour-tasting stew of salt beef and ancient, woody turnips. After the eating is over, Cavendish taps a cask of brandy and has a ration served to each man. They sullenly drink down their allotted portions and then, without asking further permission, begin taking more, until the cask is emptied and the atmosphere inside the tent is liquorous and unstable. Soon, after a period of drunken and cantankerous arguing, a fight breaks out and a knife is drawn. McKendrick, a mere onlooker, is slashed deeply in the forearm, and the blacksmith is knocked senseless. When Cavendish tries to intervene, his head is split open with a belaying pin, and Sumner and Otto have to step in to save him from a worse beating. They pull him outside for safety. Otto goes back to try to calm the men, but is himself abused and then threatened with the knife. Cavendish, back on his feet, cursing foully, face gruesomely chequered with his own blood, takes two loaded rifles from the whaleboats, gives a third to Otto and ventures back inside the tent. He fires once down into the ice to gain their attention and then declares that he will gladly put the second bullet into any cunt who fancies his chances.

'With Brownlee gone, I'm captain still, and I'll cheerfully murder any mutinous bastard who dares think otherwise.'

There is a pause, then Bannon, a loose-eyed Shetlander with silver hoops in his ears, picks up a barrel stave and rushes wildly forward. Cavendish, without raising the rifle from his hip, tilts the barrel upwards and shoots him through the throat. The top portion of the Shetlander's skull detaches and flies backwards against the steeply pitched canvas roof, leaving a broad red bull's-eye and, around it, a fainter aureole of purplish brain matter. There is a guttural roar of dismay from the other men, and then a sudden, leaden silence. Cavendish drops the empty rifle at his feet and takes the loaded one from Otto.

'You other cunts take heed now,' he tells them. 'This pox-arsed foolishness has just cost a man his life.'

He licks his lips, then looks curiously about as though selecting who to shoot next. Blood seeps off his eyebrow and beard, and spatters down onto the ice. The tent is smeared with shadows and smells fiercely of liquor and piss.

'I'm a loose fucking cannon, I am,' Cavendish tells them quietly. 'I do whatever takes my fancy at the time. You best remember that if you ever think of crossing me again.'

He nods twice in bullish confirmation of this candid self-accounting, sniffs and draws his hand across his blood-soaked beard.

'Tomorrow we make a run for Pond's Bay,' he says. 'If we don't find the *Hastings* on the way there, we'll surely find another ship to take us when we arrive.'

'It's a hundred mile to Pond's Bay if it's an inch,' someone says.

'Then you bastards best sober up and get some sleep afore-times.'

Cavendish looks down at the dead Shetlander and shakes his head.

'It's a fucking foolish way to go,' he says to Otto. 'Man's carrying a loaded rifle, you don't take him on with a barrel stave. That's simple common sense.'

Otto nods and then steps forward and, with a solemn and pontifical air, makes the sign of the cross above the corpse. Two of the men, unbidden, take the Shetlander by the boot heels and drag him out onto the floe. Off in a corner, unnoticed amid this uproar, Drax in chains sits like an idol—cross-legged, smiling, watching from afar.

18

The next day, Sumner is too feverish to steer or row. As they pull east through layers of thick fog and showers of freezing rain and sleet, he huddles in the stem covered by a blanket, shivering and stomach-sick. Every now and then, Cavendish shouts out an order or Otto commences whistling a Germanic air, but there are no other sounds except the death rattle creak of the oarlocks and the asynchronous plash of the blades in the water. Each man, it seems, is wrapped up in his own silent forebodings. The day is gloomy, the sky dun-coloured and raw. Twice before noon, Sumner has to pull down his britches and hang his arse over the gunwale to sputter out a pint or so of liquid shit into the sea. When Otto offers him brandy, he swallows it down gratefully, then retches it straight back up. The men watch all this without comment or mockery. Bannon's murder has flattened their resolve, left them stranded warily between equal but opposing fears.

At night, they camp on the floe edge, raise the blood-stained tent, attempt to dry and feed themselves. Near midnight, the bluish twilight thickens briefly to a gaudy and stelliferous darkness, then an hour later reasserts itself. Sumner sweats and shivers, dips in and out of an uneasy and dream-afflicted sleep. Around him, bundled bodies grumble and gasp like snoozing cattle; the air inside the tent feels iron cold against his cheeks and nose, and has a stewed and crotch-like reek to it. As his flesh yearns, aches and itches for the absent drug, his mind drifts and circles. He remembers the solitary journey from Delhi, the humiliations of Bombay, and then London in April. Peter Lloyd's Hotel in Charing Cross: the smell of semen and old cigar smoke; the squeals and shrieks of whores and their customers at night; the iron bed, the oil lamp, the threadbare fauteuil spitting horse hair and grimed with bear fat and Macassar oil. He eats pork chops and peas and lives on questionable credit. Every morning for two weeks, he goes out to the hospitals with his diplomas and his outdated letters of introduction; he sits in corridors and waits. In the evening, he seeks out acquaintances from Belfast and Galway—not good friends but men who will at least remember him: Callaghan, Fitzgerald, O'Leary, McCall. They reminisce over whisky and ale. When the time is right, he asks for their help and they tell him to try America, Mexico or possibly Brazil, somewhere where the past does not matter as much as it does here, where the people are more free and easy and more likely to forgive a man's mistakes since they

have made a few themselves. England is not the place for
him, they tell him, not any more, it is too rigid and severe, he
must give it up. Although they believe his story, they assure
him, others never will. Their tone is friendly enough, com-
radely even, but he can tell that they wish him away. They
greet news of his great failure as a reassuring reminder of
their own more modest success, but also, more deeply, as a
warning of what calamities might overtake them if they ever
lose their vigilance, if they ever forget who they are or what
they are about. In their worst imaginings, they see in his disgrace a garish prophecy of their own.

At night, he takes opium and walks about the city until he
is tired enough to sleep. One evening, as he scuffs lopsidedly
along Fleet Street, then past Temple Bar and the Courts of
Justice, his ferule tapping the pavement as he goes along, he
is astonished to see Corbyn coming straight towards him. He
is wearing his campaign medals and red dress uniform; his
tar-black boots are polished to a mirrored sheen and he is in
conversation with another, younger officer, moustachioed
and similarly attired. They are both smoking cheroots and
laughing. Sumner stands where he is in the shadow of a
castellated doorway, and waits for them to reach him. As he
waits, he remembers Corbyn's manner at the court martial—casual, unconcerned, *natural*, as if, even as he lied, the
truth was in his gift, as if he could make or unmake it exactly
as he chose. As Sumner remembers the scene, he feels an ava-
lanche of rage beginning to gather inside his chest; the
muscles tighten in his throat and legs; he begins to shudder.
The two officers draw closer, and he feels for a ghoulish

moment excarnated, transcendent even, as if his body is much too small and slight to contain his furious thoughts. As they pass him, smoking and laughing, Sumner steps out from the doorway. He taps Corbyn on the brass-buttoned epaulette and, when he turns round to see who it is, strikes him across the face. Corbyn topples sideways. The younger officer drops his cheroot and stares.

'What the fuck?' he says. '*What?*'

Sumner doesn't respond. He looks at the man he has just hit and realises with a jolt that it is not Corbyn at all. They are roughly similar in age and height certainly, but apart from that, there is little true resemblance—the hair, the whiskers, the shape and features of the face, even the uniform is wrong. Sumner's rage dissolves, he returns to himself, to his own body, to the deep humiliations of the real.

'I thought you were someone else,' he tells the man. 'Corbyn.'

'Who the fuck is Corbyn?'

'A regimental surgeon.'

'Which regiment?'

'The Lancers.'

The man shakes his head.

'I should find a constable and have you jailed,' he says. 'I swear to God, I should.'

Sumner tries to help him, but the man pushes him away. He touches his cheek again, winces, then looks carefully at Sumner. The cheek is reddening, but there is no blood.

'Who are you?' he says. 'I recognise that face.'

'I'm no one,' Sumner tells him.

'Who are you?' he says again. 'Don't fucking lie to me.'

'I'm no one,' he says. 'No one at all.'

The man nods.

'Come here then,' he says.

Sumner steps closer. The man places his hand on Sumner's shoulder. Sumner smells the port wine on his breath, the bandoline in his hair.

'If you're really no one,' he says, 'I don't suppose you'll object too much to this.'

He leans in six inches and drives his knee high up into Sumner's balls. The pain ricochets through Sumner's stomach and out into his chest and face. He drops to his knees on the wet pavement, groaning and wordless.

The man, who he thought was Corbyn but isn't, leans down and whispers gently into his ear.

'The *Hastings* is gone,' he says. 'Sunk. Smashed to little pieces by a berg, and every fucker in her bar none is drowned, for sure.'

The next afternoon, they find a capsized whaleboat and then, a little while later, an intermittent half-mile-long slew of empty blubber casks and shattered timbers. They row about in slow circles, picking up pieces of the debris, examining them, conferring, then dropping them helplessly back into the water. Cavendish for once is pale and silent, his normal piss and windiness crushed by the weight of unlooked-for catastrophe. He scans the nearby ice floes with the telescope but sees nothing and no one. He spits, curses, turns aside. Sumner, through the green and melancholic haze of his sickness, realises that their best hope of rescue is now gone. Some of the men begin to weep and others start clumsily praying. Otto checks the charts and takes a reading with the sextant.

'We're past Cape Hay,' he calls across to Cavendish. 'We can reach Pond's Bay before night. When we get there, we'll find another ship, God willing.'

'If we don't, we'll have to winter o'er,' Cavendish says. 'That's been done afore.'

Drax, who is chained to the rearmost rowing bench and is thus the closest man to Cavendish, who is at the steering oar, snorts at this.

'It hant been done afore,' he says, 'and it hant been done afore because it can't *be* done. Not without a ship to shelter in and ten times the provisions we have left.'

'We'll find a ship,' Cavendish says again. 'And if we don't find one, we'll winter o'er. Whichever way it goes, we'll all live long enough to see you hanged in England, you can be sure of that.'

'I'd be happier hanged than fucking starved to death or frozzen.'

'We should drown you now, you cavilling bastard. That'd be one less fucking mouth to feed.'

'You wouldn't like my dying words too well if you tried that trick,' Drax answers. 'Although there's others here might find 'em interesting enough.'

Cavendish looks at him for a time, then leans forward, takes a firm handful of his waistcoat, and replies in a fierce whisper.

'You hant got nothing on me, Henry,' he says. 'So don't ever think you do.'

'I int squeezing, Michael,' Drax says calmly. 'I'm just reminding. The time may never come, but if it comes, it'd suit you to be ready, that's all.'

Drax picks up his oar, Cavendish calls out the order, and they begin to row again. To the west, a long line of coal-dark mountains, ashen-tipped, rise up out of the hammered greyness of the sea. The two whaleboats move gradually onward. After several hours, they reach the craggy tip of Bylot Island, and enter the mouth of Pond's Bay. Rain clouds gather and disperse, the light is slowly failing. Cavendish peers eagerly through his telescope, sees first nothing, then, wobbling on the horizon, the black outline of another vessel. He waves and points. He shouts to Otto.

'A ship,' he calls. 'A fucking ship. Over yonder. See there.'

They all see it, but it is far away and seems to be steaming south already. The smoke from its stack makes a faint, angled smudge against the sky, like a thumbed-out pencil line. They give urgent chase, but the effort is futile. In another half an hour, the ship has disappeared into the haze, and they are alone again on the dark, brimful sea with only the brown snow-clad hills about them and the scuffed and mournful evening sky above.

'What kind of fucking watch are they keeping that they don't see a whaleboat in distress?' Cavendish says bitterly.

''Appen the ship is full,' someone answers him. ''Appen they're heading home with all the rest.'

'No fucker's full this year,' Cavendish says. 'If they had anything about them, any fucking thing at all, they'd still be out here fishing.'

No one answers him. They look out into the pallid, misty drabness seeking for a sign, but see nothing.

As darkness falls, they pull over to a nearby headland and raise the tent on a thin strip of gravel beach backed by low brown cliffs. After eating, Cavendish orders the men to break up one of the whaleboats with hand axes and build a beacon fire with its salvaged timbers. If there is another ship out there in the bay, he argues, they will see the blaze and come to rescue them. Although the men appear to doubt this reasoning, they do as they are told. They turn the boat over and begin to smash apart its hull, keel and stern piece. Sumner, wrapped in a blanket, shivering and queasy still, stands beside the tent and watches them at their work. Otto approaches and stands next to him.

'This is how I dreamed it,' he says. 'The fire. The broken whaleboat. Everything the same.'

'Don't tell me that,' Sumner says. 'Not now.'

'I don't fear death,' Otto says. 'I never have. We none of us have any idea of the riches that await.'

Sumner coughs violently twice, then retches onto the icy ground. The men gather the broken wood into a pyre and light it. The wind catches the flames and blows them sparkling upwards into darkness.

'You're the one who survives,' Otto tells him. 'Out of all of us. Remember that.'

'I said before, I don't believe in prophecies.'

'Faith is not important. God doesn't care whether we believe in him or not. Why should he care?'

'You really think all this is His doing? The murders? The wrecks? The drownings?'

'I know it must be someone's,' Otto says. 'And if not the Lord, who else?'

While it burns, the bonfire elevates the crewmen's spirits; its startling brightness gives them hope. As they watch it rage and fork and spit out sparks, they feel sure that somewhere out there other men are also watching, that boats will soon be lowered, help dispatched. They throw the last fragments of wood on the raucous blaze and wait expectantly for their rescuers to arrive. They smoke their pipes and squint eagerly out into the murky distance. Their talk is of women and children, of houses and fields they might still live to see again. Every minute, as the flames gradually reduce and daylight increases around them, they anticipate a boat, but none appears. After an hour more of fruitless waiting, they begin to feel their optimism curdle, and something rank and bitter take its place. Without a ship to shelter in, without enough firewood and food, how can anyone live through the winter in a place like this one? When Cavendish walks down from his seat on the cliff, holding the closed telescope in one hand and a rifle in the other, his expression remote, disgraceful, his eyes turned away, they know for certain that the plan has failed.

'Where are the boats?' someone shouts to him. 'Why don't they come?'

Cavendish ignores the questions. He goes inside the tent

and starts counting up their remaining provisions. Even reducing everyone to half-rations, two pounds of bread a week and the same of salt meat, there is barely enough to last past Christmas. He shows Otto, then calls the remaining crewmen together and explains that they will need to hunt for their food if they want to survive until the spring. Seals will do, he says, foxes, loons, auks, any kind of bird. As he speaks, it starts to snow outside and the wind picks up and shakes the canvas walls like a prelibation of the coming winter. No one answers him, and no one volunteers to hunt. They look back at him silently and when he has finished, they curl up in their blankets and drift to sleep, or sit about playing euchre with a pack of cards so ancient, limp and filthy they might have been cut from the rags of a lazar.

The snow falls steadily outside for the remainder of the day: heavy, wet flakes that sag the tent and clump like barnacles against the remaining whaleboat's upturned hull. Sumner is racked and shuddering; his bones ache and his eyeballs itch and throb. He cannot sleep or piss, although the desire for both is fierce within him. As he lies there, immobile, garbled fragments of the *Iliad* pass through his beleaguered mind—the black ships, the broken barricade, Apollo as a vulture, Zeus seated on a cloud. When he leaves the tent to shit, it is dark outside and the air is bitter cold. He crouches, pulls apart his raddled arse cheeks and lets the hot, green liquid sluice out from him. The moon's light is blurred by lines of cloud, snow sweeps across the outstretched bay, gathering on the extant floes and dissolving down into the black waters between. The cold air clamps and shrivels his bollocks. Sumner refastens his britches, turns and sees, fifty yards away along the gravel shore, a bear.

The bear's sharp, snake-like head is upraised, its broad body, heavy-shouldered and vast across the withers, stands fixed and certain. Sumner, shielding his eyes from the falling snow, takes a slow step forwards, then stops. The bear is unconcerned. It sniffs the ground, then turns in a slow pacing circle, ending where it began. Sumner stands and watches. The bear comes closer, but he doesn't move away. He can see the texture of its coat now, the dark semi-quadrants of its claws against the snow. The bear yawns once, bares its fangs, and then, without warning or obvious purpose, rears upwards on its hind limbs like a circus animal and dangles for a moment, suspended like a limestone obelisk against the pelting, moon-stained sky.

From behind him, blowing down off the mud-brown cliffs, Sumner hears a sudden uprearing bellow, a vast symphonic howl, pained, primeval, yet human nonetheless; a cry beyond words and language it seems to him, choral, chthonic, like the conjoined voices of the damned. Filled with a moment's terror, he turns round to look, but there is nothing there except the falling snow, the night, and the enormous, empty land off to the west, scarred and unimaginable, wrapping like bark around the planet's darkened bole. The bear stays poised upright a moment longer, then flops down onto its front paws, swivels and begins, implacably and without dispatch, to walk away.

19

The sea is beginning to refreeze. New ice, thin as glass, is forming between the existing floes, gluing them together. Soon enough, the bay will form into a solid white mass, rough-surfaced, immovable, and they will be locked in until the spring thaw arrives. The men sleep, smoke, play cards. They eat their meagre rations but make no efforts to improve their lot or prepare for the brutal winter to come. As the temperature falls and the nights lengthen, they burn driftwood washed in from the wreck of the *Hastings* and finish the final bags of coal they salvaged from the *Volunteer*. In the evenings, after supper, Otto reads drearily from the Bible, and Cavendish leads them all in ribald song.

Since the night he saw the bear, Sumner's symptoms have been gradually reducing. He still has headaches and night sweats, but the nausea is not so frequent and his stool is firmer. Freed to this degree from the hectoring tyrannies of his own body, he is better able to notice the condition of those around him. Without the usual healthful rigour of their shipboard duties, they have grown listless and pale. If they are to have enough strength and will to live through the depredations of the coming winter, to fend off the effects of cold and hunger, it occurs to him that they must be made to move about somehow, to invigorate themselves with exercise and labour. If not, then their current mood of melancholy will likely harden into despair and a more deadly lassitude will overtake them all.

He speaks to Cavendish and Otto, and they agree that the men should be divided into two roughly equal watches and that each morning, so long as the weather allows it, one watch will take the rifles and climb the cliffs to hunt for food and the other will spend an hour at least outside the tent tramping up and down the strand as a way of maintaining their vigour. The men, when they are told this, show little enthusiasm for the scheme. They appear unconcerned when Sumner explains that if they remain immobile and torpid their blood will thicken and clot inside their veins and their organs will become flaccid and eventually fail. It is only when Cavendish bellows at them and threatens to reduce the rations still further if they don't comply that they sourly give in.

Once begun, the daily hunting produces little that is edible—some small birds, occasionally a fox—and the trudging back and forth is much resented. After less than a month, these Spartan regularities are interrupted by two days of unceasing horizontal snow and pounding gales. Afterwards, there are drifts five feet deep all around the camp and the temperature has dropped so low that it is painful to inhale. The men refuse to hunt or walk in such conditions, and when Cavendish ventures out alone, in spite of them, he returns an hour later empty-handed, exhausted and frost-bitten. That same night they start to break up the second whaleboat for fuel, and, as the brutal cold persists and deepens, they burn more and more of it every day until Cavendish is forced to take control of the remaining wood supply and begin to ration its use. The fire, already meagre, becomes for most of the day little more than a small pile of faintly glowing embers. A layer of ice forms on the inside of the tent and the very air itself feels viscous and gelid. All night, triple-layered in wool, flannel and oilskin, clustered together like the victims of a sudden massacre, men shudder and spasm and jolt themselves awake.

Before they see the sledge, they hear the sledge-dogs' hectic barking. Sumner thinks at first that he is dreaming of Castlebar and Michael Duigan's famous pack of lurchers coursing hare, but when the other men begin to rouse and mumble, he realises that they must hear it too. He wraps a scarf tight about his head and face and goes outside. Looking west, he sees a pair of Yaks coming in at a pace across the sea ice, their brindled dogs fanned out in front of them, their rawhide whip, antenna-like, flicking and wafting in the frigid air. Cavendish rushes out of the tent, then Otto and the rest of the men. They watch the sledge gradually approaching, appearing ever more solid and real as it does so. When it reaches them, Cavendish steps forward and asks the Yaks for food.

'Meat,' he says loudly, 'fish.' He makes crude feeding gestures with his fingers and mouth. 'Hungry,' he says, pointing at his own stomach first and then the stomachs of the other men.

The Yaks look at him and grin. They are small and dark-skinned both. They have flat Gypsy faces and filthy black hair down to their shoulders. Their anoraks and boots are stitched from untanned caribou and their britches from bear fur. They point back at the loaded sledge. The dogs are barking madly all around.

'Trade,' they tell him.

Cavendish nods.

'Show me,' he says.

They undo the lashings on the sledge and show him a frozen seal carcass and what looks like the hind part of a walrus. Cavendish calls Otto over and the two men briefly confer. Otto goes back into the tent and comes out with two blubber knives and a hand axe. The Yaks examine them carefully. They give the axe back, but keep both the knives. They show Cavendish an ivory harpoon head and some soapstone carvings, but he waves them off.

'All we want is the food,' he says.

They agree to swap the frozen seal carcass for the two knives and a length of whale-line. Cavendish gives the meat to Otto, and Otto takes it inside the tent, hacks it into lumps with the hand axe and drops the lumps onto the embers of the fire. They hiss a moment, and then, after a few minutes longer, begin to broil and give off steam. While the men wait eagerly to eat, the Yaks tether and feed their dogs. Sumner hears them outside, laughing and chattering away in their own rapid, jerky tongue.

'If they give us seals,' he says to Cavendish, 'we can live until the spring. We can eat the meat and burn the blubber.'

Cavendish nods.

'Aye,' he says. 'I need a parley with them aboriginal fuckers. I need to strike up a good bargain. Problem is, they know we're fucked already. Listen to 'em out there, laughing and joking withemselves.'

'You think they'd let us starve to death?'

Cavendish sniffs.

'Happily they would,' he says. 'Heathenish fuckers such as them int burdened with the Christian virtues as men like us are. If they don't fancy what we have to offer, they'll be gone just as quick as they arrived.'

'Offer the rifles,' Sumner suggests. 'Ten dead seals for each rifle. Three rifles is thirty seals. We can live off that.'

Cavendish thinks a moment, then nods.

'I'll tell them twelve,' he says, 'twelve per rifle. Though I honestly doubt the savage bastards can even count that high.'

After they have eaten, Cavendish goes back outside, and Sumner goes with him. They show the Yaks one of the rifles, and then point back at the tent and make feeding gestures.

The Yaks examine the rifle, heft it, peer along the barrel. Cavendish loads a cartridge and lets the elder Yak shoot it off.

'That there's a fucking good weapon,' Cavendish says.

The Yaks talk to each other for a while, then slowly re-examine the rifle. When they finish, Cavendish leans down and makes twelve short marks in the snow. He points to the rifle, then he points to the marks and then to the tent. He makes the same feeding gesture as before.

For a minute, the Yaks say nothing. One of them reaches into his pocket, takes out a pipe and stuffs and lights it. The other smiles briefly, says something, then bends down and rubs out six of the marks.

Cavendish purses his lips, shakes his head and then slowly reinscribes the same six marks.

'I won't be jewed down by no fucking Esquimaux,' he says to Sumner.

The Yaks look displeased. One of them frowns, says something to Cavendish, and then quickly with the toe of his boot rubs out the same six marks again and then rubs out another.

'Shit,' Sumner whispers.

Cavendish laughs scornfully.

'Only five,' he says. 'Five fucking seals for a rifle. Do I honestly look like that much of a cunt?'

'If they leave us now, we'll starve to death,' Sumner reminds him.

'We'll survive without them,' he says.

'No, we fucking won't.'

The Yaks look back at them indifferently, point down at

the five marks on the ground, then hold out the rifle as if well prepared to give it back. Cavendish looks at the rifle steadily, but doesn't reach for it. He shakes his head and spits.

'Gouging ice-nigger bastards,' he says.

The Yaks build themselves a small snow house fifty yards away from the tent, then mount the sledge and go back out onto the ice to hunt. It is dark when they return. The black sky is dense with stars and upon its speckled blank, the borealis unfurls, bends back, reopens again like a vast and multi-coloured murmuration. Drax, still in manacles, but left unguarded now since they are all, in effect, imprisoned by the shared calamity, watches them unship their kill. He listens to the throttled grunting of their caveman speech, sniffs then smells, even through the frigid air, the sour reek of their grease-streaked armature. He weighs them up a while—their height, their weight, the speed and implication of their various shiftings—then walks towards them, clinking as he goes.

'Ye got two nice fat-looking ones there,' he says, pointing at the two dead seals. 'I can help you butcher 'em, if you'd like.'

Although they have been out hunting all day, the two men seem as fresh and lively as before. They look at him a moment, then point at his chains and laugh. Drax laughs with them, then rattles the chains and laughs again.

'Them cunts in there don't trust me, see,' he says. 'They think I'm dangerous.' He makes a distended, monster face and claws the air to illustrate his meaning. The Yaks laugh louder still. Drax reaches down and takes one of the dead seals by the tail.

'Let me butcher this one for ye,' he says again, making a cutting gesture along its belly as he does so. 'I can do it easy.'

They shake their heads and wave him off. The elder takes a knife, leans down and quickly cuts open and guts the two seals. He leaves the particoloured giblets, purple, pink and grey, steaming in a pile on the snow then separates the blubber from the meat. Drax watches on. He smells the ferric blood-tang of the innards and feels the drool begin to puddle in his mouth.

'I'll haul that over for ye, if you'd like it,' he says.

The two men ignore him still. The younger takes the meat and blubber over to the tent and gives it to Cavendish. The elder starts swiftly picking through the piles of giblets with his blade. He finds one of the livers, slices off a good-sized piece and eats it raw.

'Christ alive,' Drax says. 'I hant seen that before. I seen plenty, but I hant seen that.'

The man looks up at Drax and grins. His teeth and lips are red with seal blood. He cuts off another piece of the raw liver and offers it to him. Drax considers a moment, then takes it.

'I've eaten worse in my day,' he says. 'Plenty worse.'

He chews once, then swallows it down and smiles. The elder Yak smiles back and laughs. When the younger one comes back from the tent, they confer for a while and then beckon Drax closer. The elder reaches into the pile of giblets and pulls out a severed eyeball. He pierces its skin with the point of the knife and sucks out the inner jelly. They look at Drax and grin.

'That don't trouble me none,' Drax says. 'I've eaten eyeballs before, an eyeball's easy pickings.'

The elder finds another eyeball, pierces it as before, and gives it to him. Drax sucks out the juice, then puts the rest into his mouth and swallows it down. The Yaks start cackling wildly. Drax opens his mouth wide and sticks out his tongue to show that it's truly gone.

'I'll gobble down anything you can give me,' he says, 'any fucking thing at all—brains, bollocks, hooves. I int fussy, see.'

The elder Yak points to his chains again, growls and claws the air.

'Aye,' Drax says. 'Aye, that's about the size of it, right there.'

That night the Yaks feed their dogs with the remains of the rancid walrus meat, tether them to whalebone stakes driven into the gravel, and then crawl inside the snow house and settle down to sleep. They leave again early the next morning, but return after dark with no seals to show for their labour. The next day, it is snowing too hard to hunt and they stay inside the snow house all day. Drax hobbles through the blizzard, past the scattered humps of curled-up dogs, to visit them. He gives them each a pinch of tobacco and asks them questions. When they miss his meaning, he repeats himself more loudly and makes signs. In response, they point and laugh and trace out patterns in the air or on the rawhide surface of their reindeer sleeping bags. Occasionally, they slice off a piece of the frozen seal liver and gnaw on it like liquorice.

There are periods of silence, and periods in which the Yaks talk to each other as though he is not even there. He watches them and listens to what they say, and, after a while, he understands what he must do next. It is not a decision, so much as a slow uncovering. He feels the future gradually show itself. He smells its hot perfume hanging in the Arctic air, as a dog smells the rank requirements of a bitch.

When the blizzard abates, the Yaks go out seal hunting again. They kill one seal on the first day, and two more on the next. When they give over the final butchered carcass as agreed, Cavendish shows them the second rifle. He makes five more marks in the snow, but the Yaks shake their heads and point back in the direction they came from.

'They want to go back home,' Sumner says. They are standing outside the tent; the sky is bright and clear, but the air around is bitter cold. Sumner feels its desiccating bluntness press against his face and eyes.

'They can't go back,' Cavendish says. He points down at the ground again and waves the rifle at them.

The elder one shows him the rifle they already have, then points again to the west.

'*Utterpok*,' he says. 'No trade.'

Cavendish shakes his head and softly curses.

'We have enough meat and blubber now to last a month,' Sumner says. 'So long as they come back before the supply runs out, we can survive.'

'If that old bastard goes, the other one must stay here with us,' Cavendish says. 'If they go off together, we can't be sure they're ever coming back.'

228

'Don't threaten them,' Sumner warns. 'If you press too hard, they'll be gone for sure.'

'They may have that one rifle but they hant got no balls or powder for it yet,' Cavendish says. 'So I reckon I can threaten the bastards all I like if I have a mind to do it.'

He points at the younger man and then at the snow house.

'*He* stays here,' he says. '*You*'—pointing at the older man, then gesturing west—'can fuck off if you want to.'

The Yaks shake their heads and smile ruefully, as if they understand the suggestion, but find it both foolish and faintly embarrassing.

'No trade,' the older one repeats lightly. '*Utterpok.*'

Unafraid, amused even, they look at Cavendish for a while longer then turn away and start walking back towards the sledge. The tethered dogs uncurl from their snow holes and start to yip and howl as they approach. Cavendish reaches into his pocket for a cartridge.

'You think killing them will change their minds?' Sumner says. 'Is that your best idea?'

'I int killing anyone yet, I'm just aiming to get a little more attention, that's all.'

'Just wait,' he says. 'Put down the gun.'

The Yaks are already busy reloading their sledge, rolling up their bedding and lashing it to the wooden frame with strips of walrus hide. When Sumner walks across to them, they don't trouble to look up.

'I have something for you,' he says. 'See here.'

He holds out his gloved hand and shows them the looted

gold ring that he has been carrying, buttoned in his waistcoat pocket, since the day of Drax's capture.

The elder one looks up, pauses what he is doing and touches the younger on the shoulder.

'What use do such as they have for gold and jewels?' Cavendish asks. 'If ye can't eat it or burn it or fuck it, it int much use out here, seems to me.'

'They can trade it with other whalers,' Sumner says. 'They're not so stupid.'

The two men come closer. The elder one picks the ring from Sumner's dark woollen mitten and examines it carefully. Sumner watches him.

'If you stay here,' he says to the younger man, pointing, 'that ring is yours to keep.'

The two men talk between themselves. The younger one takes the ring, sniffs it, then licks it twice. Cavendish laughs.

'Daft bastard thinks it's made of marzipan,' he says.

The elder presses his palm onto the chest of his anorak and then points off to the west. Sumner nods.

'You can go,' he says, 'but this one stays with us.'

They look at the ring for a while longer, turning it over several times and scraping at the bright jewels with their blackened fingernails. In the flat Arctic light, blanched and unvariegated, amid the swathing landscape of snow and ice, it seems like something unearthly, an object imagined or dreamed of rather than hewn and fashioned by human hand.

'If they've been on board a whaler to trade, they've seen coins and watches before, mebbe,' Cavendish says, 'but never such a pretty thing as that.'

'It's worth five rifles or more,' Sumner tells them, holding up his fingers and pointing.

'Ten or more,' Cavendish says.

The elder one looks at them and nods. He gives the ring to the younger one who smiles and tucks it down into the hairy complication of his britches. They turn away and begin unpacking the sledge. As he walks back towards the tent, Sumner feels a disorienting lightness, a sudden unaccounted space inside him, like a cavity or abscess, where the ring used to be but isn't.

Later, when the darkness has settled around the camp, and after they have eaten their usual supper of half-scorched seal meat and ship's biscuit smeared with grease, Drax waves to Cavendish to get his attention, then beckons him over. He is sitting, apart from the other men, in a dark and frigid angle of the tent far from the fire. He is wrapped in a coarse blanket and is passing the time by scrimshawing a crude image of Britannia triumphant into a fragment of walrus ivory. Since he is not allowed the use of a knife, he employs a sharpened iron nail instead.

Cavendish sighs and lowers himself onto the rug-covered floor.

'What now?' he asks.

Drax continues scraping for a while, then turns to look at him.

'Remember that time we talked about afore,' he says. 'That time we both thought might never ever happen. Remember that one?'

Cavendish nods reluctantly.

'I remember it well enough,' he says.

'Then I 'spect you can moreless guess what I'm about to tell you.'

'That time hant come,' he says. 'It can't have. Not out here in the icy fucking wastes of nowhere.'

'It has though, Michael.'

'Bollocks to that.'

'When the Esquimaux leaves in the morrow, he'll take me with him on the sledge. It's all agreed between us. All I need from you is a file to cut these chains off, and a quick glance the other way.'

Cavendish snorts.

'You'd rather live as a Yak than hang as an honest Englishman, is that it now?'

'I'll winter over with 'em if they let me and come spring, I'll look out for a ship.'

'A ship bound for where?'

'New Bedford, Sebastopol. You won't ever see sign of me again. I'll swear to that at least.'

'We're all of us trapped here now. Why should I help you alone escape?'

'You're only keeping me alive and breathing so they can hang me later on. Where's the sense or reason in that? Let me take my chances with the Yaks. The savage bastards may stick a lance in me, but if they do, there's no man here'll mourn my passing much. '

'I'm a whaleman, not a fucking gaoler,' Cavendish says. 'That's true enough.'

Drax nods.

'Think on it,' he says. 'It's one less mouth to feed, and fuck knows there's no abundance of food around here at present. When you get back to England, there'll be no blame attached, and you and Baxter can go about your business without no trouble from me.'

Cavendish looks at him.

'You're an evil, filthy, conniving bastard, Henry,' he says, 'and I 'spect you always were one.'

Drax shrugs.

'Mebbe,' he says. 'But if I am what you call me, why would you want such a fiend living so close among you, when you have the God-given chance to cut him free?'

Cavendish stands up abruptly and walks away. Drax goes back to his carving. It is dark outside and the glow from the blubber lamp is frail and intermittent. He can barely see what he is doing, but as he works he feels the shallow lines of engravure with his fingers, as a blind man might, and imagines the glorious and patriotic pictures they will form when he is done. Cavendish comes back shortly and crouches beside him as if wishing to inspect his work.

'You can't use it inside the tent,' he says, showing him the file, then pushing it underneath the folds of Drax's blanket. 'The others will hear for sure.'

Drax nods and smiles.

'That seal meat don't agree with me none,' he says. 'I'll be in and out all night for shitting, I 'spect.'

Cavendish nods. He stays crouching, placing one hand on the floor for balance.

'I been thinking,' he says.

'Oh aye.'

'What if I come along with ye when you go?'

Drax sniffs and shakes his head.

'It's safer here.'

'We can't all winter through alive. Ten men? It int possible.'

'One or two may die, but I'd say you won't be one of 'em.'

'I'd sooner take my chances with the Yaks like you are.'

Drax shakes his head again.

'That int the agreement I made. It's me alone.'

'Then I'll make my own agreement, separate like, why not?'

Drax turns the ivory over in his hand and feels its shallow indentations with his thumb.

'You're best to stay,' he says again.

'Nay, I'll be coming with,' he says. 'And that there file's my ticket out.'

Drax thinks a moment, then reaches into the blanket and touches the file's relentless edges, feels its tight-packed rills like the cold surface of a metallic tongue.

'Ye always were a bold and blusterous fucker, Michael,' he says.

Cavendish smirks and rubs his beard eagerly.

'You'd thought to get one over on me, I 'spect,' he says. 'But you won't do it. I int staying here to die with these others. I got bigger plans than that.'

It is so cold outside the tent that Drax can only work on his manacles for twenty minutes at a time before he begins to lose feeling in his hands and feet. It takes him four separate trips spaced out across the night to free himself. Each time he leaves the tent, he picks his way carefully through the low hillocked landscape of sleeping bodies, and each time he comes back, frosted and shuddering, his clothes stiffened with ice, he does the same. The men groan and curse as he nudges into them, but no one opens their eyes to look, aside from Cavendish who watches him intently.

Freed from the chains, he feels suddenly larger and younger than before. It is as if, since the instant he murdered Brownlee, he has been asleep and now he is awake again at last. He has no fear of the future, no sense of its power or meaning. Each new moment is merely a gate he walks through, an opening he pierces with himself. He whispers to Cavendish to get himself ready and wait for his whistle. He ties his clothing into a bundle with a cord, tucks the bundle under his arm, then drops the file into his coat pocket and makes his way over to the snow house. The moon is high and waning. Its frail light turns the broad white snowscape the colour of gruel. The fierce air around him is crisp and odourless. The dogs are sleeping; the sledge is packed. He lowers himself onto his hands and knees and crawls inside the snow house. It is pitch black, but he can smell them anyway—the younger on the left, the elder on the right—and hear them softly breathing. He is surprised they do not wake up, that his very presence does not alert them. He waits a moment, gauging the position of their heads and the directions they must be lying in. It is warmer here than in the tent, he notices. The atmosphere is close and oily. He reaches out carefully, slowly, and touches with the tip of his fingers the surface of one of the sleeping bags; he pushes very slightly down and there is an answering moan. He puts his hand into his pocket and takes out the file. It is a foot long and an inch wide and one end is spiked. The spike is not especially sharp, but it is long enough for his purposes, and he thinks he will manage. He grips the end of the file in his fist and leans forward. He can see the men's faint outlines now—a thicker, denser black against the darkness of the snow house walls. He sniffs once in preparation, then reaches out and shakes the elder one awake. The man murmurs and opens his eyes. He leans up on one elbow and opens his mouth as if to speak.

Holding the file with both hands, Drax drives the spiked end into the man's neck just below the ear; there is a spurt of hot blood, and a noise somewhere between a gurgle and a gasp. He pulls out the spike and then quickly drives it in again, a little lower this time. When the younger man stirs, aroused by the noise, Drax turns, punches him twice to keep him quiet, then starts to throttle him. Being naturally scrawny and encased in a narrow, tight-fitting sleeping bag, he makes a poor fight of it and is suffocated before the elder one has finished dying. Drax pulls them both out of their bags, then strips the elder of his anorak, slits it up the side and pulls it on over his own head. He feels around for the blubber knives and the rifle, then crawls back outside.

There is no sound or movement, no indication that anyone in the tent has heard a noise. He goes over to the sledge and gets the deerskin traces. One by one, he wakes the dogs and harnesses them. He crawls back inside the snow house, takes off the dead men's boots, britches and mittens, and stuffs them inside one of the sleeping bags. When he comes out again, he sees Cavendish standing over by the sledge. He raises his right hand and walks across to him.

'I hant whistled you yet,' Drax tells him.

'I int waiting for no fucking whistle either.'

Drax looks at him, and nods.

'The case is altered. I have to show you something now.'

'Show me what?'

Drax puts the sleeping bag down on the snow, tugs it open and points inside.

'Lookee in there,' he says. 'Tell me what you see.'

Cavendish pauses, shakes his head, then moves forward and leans down to take a look in the bag. Drax steps off to the side, grabs him by the forelock, yanks his chin upwards and cuts through his windpipe with one single slice of the blubber knife. Cavendish, rendered suddenly mute, grabs his gaping neck with both hands as if hoping to reseal the opening, and drops onto his knees in the snow. He shuffles forward for a few moments, like a crippled penitent, jerking, rasping and gushing blood from his impossible wound, then topples, shudders like a hooked fish drowning in air, and stops moving completely. Drax turns him over and starts going through the pockets of Brownlee's greatcoat.

'That wont my idea, Michael,' he tells him. 'That one were yours alone.'

20

It is still half dark when they find the first mate's corpse spreadeagled on the snow, frozen hard, throat-gashed, bibbed and spewed over with blood. They assume the Yaks have murdered him until they realise that the Yaks are both dead themselves, and it is only then they notice Drax is missing. When they figure what has happened, they stand there stunned, unable to parse the world implied by such events. They look down at Cavendish, dead and rime-covered, as if expecting him to speak to them again, to offer up one last unbelievable opinion on his own demise.

Within the hour, under Otto's direction, they bury Cavendish in a shallow, scooped-out trench at the tip of the headland and cover the body over with slabs of rock and stones prised from the cliff face. Since the Yaks are heathens and their funerary rites, in consequence, obscure, they leave their bodies as they found them, only blocking the snow house entrance and collapsing the roof and walls on top to form a crude and temporary mausoleum. Once this work is complete, Otto calls the men into the tent and suggests they pray together for God's mercy in their present distress and for the souls of the recently deceased. A few kneel and bow their heads, others unfurl themselves lengthways or crouch cross-legged, yawning and picking at themselves like apes. Otto closes his eyes and tilts his chin upwards.

'Oh dearest Lord,' he starts, 'help us to understand your purposes and your mercy. Preserve us now from the grave sin of despair.'

As he speaks, a blubber lamp is still burning at the centre of the tent. A curlicue of black smoke twists up from it and meltwater drips off the canvas where the heat has risen and touched the half-inch inner layer of ice.

'Let us not give in to evil,' Otto continues, 'but give us faith in the workings of your providence even in this time of our confusion and suffering. Let us remember that your love created this world and your love sustains it still at every moment.'

Webster the blacksmith coughs loudly, then leans his head out of the tent and spits into the snow. McKendrick, who is on his knees and trembling, begins to weep softly and so does the cook and one of the Shetlanders. Sumner, who is light-headed and nauseous from a combination of fear and hunger, tries to concentrate on the question of the manacles. Since Drax could not have committed three murders with his wrists and ankles chained together, he must have

240

freed himself beforehand, he thinks, but how could he do so? Did the Yaks assist him? Did Cavendish? Why would anyone wish to help a man like Drax escape? And if they did help him, why did they all three end up dead?

'Guard and direct the spirits of those who have just died,' Otto says. 'Protect them as they travel through the other realms of time and space. And help us remember always that we are a part of your greater mystery, that you are never absent, that even if we fail to see you, or if we mistake your presence for some other lesser thing, you are still there with us. Thank you, Lord. Amen.'

The amens come back to him in ragged, grumbling chorus. Otto opens his eyes and looks about as though surprised at where he finds himself. He suggests they sing a hymn, but before he can begin, he is interrupted by Webster. The blacksmith appears angry. His dark eyes are filled with a bitter eagerness.

'We've had the Devil hisself living here among us,' he shouts out. 'The Devil hisself. I seen his footprints out there in the snow just now. The cloven hoof, the mark of Satan. I seen it clear as day.'

'I seen it too,' McKendrick says. 'Like the tracks of a pig or a goat, 'cept there int no pigs or goats alive in this forsaken hole.'

'There were no such tracks,' Otto says, 'no marks at all, except those left by the dogs. The only devil is the one inside ourselves. Evil is a turning away from good.'

Webster shakes his head.

'That Drax is Satan taken on a fleshly form,' he says. 'He int human like you or me, he just looks that way when he chooses to.'

'Henry Drax is not the Devil,' Otto tells him patiently, as if correcting an elementary confusion. 'He's a tormented spirit. I've seen him in my dreams. I've spoken to him there many times.'

'There's three dead men outside I'd weigh against your fucking dreaming,' Webster says.

'Whatever he may be, he's gone now,' Otto says.

'Aye, but where is he gone to? And who says he won't be coming back betimes?'

Otto shakes his head.

'He won't come back here. Why would he?'

'The Devil does as he wishes to,' Webster says. 'He pleases hisself, I'd say.'

The possibility of Drax's return sets the men into a hubbub. Otto tries to quiet them, but they ignore him.

'We have to leave this place,' Webster tells them all. 'We can find the Yaks' camp and they can take us down to the Yankee whaling station on Blacklead Island. We'll be safe there.'

'You don't know where the Yak camp is or how far distant,' Otto says.

'It's away off to the west somewhere. If we follow the shoreline, we'll find it soon enough.'

'You'll die before you get there. You'll freeze to death, for sure.'

'I've had about my fill of taking other men's advisements,' Webster says. 'We followed orders since we left from Hull, and it's that has brought us to this sorry fucking pass.'

Otto looks to Sumner, and Sumner thinks a moment.

'You'll have no tent,' he tells him, 'no furs or skins to wear. There are no roads or tracks of any kind here, no landmarks any of us recognise, so even if the camp is close you may not find it ever. You might survive one night out in the open air, but for sure you won't survive two.'

'Those as want to stay in this accursed place can stay,' Webster says. 'But I int staying an hour longer here.'

He stands up and starts gathering together his possessions. His face is stiff and pale, his movements jerky and enraged. The others sit and watch him, then McKendrick, the cook and the Shetlander stand up too. McKendrick's sunken cheeks are still wet with tears. He has open sores on his face and neck from his time down in the hold. The cook is shivering like an animal in distress. Otto tells them to delay, to eat dinner in the tent tonight and then leave at first light if they must, but they take no notice. When he presses them, they raise their fists against him and Webster pledges he will knock down any man who seeks to stand in their way.

The four men depart shortly afterwards, without ceremony or extended farewell. Sumner gives them each their share of the frozen seal meat, and Otto hands Webster a rifle and a handful of cartridges. They shake hands quickly, but neither party attempts to speak or soften the dread implications of their leaving. As they watch them walk away, their dark outlines shrinking into the general blankness, Sumner turns to Otto.

'If Henry Drax isn't the Devil, I can't claim to know just

what he is. If there's a word been coined for a man like him, I don't believe I've learned it.'

'Nor will you learn it,' Otto says, 'not from any human book at least. A fellow like him won't be caged in or fixed by words.'

'By what then?'

'Faith alone.'

Sumner shakes his head and laughs unhappily.

'You dreamed we'd die, and now it's coming true,' he says. 'It's getting colder every day, and we have three weeks' food at most and no hope of help or rescue. Those four bastards just gone are as good as dead already.'

'Miracles occur. If great evil exists, why not great good the same?'

'Signs and fucking wonders,' Sumner says. 'Is that the best that you can offer me?'

'I don't offer you anything at all,' Otto answers calmly. 'It's not in my power to do so.'

Sumner shakes his head again. The three remaining men have retreated into the tent for warmth. It is too cold to linger outside for long, but he cannot bear the thought of returning to their dreary, hopeless company, so instead he sets off walking east, past Cavendish's new-dug grave and out onto the frozen bay. The sea ice has been cracked by winds, buckled and then refrozen into a rubbled landscape of crazed and tilted blocks, fissured and motionless. Black mountains, gargantuan and sumptuous, rise off in the distance. The dangling sky is the colour of milky quartz. He walks until he is breathless and his face and feet are numb, and then turns about. The wind is blowing against him as he begins to walk back. He feels it seeping through his layers of clothing, nudging and chilling his chest, groin and thighs. He thinks of Webster and the others walking west, and feels suddenly sickened and wretched at his core. He stops, groans, then leans over and vomits out gobbets of half-digested seal meat onto the frozen snow beneath. He feels a sharp pain like a lance jabbing in his stomach and releases an involuntary squirt of shit into his trousers. For a moment, he cannot breathe at all. He closes his eyes and waits, and the feeling passes. The sweat is frozen on his brow, and his beard is hard now with saliva and bile and fragments of tooth-ground meat. He looks up at the snow-packed sky and opens wide his mouth, but no sounds or words come out of it, and, after a short while longer, he closes it again and walks on silently.

They divide up evenly the scanty rations that remain and allow each man to cook and eat them as and when he pleases. They take turns to feed and tend the fitful blubber lamp. The remaining rifle lies near the entrance of the tent for anyone who wishes to hunt with it, but although they pass to and fro to shit and piss and bring back snow to melt for water, no one picks it up. There is no one in command any longer: Otto's authority has gone and Sumner's role as surgeon, without his medicines, means nothing. They sit and wait. They sleep and play cards. They tell themselves that Webster and the others will send help, or that the Yaks themselves will surely come out searching for the two who are dead. But no one arrives, and nothing changes. The only book they have is Otto's Bible and Sumner refuses to read from it. He cannot bear its certainties, its rhetoric, its all-too-easy hope. Instead, he silently recites the *Iliad*. Whole sections return to him at night, unbidden, near-complete, and in the morning, he tells them over line by line. When the other men see him mumbling to himself like that they assume he is at prayer, and he doesn't seek to disabuse them since this is as close to honest prayer as he is ever likely to come.

A week after the departure of Webster and the others, a fierce storm blows in off the bay, and the tent is lifted away from its moorings and ripped along one seam. They spend a wretched, bone-chilled night clustered together, gripping the sagged and flapping remnants, and in the morning, as the weather clears, they commence, glumly, to make what repairs they can. With his jackknife, Otto whittles and bores some rough needles out of seal bone, hands them to the men, then commences pulling lines of thread from the frayed cuffs of one of the blankets. Sumner, stiff and dazed from lack of sleep, walks off in search of rocks suitable for re-anchoring the edges of the tent. The wind is bitter and blustery, and in places he has to wade through thigh-deep drifts of snow. As he passes by the tip of the headland, with the rough ice stretching out before him and the wind whipping crystalline spindrift from its angled peaks, he notices Cavendish's gravesite in a state of ghastly disarray. The covering stones have been scattered and the corpse itself has been half consumed by animals. All that is left is a grotesque and bloody gallimaufry of bones, sinew and innards. Pieces of shredded undergarment are strewn about haphazardly. The right foot, gnawed off above the ankle but with toes intact, lies off to one side. The head is missing. Sumner comes closer and slowly crouches down. He takes his knife from his pocket and levers out a rib from the frozen mass. He pokes and peers at it a while, touches its broken end with his fingertip, then looks off into the white distance.

When he gets back to the tent, he takes Otto to one side and explains what he has just seen. They talk together for a while, Sumner points, Otto crosses himself, then they walk across to where the snow house used to be and begin digging down into the icy ruins with their bare hands. When they reach the stiff and frozen bodies of the two Yaks, they pull them free and strip off the remains of their sealskin undergarments. Lifting the bodies up by the heels like wheelbarrows, they drag them further away from the tent. When they judge the distance and angle is right, they place them down again. They are panting from the effort of the pull, and steam is rising up from their heads and faces. They stand talking a while longer and then walk back to the ramshackle tent. Sumner loads the rifle, then explains to the other men that there is a hungry bear somewhere out on the ice and the dead Yaks are bait for it.

'There's enough good meat on a beast like that to last the five of us a month or more,' he says. 'And we can use the hide for extra clothing.'

The men look back at him, empty-eyed, indifferent, strained beyond their limits. When he suggests they share the effort—that each man take the rifle for two hours at a time and keep a watch out for the bear while the others rest or repair the tent—they shake their heads.

'Dead Yaks int good bait for a bear,' they tell him, with a sureness which suggests they have tried such a thing before and found it disappointing. 'Such a plan won't work.'

'Help me anyway,' he says. 'What harm can it do?'

They turn away and begin to deal out the cards: *one, one, one; two, two, two; three, three, three.*

'A cock-eyed plan like that won't work,' they say again, as if their gloomful confidence itself provides them comfort. 'Not now, not ever.'

He sits at one side of the tent with the loaded rifle at his feet and peers out through a spyhole cut into the grey canvas. Once, while he is watching, a rook comes down and settles on the forehead of the elder Yak, pecks briefly at the matted tanglement of his frozen hair, and then extends its wings and jerks upwards and away. Sumner considers firing at it, but saves his powder. He is patient, hopeful. He is sure the bear is close. Perhaps it is asleep after its recent feasting, but when it wakes, it will be hungry again. It will sniff the air and remember the treasures nearby. As it gets darker, Sumner hands the rifle across to Otto. He cuts a two-inch cube of seal meat from his cache of provender, skewers it on the point of his knife and holds it over the blubber lamp to cook. The other three, without pausing from their endless game of euchre, observe him carefully. When he has eaten, he lies down and covers himself.

After what seems like barely a moment, Otto nudges him awake again. There is ice on the outside of his blanket where the moisture from his breath has seeped through its weft. Otto tells him there is still no sign of any bear. Sumner shuffles across to the spyhole and looks out again. The moon is gibbous, the arcing sky garrulous with stars. The two dead bodies lie just as they were, exposed and recumbent, like the eerie *gisants* of a long-forgotten dynasty. Sumner props himself against the rifle and wills the bear to come to him. He tries to picture its arrival, its slow-footed emergence from the murk. He imagines its curiosity, its wariness. The smell of dead flesh pulling it forward; a sense of strangeness, foreignness, holding it back.

He falls asleep while seated. He dreams of trout fishing on Bilberry Lough: it is summer and he is wearing shirtsleeves and a boater, above and below him is a blue expanse of sky and water, and all around the lake is edged with elms and oak. He is empty-headed, happy. When he wakes, he sees movement in the distance. He wonders if it is the wind against the snow, or if the ice is shifting out in the bay, but then he sees the bear, starkly white against the ashen darkness. He watches it approach the dead bodies, moving, low-headed and rhythmical, without eagerness or urgency. He pushes the tent flap slowly to one side with one hand, checks the percussion cap, cocks the rifle and raises it partway up to his shoulder. The bear is tall and broad, but spindle-shanked and gaunt around the ribs. He watches it sniff at the two bodies, then raise its paw and place it atop the chest of the elder. No one else is awake. Otto is snoring softly. Sumner kneels. He rests his left elbow on his knee and presses the rifle stock into the softness of his right shoulder. He raises the sight and looks along the barrel. The bear is a rag of whiteness in the larger dark. He breathes in once, exhales, then fires.

The bullet misses the head, but hits high on the shoulder. Sumner grabs the bag of cartridges and rushes out of the tent. The snow is deep and uneven, and he stumbles twice, then rights himself. When he reaches the bodies, he sees a large patch of blood and then a spattered trail leading onward. The bear is nearly a quarter-mile ahead now, running lopsidedly, favouring the right foreleg as if the left is maimed or numb. Sumner runs after it. He is sure it cannot escape. That soon it will either collapse and die or turn round to fight.

Away to the east, the sky is faintly whitening. Narrow pearlescent fissures open in the dark ranks of close-packed cloud; the taut and featureless horizon turns grey, then brown, then blue. As he reaches the tip of the headland, Sumner's lungs and gullet are aching from the cold; he is panting, and the blood is thrumming in his ears. The bear passes the desecrated gravesite without pause, and then veers north out onto the ice field. Sumner loses sight of it briefly, then sees it again emerging from behind the heaped-up rubble of a pressure ridge. He clambers after, up and over, slipping and scrambling as he goes, dropping his rifle, then picking it up again. He follows the deep set tracks, the blood spots. His leg aches, and his heart is thumping, but he tells himself that it is a matter of time only, that every minute that passes weakens the bear a little more. He wades on through the snow. On either side, high, hard-frozen shards rear up like the pitched roofs of a half-drowned village. Grainy shadows gather in their lee and spill out sideways.

The bear, despite the wound, moves steadily and surely, as though set on a course plotted long before. The sky is filled by narrow rolls of cloud, grey and brown on top, gilded below by the breaching sun. They move on, man and animal in primitive procession, through a landscape so smashed up and uneven it might have been constructed by a simpleton from the shattered pieces of some previous intactness. After an hour, the ice flattens into a mile-wide plain, its surface gently ribbed like the palate of a hound. Halfway across, as if suddenly aware of its new environment, the bear slows, then stops and turns about. Sumner can see the smear of red blazoned on its flank and the gouts of steam rising from its muzzle. After a moment's pause, he takes a waxed paper cartridge from his pocket, bites off the end and pours the black powder into the bore of the rifle; he pushes the ball-end of the cartridge in also, tears off the excess paper and presses it home with the ramrod. His hands are trembling as he does this. He is dripping sweat, and he can feel his lungs wheezing and roaring inside his chest like bellows in an iron-forge. He fumbles in his pocket for a percussion cap, finds one and fits it over the steel nipple. He paces forwards slowly until the gap between them is no more than three hundred feet, then lowers himself down onto the ridged ice. He feels its coldness against his stomach and thighs. His head is wreathed in steam. The bear watches carefully but does nothing. Its flanks are heaving. Strings of drool are dripping down from its jaw. Sumner raises and adjusts the sights, cocks the hammer and, remembering the previous shot, aims a foot to the left. He blinks the sweat away from his

251

eyes, squints and pulls the trigger. There is the sharp crack of the percussion cap exploding, but no recoil. The bear snorts at the sudden noise, then wheels about and starts to run again. Scuds of snow spume out from under it. Sumner, cursing the misfire, scrambles to his feet, tosses the old percussion cap away and fits another one. He steadies himself, takes aim again and shoots, but the bear is too far gone and the shot falls shy. He watches it a while, then re-shoulders the rifle and begins to follow after.

21

Beyond the ice plain's edge, another pressure ridge rears up, brown-edged and haggard at the peaks, its steep flanks bermed and bastioned like an antique siegework. The bear tracks west until it finds a gap, then leaps up into it and clambers through. The risen sun, smeared by cloud, gives off no noticeable heat. Sumner's sweat drips down into his beard and eyebrows and freezes into hard spangles. The bear has slowed down to a walk now, but so has Sumner. As he follows it up and across the ridge and onto another undulant snow field, the gap between them barely alters. He gains twenty yards, then loses them again. The aching in his legs and chest is sharp and hot but regular. He thinks of turning back but doesn't. The chase has found a rhythm already, a pattern he can't easily disrupt. When he is thirsty, he reaches down and eats the snow; when he is hungry, he lets the feeling rise, peak, then pass away. He breathes, he walks, the bear precedes him always, badged high with blood, steam-bound, its tracks as broad and round as soup bowls.

Every minute he expects the bear to fail, to weaken, to begin to die, but it never does so. It persists. Sometimes he feels a fierce and violent hatred for it, at other times a sickly kind of love. Rump muscles roil beneath the bear's slack fur. Its giant legs lift and fall like drop hammers. They pass by a berg embedded in the floe—two hundred feet high, half a mile long, starkly vertical and flat-topped like the rhomboid plug of an extinct volcano. Its steep and shear-marked sides are veined with blue and gaitered at their base with drifted snow. Sumner has no pocket watch, but guesses it is now past noon. He realises that he has come too far, that even if he kills the bear, he will not be able to carry its meat back to camp. This truth disturbs him for a moment, but then, as he walks onwards, its power thins and fades, and all he is aware of is the lift and press of his feet across the snow and the hollow roar of his own quick breathing.

An hour or so later, they reach a long line of high black bluffs, their dark faces soil-less and switchbacked with pale grey threads of ice. The bear pads steadily alongside, until it reaches a narrow, shadow-draped breach in the cliff face. It glances rearwards once, then turns sharply and disappears from sight. Sumner follows after. When he reaches the opening, he turns as the bear turned, and sees before him a long narrow ice-choked fjord, steep-sided and without apparent egress. To left and right, high grey rocks gashed with couloirs grope up towards the pallid sky. The ice underfoot is as flat and pure as marble. Sumner, pausing at the threshold and looking about, senses he has been here before, that this place is already known to him somehow. Prefigured in a dream perhaps, he thinks, or in some opiated flight of fancy. He steps across the threshold and continues walking forward.

Along the bone-white valley floor, between looming walls of gneiss and granite, beast and man proceed in loose-knit tandem—separate yet eerily conjoined—as if along a corridor or hallway paved with snow and canopied with sky. Sumner feels the weight of the rifle pulling down against his shoulder, and the stubborn ache of his malunited leg. He is light-headed now, and sorely weakened by hunger. Presently, it starts to snow: light at first, but then thicker and more forceful.

As the wind and cold increase, and the snow drops down in dense diagonal gusts, Sumner loses sight of the bear. It appears and disappears from his view in awkward, flickering glimpses like an image in a zoetrope. Its outline blurs, then complicates and finally dissolves. Soon, the sky and the cliffs disappear also, and all he can see is the blizzard's ashen iterations—everything swirling and shifting—nothing clear or separate or distinct. Enclosed in this bewildering mesh, he loses all sense of time and direction. He staggers back and forth, witless and nearing exhaustion, for what feels like hours, but could be only minutes or even seconds. Eventually, by chance, he stumbles onto the rumbled scree slope and takes shelter in the lee of a brindled boulder. Waves of fear and panic gather and break inside him as he crouches there. He is shuddering with cold, and he feels his sweat-soaked clothes beginning to harden around him like a suit of mail. He has no sensation left in either feet or hands. Snow gathers along the creases of his face and lips but doesn't melt. He has walked much too far, he knows it: he has strayed from his true purposes, he is lost and bewildered, and his failure is complete.

Looking up through the hazy downfall, he sees a dead boy standing before him, grubby and bare-footed, clad in a *dhoti* and blood-soaked tabard. He is holding a limp cabbage leaf in one hand and a tin cup of water in the other. The bubbling bullet-wound in his chest goes all the way through to the other side now. A yellow, coin-sized patch of light is just visible where his heart should rightly be. It is like a narrow loophole in the thickness of a castle wall. Sumner raises his right hand in awkward greeting, but the boy offers no response. Perhaps he is angry with me, Sumner thinks. But no, the boy is weeping, and, seeing this, he starts to weep himself for sympathy and shame. The warm tears course down his cheeks, and then harden and freeze amid the tangled edges of his beard. As he sits and weeps, he feels himself liquefying, losing form, sliding away into a stew of sadness and regret. His body starts to shake and shudder. His breathing slows and his heartbeat becomes languid and unwilling. He senses death, feels its leaden presence, scents its faecal perfume on the whipping air. The boy reaches out for him and Sumner sees, through the spyhole in his chest, another world in miniature: perfect, complete, impossible. He stares for a moment captivated by the brilliance of its making, then turns away again. He grabs himself tightly, breathes in and looks about. The child is gone: there is nothing in existence but the raging storm and, concealed somewhere inside it, the bear he must kill if he is to live. He pulls his legs up to his chest and hugs them for a moment. He stands with difficulty and loads the rifle with numb and trembling fingers. When he is finished, he steps away from the boulder and shouts out into the freezing air.

'Come on out here now,' he yells. 'Come on out here now, you baleful bastard, and let me shoot you dead.'

There is no response, nothing except the wind-driven snow and the silent slabs of rock and ice. He peers blindly forwards and yells again. The storm continues unabated; the high wind wails. He could be standing alone on the surface of a far-flung, bitter moon— ice-choked, sunless and unpeopled. He yells a third time and, like a sudden ghost, conjured against its will, the bear appears before him, less than thirty yards away, part-veiled by thickly wafting snow but clearly visible. He sees the ragged edges of its shoulder wound, the thin white saddle of snow settled across its spine. The bear looks blankly back at him; steam leaks from its nostrils like smoke from a cooling campfire. Sumner raises his rifle and takes unsteady aim at its enormous chest. His head is clear. There is nothing left to decide or hope for. All that exists is this single moment, this event. He breathes in, then out again, his heart fills up with blood, then empties. He pulls the trigger, hears the powder catch and roar and feels the recoil.

The bear drops down onto its knees, and then falls sideways. The report echoes off the high rocks—loud, then quieter, then quieter still. Sumner lowers the rifle and runs over to the body. He crouches down, puts both his palms on the bear's still-warm flank and pushes his face and fingers deep into the fur. His lips are parted, and he is gasping. He takes a blubber knife from his belt, hones its edge with a whetstone and tests the sharpness against his thumb. He makes the first incision near the groin, and then cuts up through the soft flesh of the belly until he meets the sternum. He starts sawing through bone until he reaches the throat. He cuts the windpipe, then jams his boot heel against one side of the severed ribcage, grips the other with both hands and breaks it open. He feels the sudden kitchen-heat of the bear's inner organs, and tastes the heady, carnal fetor that rises out of them. He drops the blubber knife onto the snow and pushes both his bare hands down into the dead bear's steaming guts. His frozen fingers feel like they might burst apart from the warmth. He grinds his teeth and pushes his hands in deeper. When the pain reduces, he pulls them out, dripping with red, rubs his face and beard with the hot blood, then picks up the knife again and begins to sever and remove the bear's innards. He tugs out the heart and lungs, the liver, intestines and stomach. The deep cavity that remains is half filled with a steaming pool of hot black liquid—blood, urine, bile. Sumner leans forward and starts to drink it, ladling it up quickly into his open mouth with both hands. As he drinks, and as the bear's heat passes directly into him like an elixir—down his throat, into his empty stomach and outwards—he starts to tremble, then twitch. After a minute, he begins to spasm uncontrollably, his eyes roll back into his skull, and blackness overtakes him.

When the fit passes, Sumner is lying prone and half covered by drifting snow. His beard is stiff with ursine gore, both hands are dyed dark red, and the arms of his pea coat are soaked up to the elbows. His mouth, teeth and throat are caked with blood, both animal and human. The tip of his tongue is missing. He pulls himself to his feet and looks about. The wind howls, and the gelid air is dense with close-set waves of gusting ice. He can no longer see the cliffs, or the scree slope, or the boulder where he sheltered previously. He looks down at the bear's eviscerated corpse, its split and opened ribcage yawning like an empty tomb.

He pauses a moment, considers, then, as if stepping into a bath, he bends and lowers himself down into the striated, crimson cavity. The severed bones close over him like teeth. He feels the stiffened muscle compress and spread beneath him. There is the clean, wet smell of butchery, a faint but marvellous residue of animal warmth. He tucks his sea boots up into the hollowed-out abdomen and pulls the dead flesh tight around him like an overcoat. He hears the howling wind still, but doesn't feel it. He is enclosed, encoffined, in a tight and vasculated darkness. Lying there, his mutilated tongue begins to swell inside his mouth, blood and saliva bubble out from his lips and dribble down into his beard. He wishes to pray, to speak, to make himself known somehow. He remembers Homer—a hero's corpse, the funeral games, the armour bent and broken—but when he tries to murmur out the opening dactyls, instead of words what burbles from his brutalised mouth are the inchoate grunts and gaspings of a savage.

22

The stranger is covered in blood, drenched and laved in it from head to foot. He resembles a skinned seal or a stillborn child newly pushed from his mother's womb. He is breathing, just, but his blood-caked eyes are closed up, and he is half-frozen. They drag his body off to the side, and leave it there while they skin and butcher the bear, then pack the meat and hide onto the sledge. One hunter takes the stranger's rifle, and the other takes his knife. They debate whether to kill him where he lies or take him back to the camp. They argue a while, then agree to take him back. Whatever else he is, they reason, he is a lucky bastard, and a man who is that lucky deserves another chance. They pick him up and lay him on the sledge. He groans a little. They prod and shake him but he doesn't wake. They push snow into his mouth, but the snow merely melts on his ravaged tongue and drools out onto his chin in pinkened rivulets.

At the winter camp, the wives give him water and warmed seal blood to drink. They wash his face and hands, and pull off his blood-stiffened garments. When word gets out, the children come to stare. They peer and prod and giggle. If he opens his eyes, they squeal and run away. Soon the rumours begin. Some say he is an *angakoq*, a spirit guide, sent direct from *Sedna* to help with their hunting, while others say he is an evil ghost, a shabby *tupilaq*, whose touch will kill, and whose very presence causes sickness. The hunters consult the shaman who advises them that the stranger will not recover until he is returned to his own people. They should take him south, the shaman says, to the new mission on Coutts Inlet. They ask him if the stranger is lucky, as they supposed he must be, and whether any of his luck will pass to them. The shaman tells them that he is indeed lucky, as they supposed, but his luck is of a particular, alien kind.

They carry him, wrapped in hides and palely shivering, back onto the sledge and take him south, past the frozen lake and the summer hunting grounds, to the mission. The red-painted cabin is set on a shallow rise, with the frozen sea below it and the tall mountains behind. There is a large igloo standing adjacent, with a line of black smoke rising through the opening in the roof, and a set of tethered sledge-dogs curled asleep in front. The hunters are greeted on their arrival by the priest, a bright-eyed, wiry Englishman with greying hair and beard, and an expression earnest but fiercely sceptical. They point to Sumner and explain where they found him and how. When the priest looks doubtful, they trace a map of the shoreline with their fingers in the snow and point to the place. The priest shakes his head.

'A man can't just appear from nowhere,' he says.

They explain that, in that case, he is most likely an *angakoq* and that, until now, he has been living in a house at the bottom of the sea with *Sedna* the one-eyed goddess and her father *Anguta*. At this, the priest becomes irritable. He starts telling them again (as he always does) about Jesus, and then goes into the cabin and brings out the green book. They stand by their sledges and listen to him read in clumsy Inuktitut. The words make a kind of sense, but they find the stories far-fetched and childlike. When he's finished, they smile and nod.

'Then perhaps he is an angel,' they say.

The priest looks at Sumner and shakes his head.

'He's not an angel,' he says. 'I will guarantee you that.'

They carry Sumner inside and lay him on a cot near the stove. The priest covers him in blankets, then crouches down and tries to shake him awake.

'Who are you?' he says. 'What ship do you come from?'

Sumner half opens one eye, but doesn't attempt to answer. The priest frowns, then leans forward and examines Sumner's frost-blackened countenance more closely.

'Deutsch?' he asks him. 'Dansk? Ruski? Scots? Which one is it now?'

Sumner gazes back at him for a moment without interest or recognition, then closes his eye again. The priest stays crouching beside him for a moment, then nods and stands up.

'You lie there a while and rest yourself,' he says, 'whoever you are. We'll talk more after.'

The priest makes coffee for the hunters and asks them more questions. When they have gone, he feeds Sumner brandy with a teaspoon and rubs lard into his frostbite. When Sumner is settled, the priest sits at a table by the window and writes in the green book. There are three other thick leather-bound volumes by his elbow, and now and then he opens one, looks into it and nods. Later, an Esquimaux woman comes in with a pan of stew. She is wearing a deerskin anorak cut longer at the rear and a black wool hat; she has V-shaped blue lines tattooed in parallel across her forehead and the backs of both hands. The priest takes two thick white bowls from the shelf above the door and pushes back his papers and books. He spoons half the stew into one bowl and half into the other, then gives the pan back to the woman. The woman points at Sumner and says something in her native language. The priest nods, then says something in reply which makes her smile.

Sumner, lying motionless, smells the hot food. Its soft scent reaches him through the nerveless weft of his exhaustion and indifference. He is not hungry, but he is beginning to remember what hunger might be like, the particular, hopeful nature of its aching. Is he ready to return to all that? Does he want to? Could he? He opens his eyes and looks around: wood, metal, wool, grease; green, black, grey, brown. He turns his head. There is a grey-haired man sitting at a wooden table; on the table there are two bowls of food. The man closes the book he is reading, murmurs out a prayer, then stands up and brings one of the bowls over to where Sumner is lying.

'Will you eat something now?' he asks him. 'Here, let me help you.'

The priest kneels down, puts his hand behind Sumner's head and raises it up. He scoops a piece of meat onto the spoon and brings the spoon to Sumner's lips. Sumner blinks. A wave of feeling, dense and unnameable, sweeps through his body.

'I can feed you better if you'd open up your mouth a little,' the priest says. Sumner doesn't move. He understands what is being asked of him, but makes no effort to comply.

'Come on now,' the priest says. He puts the very tip of the metal spoon onto Sumner's lower lip and gently presses down. Sumner's mouth opens a little. The priest tips the spoon up quickly, and the meat slides onto Sumner's lacerated tongue. He lets it sit there a moment.

'Chew,' the priest tells him, making a chewing motion himself and pointing up at his jaw so Sumner is sure to see. 'You won't get any of the goodness out if you don't chew it right.'

Sumner closes his mouth. He feels the meat's taste seeping into him. He chews it twice, then swallows. He feels a sharp pain and then a duller ache.

'Good,' the priest says. He scoops another piece of meat and does the same again. Sumner eats three more pieces but lets the fourth drop out onto the floor unchewed. The priest nods, then lowers Sumner's head back down onto the blanket.

'We'll try you with a mug of tea later on,' he says. 'See how you do with that.'

After two days more, Sumner is able to sit up and eat by himself. The priest helps him up into a chair, puts the blanket over his shoulders and they sit together on two adjacent sides of the small wooden table.

'The men who found you consider you what they call an *angakoq*,' the priest explains, 'which means wizard in the Esquimaux language. They believe that bears have great powers, and that certain, chosen men partake in them. The same thing is true of other animals too, of course—deer and walrus, seals, even certain sea birds, I believe—but in their mythology, the bear is the most powerful beast by far. Men who have the bear as their genius are capable of the greatest magic—healing, divination and so on.'

He glances at the stranger to see if there is any sign that he has understood, but Sumner looks impassively down at his food.

'I've seen some of their *angakoqs* in action and they're naught but conjurers and charlatans, of course. They dress themselves up in gruesome masks and other audacious gewgaws; they make a great song and dance in the igloo, but there's nothing to it at all. It's nasty heathenish stuff, the crudest kind of superstition, but they know no better and how could they? They'd never seen the Bible before I got here, most of them, never heard the gospel preached in earnest.'

Sumner looks up at him briefly but doesn't pause from his chewing. The priest smiles a little and nods encouragement, but Sumner doesn't smile back.

'It's slow and painful work,' the priest goes on. 'I've been here alone since the early spring. It took months to win their trust—through gifts at first, knives, beads, needles and so on, and then through acts of kindness, giving help when they needed it, extra clothes or medicines. They are kindly people, but they are very primitive and childlike, almost incapable of abstract thought or any of the higher emotions. The men hunt and the women sew and suckle children, and that forms the limit of their interests and knowledge. They have a kind of metaphysics, true, but it is a crude and self-serving one and, so far as I can tell, many don't even believe in it themselves. My task is to help them grow up, you might say, to develop their souls and make them self-aware. That is why I am making the translation of the Bible here.' He nods at the piles of books and papers. 'If I can get it right, find the correct words in their language, then they will begin to understand, I'm sure. They are God's creatures after all, in the end, just as much as you or I.'

The priest spoons up a piece of meat and chews it slowly. Sumner reaches for his mug of tea, picks it up, sips, then puts it back down on the table. For the first time in days, he feels the words gathering inside him, dividing, accumulating, taking on strength and form. Soon, he knows, they will begin to rise up his throat, and then they will spill out onto his bruised and ulcerated tongue, and then, whether he likes it or not, whether he wants it or not, he will speak.

The priest looks at him.

'Are you ill?' he asks.

Sumner shakes his head. He raises his right hand a moment, then opens his mouth. There is a pause.

'What medicines?' he says.

It comes out in a blurred mumble. The priest looks confused, but then smiles and leans eagerly forward.

'Say that again,' he says. 'I didn't quite catch . . .'

'Medicines,' Sumner repeats. 'What *medicines* do you have?'

'Oh, *medicine*,' the priest says. 'Of course, of course.'

He stands up, goes into the storeroom at the rear of the cabin and comes back with a small medicine chest. He places it down on the table in front of Sumner.

'This is all I have,' he says. 'I've used the salts a good deal, of course and the calomel for the native children when they have the flux.'

Sumner opens the box, and begins taking out the bottles and jars, peering at the contents and reading the labels. The priest watches him do it.

'Are you a doctor?' he asks. 'Is that what you are?'

Sumner ignores the question. He takes out everything in the chest, and then tips the chest upside down to make sure it is truly empty. He looks at the collection arrayed on the tabletop and shakes his head.

'Where's the laudanum?' he says.

The priest frowns, but doesn't answer.

'The laudanum,' Sumner says again more loudly. 'The fucking laudanum, where is it gone to?'

'We have none of that left,' the priest says. 'I had one bottle but it's used up already.'

Sumner closes his eyes for a moment. When he opens

them again, the priest is putting the medicines carefully back into the chest.

'I see you can talk plain English, after all,' he says. 'For a while there, I was fearing you were a Polack or a Serb or some other strange denomination.'

Sumner takes up the bowl and spoon, and starts eating again as if nothing has happened.

'Where are you from?' the priest asks him.

'It doesn't matter so much where I'm from.'

'Perhaps it doesn't to you, but if a man is being fed and kept warm in a spot where he would likely die if left to fend for himself, you might expect a little courtesy is due to the people who are doing it for him.'

'I'll pay you back for the food and the fire.'

'And when will you do that, I wonder?'

'In the spring, when the whaling ships come back.'

The priest nods and sits down again. He rakes his fingers through the edges of his grey beard, then scratches the point of his chin with his thumbnail. His cheeks are flushed, but he is struggling to remain charitable in the face of Sumner's insults.

'Some might call it a kind of miracle what happened to you,' he says, after a pause, 'being found preserved alive on the ice inside the body of a dead bear.'

'I wouldn't call it that myself.'

'Then what would you call it?'

'Perhaps you should be asking the bear.'

The priest stares back at him for a moment, then yaps out a laugh.

'Oh, you're a clever kind of fellow, I can see that,' he says. 'Three days lying over there silent as the grave, not a single word from your lips, and now you're up and making merry with me.'

'I'll pay you back for the food and the fire,' Sumner says again flatly. 'Just as soon as I get another berth.'

'You're sent here for a reason,' the priest says. 'A man doesn't just appear like that from nowhere. I don't know what the reason is yet, but I know the Good Lord must have one.'

Sumner shakes his head.

'No,' he says. 'Not me. I want no part of that rigmarole.'

Half a week later, a sledge arrives carrying two hunters the priest has not seen before. He pulls on his anorak and mittens and goes outside. The woman, whose Christianised name is Anna, comes out of the igloo at the same time, greets the men and offers them food. They talk to her for several minutes and then, speaking more slowly so he will understand them, they talk to the priest. They explain that they have found a ruined tent a day's journey away with four dead white men lying frozen within it. They show him, as proof, the items they have salvaged—knives, ropes, a hammer, a grease-stained copy of the Bible. When he asks if they will go back there to retrieve the bodies, so they can be buried with the proper rites, they shake their heads and say they must continue on with their hunting. They feed their dogs on walrus meat, then eat in the igloo and rest a while but do not stay overnight. They try to sell him the Bible before they leave, but when he refuses to trade for it, they hand it to the woman Anna as a gift. After they have gone, Anna comes to the cabin and explains that the hunters told her they also found two dead Esquimaux at the white men's camp. They were both stripped naked, she reports, and one had been murdered with a knife. She points to her own neck and indicates the location of the wounds.

'One here,' she says, 'and the other here.'

Later, when the two of them are alone, and after he has thought on it a little while, the priest tells the hunters' story to Sumner. He watches his reactions.

'As I understand it, the place they found the bodies is not so very far from where you were found yourself,' he says. 'So I'm guessing you will know the men who died; I'm guessing that they were your own shipmates.'

Sumner, who is seated by the stove whittling at a piece of driftwood, scratches his nose and nods once in agreement.

'Were they dead when you left them?' the priest asks him.

'Only the Yaks.'

'And you didn't think to go back there?'

'I knew that blizzard would have killed them.'

'It didn't kill you.'

'I'd say it tried its damnedest.'

'Who murdered the Esquimaux?'

'A man named Henry Drax, a harpooner.'

'Why would he do such a thing?'

'Because he wanted their sledge. He wanted to use it to escape.'

Frowning and shaking his head at this extraordinary intelligence, the priest picks up his pipe and fills it with tobacco.

His hand is trembling as he does so. Sumner watches him. Charcoal ticks and crackles in the stove beside them.

'He must have travelled north,' the priest says, after a pause. 'The northern tribes of Baffin Land are a law unto themselves. If he fell among them, there is no way of us ever finding out where he is or what has become of him. He may be dead, but more likely he has traded the sledge for shelter and is waiting for the spring.'

Sumner nods. He watches the candle's shimmering ghost hovering in the darkened windowpane. Beyond it, he sees the pale template of the igloo and, beyond that, the high hard blackness of the mountains. He thinks of Henry Drax still alive somewhere, and shudders.

The priest stands up. He takes a bottle of brandy from the cabinet near the door and pours them both a glass.

'And what is your name?'

Sumner looks up at him sharply, then turns back to the driftwood and continues whittling.

'Not Henry Drax,' he says.

'Then what?'

'Sumner. Patrick Sumner from Castlebar.'

'A Mayo man,' the priest says lightly.

'Aye,' he says. 'Once upon a time.'

'And what is your history, Patrick?'

'I have none to speak of.'

'Come,' he says, 'every man has his history, surely.'

Sumner shakes his head.

'Not me,' he says.

*

On Sundays, the priest holds Communion in the main room of the cabin. He pushes the table to one end of the room, clears off the books and papers, and puts a linen table-cloth, a crucifix and two candles in brass candlesticks down in their place. There is a pewter jug and chalice for the wine, and a chipped china plate for the wafers. Anna and her brother attend always and sometimes four or five others come down from the camp nearby. Sumner acts as altar boy. He lights the candles, then blows them out again. He dabs the lip of the chalice with a rag to keep it clean. When required, he even reads the lesson. The whole thing is a non-sense, he believes, a crude human circus with the priest as ringmaster and lion tamer combined, but it is easier to go along with it once a week, he thinks, than argue the toss on each separate occasion. What the Esquimaux make of it all, though, he can't imagine. They stand and kneel as required, even sing the hymns as best they can. He suspects they find it secretly amusing, that it serves them as a form of exotic entertainment in the otherwise dull expanses of winter. When they get back to their igloo, he imagines them laughing at the priest's solemnity and gaily mimicking his pointless, ponderous gestures.

One Sunday, after the service has concluded and the tiny congregation is standing smoking pipes or sipping mugs of sugared tea, Anna tells the priest that one of the Esquimaux women from the camp has a sickening infant and is asking her for medicine. The priest listens, nods, then goes to the storeroom and selects a bottle of calomel pills from the med-icine chest. He gives the woman two of the white pills and tells her to divide them in half and to give the child one half each morning and keep it tightly swaddled in the meantime. Sumner, who is sitting by the stove in his usual place, watches on, but doesn't speak. When the priest has moved away, he stands up and walks over to the Esquimaux woman. He gestures to look at her child. The woman says something to Anna and then, after Anna replies, removes the child from the hood of her anorak and hands it to Sumner. The child's eyes are dark and sunken, and its hands and feet are cold. When Sumner pinches its cheek, it doesn't cry or complain. He gives the child back to his mother then reaches behind the stove and takes a small piece of charcoal from the galvanised bucket. He twists it beneath his boot heel, then licks his index finger and dabs it down into the black powder. He opens up the infant's mouth and smears the charcoal powder on its tongue, then gets a teaspoon of water and washes it down. The infant turns red, coughs, then swallows. Sumner takes a larger piece of charcoal from the bucket and hands it to Anna.

'Tell her to do what I just did,' he says. 'She should do it four times each day, and she should feed the baby as much water as she can in between.'

'And the white pills too?' she says.

Sumner shakes his head.

'Tell her to throw away the pills,' he says. 'The pills will make it worse.'

Anna frowns and then looks down at her feet.

'Tell the woman I am an *angakoq*,' Sumner says. 'Tell her I know a lot more than the priest ever will.'

Anna's eyes widen. She shakes her head.

'I cannot tell her that,' she says.

'Then tell her she must choose for herself. The pills or the charcoal. It is up to her.'

He turns away, unfolds his pocketknife and starts up again with the whittling. When Anna tries to speak to him again, he waves her away.

The two Esquimaux hunters who rescued Sumner return to the mission a week later. Their names are Urgang and Merok. They are ragged, cheerful men both, lank-haired and boyish. Their ancient anoraks are torn and shabby, and their bulbous bearskin trews are darkened in patches by seal grease and baccy juice. On arrival, after tethering the dogs and doing the decencies with Anna and her brother, they draw the priest aside and explain they want Sumner to come with them on their next hunting trip.

'They don't need you to hunt,' the priest tells Sumner shortly afterwards. 'They just want you to be there. They suspect you have magical powers, and they think the animals will be drawn to you.'

'How long would I be gone?'

The priest goes outside to check.

'They say a week,' he says. 'They're offering you a new set of furs to wear and a fair portion of the catch.'

'Tell them yes,' Sumner says.

The priest nods.

'They're good-hearted fellows, but crude and backward, and they speak not a word of English,' he says. 'You'll be able to act as a good example of the civilised virtues while you're in among them.'

Sumner looks at him and laughs.

'I'll be no such fucking thing,' he says.

The priest shrugs and shakes his head.

'You're a finer man than you think you are,' he tells him. 'You hold your secrets tight, I know that, but I've been watching you a while now.'

Sumner licks his lips and spits into the stove. The blob of khaki phlegm bubbles a moment, then disappears.

'Then I'd thank you to stop watching. What I may or mayn't be is my business, I think.'

'It's between you and the Lord, true enough,' the priest replies, 'but I hate to see a decent man miscount himself.'

Sumner looks out of the cabin window at the two slovenly-looking Esquimaux and their piebald pack of hounds.

'You should save your good advice for those who need it most,' he says.

'It's Christ's advice I'm giving out, not my own. And if there's a man alive who doesn't need that, I've yet to meet him.'

In the morning, Sumner dons his new suit of clothes and perches himself on top of the hunters' sledge. They carry him back to their winter campground, a low complex of inter-linked igloos with sledges, tent poles, drying frames and other pieces of wood and bone scattered about on the tram-pled and piss-marked snow. They are greeted by an eager cluster of women and children and an uproar of barking dogs. Sumner is led into one of the larger igloos and shown a place to seat himself. The igloo is lined, top and bottom, with reindeer hides, and warmed and lit by a soapstone blubber lamp at its centre. It is dank and gloomy inside, and reeks of old smoke and fish oil. Others follow him in. There is laughter and talking. Sumner fills his pipe bowl and Urgang lights it for him with a taper made of whaleskin. The dark-eyed children chew their finger-ends and silently stare. Sumner doesn't speak to anyone or attempt to communicate by glance or gesture. If they believe he is magic, he thinks, then let them. He has no obligation to set them right, to teach them anything at all.

He watches as one of the women heats a metal saucepan full of seal blood over the lamp. When the blood is steaming hot, she removes the pan from the low flame and passes it around. Each person drinks, then passes it on. It is not a rite or ritual, Sumner understands, it is just their way of taking food. When the pan reaches him, he shakes his head; when they press it on him, he takes it, sniffs, then gives it to the man on his right. They offer him a piece of raw seal liver instead, but he turns it down also. He realises that he is offending them now, he notices the flickers of sadness and confusion in their eyes, and wonders whether it would be easier, better, to concede. When the pan comes round again, he accepts it and drinks. The taste is not unpleasant, he has eaten worse. It reminds him of an oily and saltless version of oxtail soup. He drinks again to show himself willing, then passes the pan on. He senses their relief, their pleasure that he has accepted their proffered gift, that he has joined them somehow. He doesn't begrudge these beliefs, although he knows they aren't true. He hasn't joined them—he is not an Esquimaux any more than he is a Christian or an Irishman or a doctor. He is nothing, and that is a privilege and a joy he is loath to give up. After the eating is finished, they play games and make music. Sumner watches them and even joins in when he is asked to. He throws up a ball made of walrus bone and tries to catch it in a wooden cup; he artlessly mimics their singing. They smile and pound him on the shoulder; they point at him and laugh. He tells himself he is doing it for the new set of furs, for the promised portion of the seal meat, both of which he will give to the priest. He is busy paying his way.

They sleep, all together, on a platform built up of snow and covered over with branches and hides. There are no distinctions or barriers between them, no attempt to create privacy or hierarchy or enclosure of any kind. They are like cattle, he thinks, lying together in a cattle shed. Sometime in the night, he wakes and hears two people fucking. The noises they make suggest not pleasure or release but a kind of unwilling and guttural need. In the morning, he is woken early and given water by Punnie, one of Urgang's two wives—a square-shouldered, stocky woman with a broad face and a fierce expression. Urgang and Merok are already outside preparing the sledge for the hunting. When he goes to join them, he notices they are quieter and less boisterous than before, and he guesses they are nervous. Probably they have boasted wildly about the white man's magical powers, and they are wondering if they have said too much.

When everything is ready, Sumner gets onto the sledge again, and they drive it out onto the sea ice. They track along the coastline for several miles before stopping at a place which seems to Sumner no different from the hundred others they have already seen and passed without pausing. They take the spears off the sledge and tip the sledge over, jamming it hard down into the snow to prevent the dogs pulling it away, then they unharness one of the dogs and let it loose to sniff around for a breathing hole. Sumner watches them and follows after, but they pay him no attention and he wonders after a while if they have already discounted him, whether something he has done or said already has made them doubt his supernatural influence. When the dog starts circling then barking, Merok grabs it by the mane and pulls it away. Urgang gestures for Sumner to stay where he is, then, holding the spear upright in one hand like a pilgrim's staff, he slowly approaches the breathing hole. When he gets close to it, he kneels down and scrapes away the covering of snow with his knife. He peers into the hole, tilts his head to listen, then pushes the snow back on top, closing the gap he has just made. He takes a piece of sealskin from inside his anorak, lays it down on the ice and stands on top of it. He bends his knees and leans towards the hole with his hands holding the long iron-tipped spear horizontal against his thighs and his body tilted forward.

Sumner lights his pipe. For a long time, Urgang stands motionless, then suddenly, as if stirred into action by the silent hailing of some mystical and Quakerish inner voice, he straightens up and in one rapid and indivisible flash of movement raises the spear and plunges it down through the loose-packed snow and into the body of the seal that has just risen to breathe. The barbed iron head, with a looped line reeved to it, detaches from the spear shaft. Urgang grips the line with both hands, digs his heels into the snow and yanks up against the hidden downward thrashings of the wounded seal. As they wrestle each other, spumes of water pulsate upwards through the cleft in the ice. The water is clear at first, then pink, then bright red. When the seal finally dies, a gout of its blood, thick and dark, rises up out of the breathing hole and spatters across the ice at Urgang's feet. He kneels down and, keeping hold of the line with one hand, takes his knife in the other and chips away at the sides of the hole. Merok runs across and helps to pull the dead seal out onto the surface of the ice. When it is clear, they push the iron spearhead out through the underside of the seal's body, re-attach it to the shaft and then plug the open wounds with ivory toggles to avoid losing any more of the precious blood. The seal is large, a giant, almost twice as big as the norm. The hunters' movements as they work around it are urgent and joyful. Sumner senses their elation, but also their wish to subdue it, to ensure their pleasure does not confuse the purity of this moment. As the three of them walk back to the sledge together across the corrugated surface of the ice, with the dead seal dragging along behind like a sack of bullion, he feels, deep in his chest, as if in answer to an unasked question, the flickering warmth of an unearned victory.

Later, while the two hunters butcher the seal and pass out portions of the meat and blubber to the other families in the camp, the children gather round Sumner where he stands, tugging at his bearskin pantaloons, touching and rubbing themselves against his thighs and knees, as if hoping for a share of the good luck he has brought. He tries to shoo them away, but they ignore him and it is only when the women come out of the igloos that they disperse. The size of the seal, it seems, has confirmed his status. They believe he has magic powers, that he can conjure the animals up from the depths and draw them onto the hunters' spears. He is not a full-blown god, he supposes, but he is a kind of minor saint at least: he assists and intercedes. He thinks of the chromolithograph of St Gertrude hung on the parlour wall in William Harper's house in Castlebar—the golden halo, the quill pen, the sacred heart lying like a holy beetroot on the flat of her outstretched palm. Is this any more absurd or improbable, he wonders, any more sinful even? The priest would have a thing or two to say on the matter, of course, but he hardly cares. The priest is in another world altogether.

Later, under the deerhides, Punnie presses herself up into him, rump against groin. He thinks at first that she is only rearranging herself, that she must be asleep like the others are, but then, when she does it again, he understands what is intended. She is short and thick-limbed, broad in the hips and no longer young. Her square-topped head reaches only up to his chest and her hair smells of dirt and seal grease. When he reaches out to touch her shallow breasts, she doesn't speak or turn round. Now she is sure he is awake, she lies there waiting for him, the way her husband waited for the seal earlier out on the ice, poised but without expectation, both desirous and cleansed of all desire, like everything and nothing held together in silent balance. Her hears her breathing and feels the soft heat her body radiates. She twitches once, then settles again. He thinks of saying something then realises there is nothing he can say. They are two creatures coupling. The moment has no greater meaning, no further implications. When he pushes into her, his mind empties out and he feels a purifying surge of inner blankness. He is muscle and bone, blood and sweat and semen, and, as he jerks and jitters to a rapid and inelegant conclusion, he needs and wants to be nothing else.

Each day, the hunters go out and catch another seal, and each night, under the deerhides, while the others are sleeping, he couples with Punnie. She keeps her back turned against him always; she neither resists nor encourages; she never speaks. When he is finished, she rolls away. When she gives him breakfast in the morning—warm water, raw seal liver—she treats him coolly, and there is no sign that she remembers anything that has occurred between them. He imagines she is acting out of a heathenish model of *politesse*, and that Urgang himself has encouraged or commanded this. He accepts the offering for what it is: no more or less. After a week, when it is time for him to return to the mission, he decides he will miss the vacancy of the ice, and the incomprehensible jabber of the igloo. He has not spoken English since he left the mission, and the thought of the priest sitting in the cabin waiting for him with his books and papers, his opinions and plans and doctrines, fills him with irritation and gloom.

On the final night, instead of moving away when they have finished, Punnie turns back towards him. He sees, through the lamp-leavened gloom, her blunt and pock-marked face, her dark eyes and small upturned nose, the line of her mouth. She is smiling at him, and her expression is eager and curious. When she opens her lips to speak, he doesn't realise, at first, what is happening. The words sound to him like noises only, like the low guttural clucks the hunters make when they are soothing their dogs at night, but then, with a shudder of dismay, he understands she is talking to him in a crude but recognisable form of English, that she is trying to say 'goodbye'.

'*Gud bye,*' she says to him, smiling still. '*Gud bye.*'

He frowns at her, then shakes his head. He feels exposed and sullied by her efforts. Ashamed. It is as if a bright, burning light has been flashed upon the two of them and their pitiful nakedness has been revealed to the world. He wants her to be quiet again, to ignore him now as she has always ignored him before.

'No,' he whispers fiercely back at her. 'No more of that. No more.'

Next day, when he arrives at the mission, it is dark and cold, and the borealis is unwinding across the night sky in peristaltic bands of green and purple, like the loosely coiled innards of a far-fetched mythic beast. Inside the cabin, he finds the priest stretched out on his cot, laid low and complaining of stomach pains. Anna, under the priest's instruction, has placed a warm poultice on his abdomen and brought him castor oil and jalap from the medicine chest. He is badly bunged up, he explains to Sumner, and may require an enema if there is no movement presently. Sumner makes tea for himself and heats a can of bouillon soup. The priest watches him eat. He asks about the hunting trip, and Sumner tells about the seals and about the feasting.

'You encourage their superstitions then, I see,' the priest says.

'I let them believe what they want to. Who am I to interfere?'

'You do them no service by keeping them in ignorance. They lead a brutish kind of life.'

'I have no better truths to tell them.'

The priest shakes his head, then winces.

'Then what are you exactly?' he says. 'If that is the case?'

Sumner shrugs.

'I am tired and hungry,' he tells him. 'I am man who is about to eat his dinner and go to bed.'

In the night, the priest has a fierce bout of diarrhoea. Sumner is woken by the sounds of loud groans and splattering. The cabin air is dense with the velvet reek of liquid faeces. Anna, who has been sleeping curled on the floor, rises to assist. She gives the priest a clean cloth to wipe himself and takes the pot outside to empty. When she comes back inside, she covers him with blankets and helps him drink some water. Sumner watches, but doesn't move or speak. The priest strikes him as robust and healthy for a man of his age, and he assumes the constipation is a result of nothing more than the usual deficiencies of the Arctic diet, bereft as it is of plants, vegetable matter or fruit of any kind. Now the purgatives have had their effect, Sumner is sure he will be back to his normal self soon enough.

In the morning, the priest declares he is much improved. He breakfasts sitting upright in the bed and asks Anna to carry over his books and papers, so he can continue with his scholarly work. Sumner goes outside to say a last farewell to Urgang and Merok, who have spent the night in the igloo. The three of them embrace like old friends. They give him one of the seals, as agreed, but they also offer him one of their old hunting spears as a souvenir. They point at the spear, then at Sumner, then out onto the ice. He understands they mean him to go hunting by himself once they are gone. They laugh, and Sumner nods and smiles at them. He takes the spear and mimes the action of striking a seal through the ice. They cheer and laugh, and then when he does it again, they cheer even louder. He realises they are mocking him a little now to ease their parting, gently putting him in his place before they leave; they are reminding him that although he has magical powers, he is a still a white man, and the idea of a white man knowing how to use a spear is comical indeed. He watches as their sledge disappears beyond the granite headland, then he goes back into the cabin. The priest is making notes in his journal. Anna is sweeping up. Sumner shows them the spear. The priest examines it, then passes it to Anna, who declares it is a well-made spear but too old to use.

They have crumbled hard tack and bouillon soup for lunch. The priest eats everything that is in front of him, but then, almost as soon as he has finished, he vomits it out again onto the floor. He stays in the chair for a while, bent over coughing and spitting, then climbs back into the bed and calls for brandy. Sumner goes into the storeroom and takes the bottle of Dover's powder from the medicine chest, dissolves a spoonful in water and gives it to the priest to drink. The priest drinks it, then falls into a doze. When he wakes, he appears pale and complains of a more severe pain in his lower abdomen. Sumner feels his pulse and looks at his tongue, which is furred. He presses his fingertips into the priest's abdomen. The skin is tense, but there is no sign of a hernia. When he presses just above the line of the ilium, the priest cries out and his body jackknifes. Sumner takes his hand away and looks out of the cabin window—it is snowing outside and the panes are thick with frost.

'If you keep the brandy down, that should help a little,' he says.

'I wish to God I could piss,' the priest says, 'but I can barely squeeze out a drop.'

Anna sits by the bed and reads out St Paul's Letters to the Corinthians in her quiet and halting English. As the afternoon moves into evening, the priest's pain worsens and he starts to moan and gasp. Sumner makes up a warm poultice and finds some paregoric in the medicine chest. He tells Anna to continue giving him brandy and the Dover's powder, and to use the paregoric whenever the pain gets worse. During the night, the priest wakes up every hour, his eyes bulging, and howls with pain. Sumner, who is asleep at the table, his head resting on his folded arms, jolts awake each time, his heart pounding and his own guts twisting in sympathy. He goes over to the bed, kneels and gives him more brandy to drink. As he sips from the glass, the priest grasps onto Sumner's arm as if scared he might suddenly leave. The priest's green eyes are wild and rheumy; his lips are crusted, and his hot breath is foul.

In the morning, when they are out of earshot, Anna asks Sumner whether the priest is going to die.

'He has an abscess inside him here,' Sumner explains, pointing to the right side of his belly just above the groin. 'Some inner part has ruptured and his belly is filling up with poison.'

'You will save him though,' she says.

'There's nothing I can do. It's impossible.'

'You told me you are an *angakoq*.'

'We are a thousand miles or more from any hospital, and I have no medicines to speak of.'

She gives him a disbelieving look. Sumner wonders how old this Anna is—eighteen? Thirty? It is difficult to judge. All the Esquimaux women have the same leathery brown skin, the same small dark eyes and quizzical expression. A different man would have taken her to his bed, he thinks, but the priest has tutored her to read the Bible and answer back.

'If you can't save him, then why are you here?' she asks. 'What are you for?'

'I'm here by accident. It doesn't mean anything.'

'Everyone died except for you. Why did you live?'

'There is no why,' he says.

She glares at him, then shakes her head and goes back to the priest's bedside. She kneels down and starts to pray.

After a few more hours, the priest begins having violent shivering fits and his skin turns cold and clammy. His pulse is faint and irregular, and his tongue has a large streak of brown along its centre. When Anna tries to give him brandy, he throws it up. Sumner watches for a while, then pulls on his new set of furs and steps outside the cabin; it is bitterly cold and only semi-light, but he is glad to escape from the sour stench of mortal illness and the priest's constant, grating howls of complaint. He walks past the igloo and looks out east across the immense desert of sea ice to the faint white parabola of the far horizon. It is noon, but the stars are visible overhead. There is no sign of life or movement anywhere, everything is still and dark and cold. It is as if the end of the world has already happened, he thinks, as if he is the only man left alive on the frigid earth. For several minutes, he stands where he is, listening to the shallow wheeze of his own breathing, feeling the red muscle of his heart gently thudding in his chest, then, remembering himself at last, he turns slowly round and goes back inside.

Anna is laying another poultice on the priest's belly. She gives him a fierce look, but he ignores it. He goes to the medicine chest and takes out a large bottle of ether, a wad of lint and a lancet. He spends a few minutes sharpening the lancet to an edge with a whetstone, then he clears the remaining books off the table and wipes it clean with a damp rag. He walks over to the bed and looks down at the priest. The elder man's skin is waxen and damp, and his eyes are filled with pain. Sumner places his hand on his forehead and then peers into his mouth for a moment.

'Your caecum is abscessed,' he tells him, 'or possibly ulcer-ated—the difference is unimportant. If we had any amount of opium in the medicine chest, that would help, but since we have none at all, the best thing to do is make a cut in your belly here, to allow the diseased matter to flow out of you.'

'How do you know such things?'

'Because I'm a surgeon.'

Since he is in too much pain to comment or express sur-prise, the priest merely nods. He closes his eyes a moment to think, then opens them again.

'So you've done the thing before?' he asks.

Sumner shakes his head.

'I've neither done it myself, nor seen it done. I read about it being performed by a man named Hancock in the Charing Cross Hospital in London some years ago. On that occasion, the patient lived.'

'We're a good way from London,' the priest says.

Summer nods.

'I'll do all I can in these conditions, but we'll need a large amount of luck.'

'You do your best,' the priest says, 'and I expect the Lord will take care of the remainder.'

Sumner asks Anna to fetch her brother in from the igloo and, when the brother arrives, he tips some of the ether onto the wad of lint, and places it over the priest's nose and mouth. They remove his clothes, then lift his naked, lolling body off the cot and lay it out on the table. Sumner lights an extra candle and places it on the windowsill to illuminate his work. Anna starts praying and rapidly crossing herself, but Sumner interrupts her pieties and instructs her to stand at the end of the table and apply more ether whenever the priest shows any sign of reviving. The brother, who is tall and has a genial, oafish air, is given a metal bucket and a towel, and told to stand by Sumner's shoulder and stay alert.

He palpates the abdomen again, feeling its lines of hardness and give. He wonders for a moment if he has made a mistake, if this is a hernia or a tumour rather than an abscess, but then reminds himself why that can't be true. He tests the sharpness of the lancet against his thumb, then presses the blade's edge down into the priest's flesh and makes a lateral cut from the top of his hip bone, halfway to the navel. It takes him several attempts to penetrate the layers of sheath, muscle and fat and get into the abdomen proper. As he presses deeper, blood wells up, and he wipes it away with a cloth and continues cutting. As soon as he pierces the cavity wall, a pint or more of foul and flocculent pus, turbid and pinkish grey, squirts unhindered out of the newly made breach, spattering across the table and coating Sumner's hands and forearms. The roaring stench of excrement and decay instantly fills the cabin. Anna yelps out in horror and her brother drops the metal bucket. Sumner gasps and jolts backwards. The discharge is fibrinous, bloody and thick as Cornish cream; it pulses out from the narrow opening like the last twitching apogee of a monstrous ejaculation. Sumner, squinting against the reek, curses, spits onto the floor, then, breathing through his mouth, cleans the muck from his hands and arms, and tells the brother to wipe the table down and throw the soiled rags into the stove. The three of them, working together, tip the priest over onto his side to further speed the drainage. He makes a low moan as they move him. Anna, with shaking hands, reapplies the etherised lint to his face until he settles. Sumner presses down on the skin and muscle around the edges of the wound with his fingertips, pushing out as much of the remaining foulness as he can. It is hard to believe that the priest's body could contain such an abundance of pus. He is not tall and, stripped naked as he now is, he appears slight, bony and almost boyish, yet it gurgles out of him like water from a rock. Sumner presses down and the brother wipes up the outflowings. They press and wipe, press and wipe until eventually the stinking stream slows, then ceases altogether.

They carry the priest back to the bed and cover him over with blankets and a sheet. Summer cleans and puts a dressing on the wound, then washes his hands with oil soap and opens the window. The air that rushes in is flecked with snow, odourless and starkly cold. It is dark outside and the wind is whistling in the eaves. He doubts the priest will live more than a day. With an abscess that severe, there is almost certain to be some form of perforation in the gut, he thinks, and once the shit starts leaking out, that is generally the end of it. He gathers the few medicines they have that might relieve or moderate the pain and instructs Anna how and when to use them. He lights his pipe and goes outside to smoke it.

That night, asleep in his own bed, he dreams he is afloat

again on the iceless reaches of the North Water. He is alone and drifting in his pal Tommy Gallagher's leaky old currach, its hull patched, and its thwarts smoothed and worn to a shine by usage. He has no oars that he can see, and there is no sign of another vessel, but he doesn't feel afraid. He spots an iceberg on his larboard side and standing, perched high on one of its ledges, clad in a green tweed suit and brown felt hat from Dames of Temple Bar, is William Harper the surgeon, the man who found him and took him in. He is smiling and waving. When Sumner calls out for him to come down, he laughs as if the very thought of swapping the majestic iceberg for the pathos of the currach is absurd. William Harper's face appears quite normal, Sumner notices, and he is moving his right arm freely enough. There is no sign of paralysis or injury, no evidence of the hunting accident that drove him to the drink. He has been wholly restored, it seems, and now he is perfect again, entire. Sumner wishes, more than anything, to ask him how this remarkable feat was achieved, what methods were used, but the currach has drifted too far away, he realises, and his voice is too weak to carry across the water.

In the morning, to his surprise, the priest is still breathing and he looks no worse than he did before. 'You're a tough old fucker, you are,' Sumner says to himself, as he removes the dressing and inspects the wound. 'For a man who puts his faith in the life everlasting, it appears you're awful keen to linger on amid the toil and strife of this one.' He wipes around the incision with a rag, sniffs the seepage, then throws the old dressing into the bucket to be washed and makes up a new one. As he works, the priest opens his eyes a crack and looks up at him.

'What did you find inside me?' he asks. The voice is grainy and faint, and Sumner has to lean down to hear it.

'Nothing good,' he answers.

'Then best be rid of it, I'd say.'

Sumner nods.

'You try to get your rest now,' he tells him. 'And if you need help, just call out for it or raise your hand. I'll be seated at the table.'

'You'll be watching over me, will you?'

Sumner shrugs.

'There's precious little else to do around here until the spring arrives,' he says.

'I thought you might be off hunting seal with your new spear and anorak.'

'I'm not a seal hunter. I don't have the patience for it.'

The priest smiles, nods then closes his eyes. He seems to be drifting back to sleep, but then, a minute later, he opens his eyes again and looks up as if remembering something else.

'Why did you lie to me before?' he says.

'I never lied to you. Not once.'

'You're a strange fellow though, aren't you? And a source of great mystery to all who know you.'

'I'm a surgeon,' he tells him quietly. 'A surgeon now, and that's the all of it.'

The priest thinks a while before he speaks again.

'I know you have suffered, Patrick, but you are not alone in that,' he says.

Sumner shakes his head.

'I've brought the sufferings on myself, I'd say. I've made mistakes aplenty.'

'Show me a man who hasn't, and I will show you a saint or a great liar. And I haven't met too many saints in my long lifetime.'

The priest looks at Sumner for a moment and smiles. There are green-grey clots of mucus in both corners of his mouth and his milky eyes look swollen in their sockets. He reaches out his hand, and Sumner holds onto it. It is cool to the touch and almost weightless. The skin is puckered above the joints, and at the fingertips it has the dull sheen of worn leather.

'You should rest,' Sumner tells him again.

'I will rest,' the priest agrees. 'That's what I will do.'

23

Baxter's man is waiting at the quayside. His name is Stevens and he says he is an office clerk, though he doesn't much resemble one. He is close to six feet tall, broad in the chest and belly, with dark pinprick eyes, mutton-chop whiskers and a paucity of teeth. Sumner packs his meagre necessaries in a sack and says his farewells to Captain Crawford and the crew of the *Truelove*, then he and Stevens walk south together towards Baxter's chambers on Bowlalley Lane. They turn down Lowgate, past the Mansion House and the Golden Galleon Inn, past George Yard and Chapel Lane. After the long weeks at sea, the simplicity and sureness of the land strikes Sumner as an aberration, a sleight of hand. He tries to tell himself that all this—the cobblestones, the wagons, the warehouses, and shops and banks—is real, but it feels like an elaborate pantomime, a sham. Where is all the water? he thinks giddily. Where is all the ice?

When they reach Bowlalley Lane, Stevens raps hard on the double doors and Baxter opens one of them. He is wearing a navy frock coat piped with lace, a green felt waistcoat and pinstriped trousers; his teeth are amber and skew-whiff, and his grey hair dangles untrimmed over his ears in a lank and perfumed page-boy. They shake hands and Baxter, smiling, looks at him intently.

'I hardly believed it when I read your letter from Lerwick,' he says, shaking his head. 'Yet here you are, Mr Patrick Sumner, alive and in the fucking flesh. We thought we'd lost you, drowned or frozzen with all the other poor bastards, yet here ye are indeed.' Baxter laughs and slaps him on the shoulder. 'Would you take something to eat now?' he says. 'Can I get you a plate of oysters or a pork sausage or a nice morsel of calf's tongue at least?'

Sumner shakes his head. Beneath Baxter's eager bonhomie, he senses an edge of wariness, fear even. His presence here is disturbing, he imagines, and unnatural. He's the man who should be dead, but isn't.

'I've come for my wages only,' he says. 'Then I'll be on my way.'

'Your wages? On your way? Oh no, you fucking won't,' Baxter says, a look of mocked-up outrage slewed across his face. 'You're not leaving here till you've sat and taken a drink with me. I won't allow it.'

He leads them up the stairs into his first-floor offices. There is a low fire crumbling in the grate and two identical armchairs set on either side of it.

'Sit your arse down there,' Baxter tells him.

Sumner hesitates a moment, then does as he is bidden. When Baxter pours two glasses of brandy and gives one to him, he takes it. They say nothing for a minute, then Baxter speaks again.

'Both ships sunk by ice and you miraculously saved by passing Yaks,' he says. 'That's quite a story you have to tell the waiting world.'

'Maybe so, but I won't be telling it any time soon.'

Baxter raises his eyebrows and takes a quick sip of his drink.

'And why is that?' he asks.

'I don't wish to become known as the one man who survived the *Volunteer*. I should never have been on that ship. I should never have seen what I saw there.'

'There are widows and orphans aplenty in this town who would like nothing better than to meet a man who could tell them the first-hand truth about what happened. You'd be doing them a great kindness, I'd say.'

Sumner shakes his head.

'The truth won't help them any. Not now.'

Baxter licks his lips and curls a strand of grey hair behind his darkly bristled ear. He smiles briefly, as if entertained by this idea.

'You may be right,' he says. 'Keeping quiet may be the greater kindness, I suppose. Since the men are long dead, the details of their deaths hardly matter. What purpose will it serve to stir things up? Let the poor bastards rest in peace, I say. It was a terrible accident, but such things must be endured.'

Sumner shifts about in his seat. He rubs the nerveless tip of his healed-up tongue against his lips and teeth.

'Some of it was accident and some wasn't,' he says. 'You read my letter. You know about the killings.'

Baxter sighs and glances sideways across the room. He takes a drink and then peers down for a while at the gleaming toe-ends of his patent-leather pumps.

'Horrifying,' he whispers. 'Just horrifying. I couldn't believe what I was reading. Cavendish? Brownlee? A fucking *cabin boy?*'

'When he signed on, you had no idea?'

'About Drax? Fuck, no. What do you take me for? The man was a great heathen, of course, but he seemed no worse than average for a Greenland harpooner and a good deal better than some I've known.'

Sumner looks at Baxter and nods. He remembers Joseph Hannah and feels a sudden tightening in his chest.

'Someone should search for him,' he says. 'Perhaps I should try it myself. He may still be alive.'

Baxter frowns and shakes his head.

'Henry Drax is either dead or he's in Canada, which if you ask me is near enough the same thing. And you're a surgeon, not a detective. What business do you have chasing after murderers?'

Baxter waits for his answer, but Sumner stays silent.

'You put Henry Drax behind you now, Patrick,' Baxter says, 'far behind you, just like you've put the rest of it. That's the wisest course for you by far. He'll be judged soon enough one way or the other.'

'If I ever see him again, I expect I'll know what to do,' Sumner says.

'Aye, but you *won't* see him again,' Baxter says. 'He's gone for good now, and we should both be fucking grateful for that mercy.'

Sumner nods and reaches into his pocket for his clay pipe and tobacco pouch. When Baxter sees what he is doing, he goes to his desk and brings back a box of cigars. They take one each and light them.

'I need employment,' Sumner tells him. 'I have a letter here.'

'Show me.'

He takes the priest's letter from his pocket and passes it to Baxter. Baxter reads.

'And this is the missionary you wintered with?'

Sumner nods.

'Says here you saved his life.'

'I did what I could. Most of it was raw luck.'

Baxter refolds the letter and hands it back.

'I know a man down in London,' he says. 'A surgeon name of Gregory, James Gregory, ever heard of him?'

Sumner shakes his head.

'He's a good fellow. He'll find you something that pays,' Baxter says. 'I'll write to him today. We'll get you a bed in the Pilgrim's Arms for tonight, then when we hear back from Gregory, we can put you on the train. There's fuck-all for a man like you to do around here. The whaling trade is dying on its feet. You're too young and bright for Hull. London's the place for your kind.'

'I'll need my wages from you,' Sumner says.

'Aye, aye, of course you will. I'll get them now and when you're settled in at the Pilgrim's, I'll have Stevens send you round a pint of good brandy and a nice plump whore to ease you back into the ways of civilised living.'

After Sumner is gone, Baxter sits at his desk and ponders. His tongue, pink at the edges and yellow down the middle, flickers around inside his mouth, as if each of his ideas has a distinctive flavour, and he is tasting each one in turn. Eventually, after nearly half an hour of thinking, he stands up, looks around the room quickly as if to check everything is in its place, then walks to the door and opens it. Out on the shadowed landing, instead of descending to the ground floor as he normally would, he climbs the narrow uncarpeted staircase up to the attic. When he reaches the top, he knocks once and enters. The room he steps into is small and steeply pitched; there is a circular window in the gable end, and a dusty skylight cut into one side of the roof. The floorboards are splintery and unpolished and the walls lack plaster. There is a wooden chair and a metal camp bed for furniture, some empty brandy bottles on the floor and a thunderpot brimming with dark brown piss and curled fragments of floating turd. Baxter, stooping and covering his nose, walks to the bed and shakes awake the man who is lying on it. The man grumbles and gasps, farts lengthily then turns over and slowly shows an eyeball.

'So tell me,' he says.

'It won't do, Henry,' Baxter answers. 'He knows too much, and what he doesn't know he can piece together easy enough. It was all I could do to stop him running off to the fucking magistrate.'

Drax swings his feet onto the rugless floor and pushes himself up into a sitting position. He yawns and scratches himself.

'He don't know about the sinking,' he says. 'He can't know that.'

'He may not know, but he suspects. He knows it wasn't right. Why turn the ship north when every other fucker's sailing south?'

'He said that?'

'He did.'

Drax reaches under the bed, finds a nearly empty brandy bottle and drinks it off.

'And what does he say about me?'

'He swears he'll search until he finds you. He says he'll hire a man if need be.'

'What man?'

'In Canada. To find out what became of you, to track your movements since.'

Drax licks his lips and shakes his head.

'He won't find me,' he says.

'He won't stop looking. He swore to it on his mother's grave. I told him you were most likely dead by now, but he wouldn't believe me. A man like Henry Drax doesn't just die, he said, he must be killed.'

'*Killed?* He's just a fucking surgeon.'

'He was in the army though, remember. The siege of Delhi. He's got some vinegar in him, I'd say.'

Drax peers into the empty bottle and sniffs. His skin is

puce and his eyes are sunk down into his face. Baxter wipes off the chair seat with his handkerchief and gingerly sits down.

'And where is he now?' Drax says.

'I've got him a room in the Pilgrim's Arms. I'll send a whore up to keep him occupied, but we need to do this tonight, Henry. We can't delay. If he gets to the magistrate in the morning, there's no telling what trouble he'll cause for us.'

'I been drinking all day,' he says. 'Get that lazy fucker Stevens to do it for you.'

'I can't trust Stevens with a task like this one, Henry. All our fortune is riding on it, don't you see that? If Sumner blabs, there'll be no more money coming to either of us, they'll hang you up by the neck and throw me into gaol.'

'What the fuck do you pay him for?'

'Stevens is a good man, but he doesn't have your experience nor your coolness under pressure. You've had a drop or two of brandy, but that makes no odds. If you do it right, there won't be any struggle.'

'It can't be in the Pilgrim's though,' he says. 'Too many people about.'

'We'll lure him out then. That's easily done. I'll send Stevens over with a message. You wait for them somewhere else. Wherever you want it to be.'

'Down by the river. The old timber yard on Trippet Street, past the foundry.'

Baxter nods and smiles.

'There aren't too many men like you out there, Henry,' he

says. 'There's plenty who will talk, but precious few who will pull the trigger when required.'

Drax blinks twice. His mouth drops open, and his thick tongue swells and stretches like some eyeless creature newly birthed.

'I'll be needing a bigger share,' he says.

Baxter sniffs and picks a tangling piece of cobweb from the thigh of his pinstriped trews.

'Five hundred guineas is what we agreed on,' he says. 'It's more than I offered Cavendish. You know it is.'

'But this is extras, int it?' Drax says. 'Above and beyond.'

Baxter thinks for a moment, then nods and gets to his feet.

'Five and a half then,' he says.

'I like the sound of six better, Jacob.'

Baxter makes to speak but doesn't. He looks at Drax, then checks his pocket watch.

'Six then,' he says. 'But six is the fucking end of it.'

Drax nods complacently, then picks up his feet and lies back down on the greasy and pungent camp bed.

'Six is the end of it,' he echoes, 'and if you could send that cunt Stevens up with another bottle of brandy, and get him to empty out this piss pot while he's at it, I'd be monstrous fucking grateful, I'm sure.'

Baxter descends to the first-floor landing. He waits there a moment and then calls down to Stevens, who is sitting in the hallway with his bowler on his knees reading the Hull and East Riding *Intelligencer*. They go into the study together and Baxter gestures for him to close the door.

'You have the revolver I gave you,' Baxter says, 'and you have the bullets also?'

Stevens nods. Baxter asks to see the gun, and Stevens takes it from his pocket and places it on the desk between them. Baxter looks it over, then gives it back.

'I have a task for you tonight,' he says. 'You listen carefully now.'

Stevens nods again. Baxter notes with pleasure his docility, his doggish eagerness to please. If only, Baxter thinks, they were all like that.

'At midnight you go to Patrick Sumner's room in the Pilgrim's Arms, and you tell him I need to see him urgently at my house. Tell him I have important news about the *Volunteer* and it can't wait until the morning. He doesn't know the town, and he doesn't know where my house is neither, so he'll follow wherever you lead him. Lead him towards the river. Go up Trippet, past the foundry until you reach the old timber yard. If he asks what you're doing, tell him it is a short cut—it makes no difference whether he believes you or not, just get him inside somehow. Henry Drax will be waiting in the yard. He'll shoot Sumner and after he shoots Sumner, you'll shoot him. You understand me?'

'I don't need Drax there,' he says. 'I can shoot the surgeon myself.'

'That's not to the purpose. I need Drax to shoot Sumner and you to shoot Drax. After you've shot him, you put this revolver in Sumner's hand, empty out his pockets and Drax's too, and then you make yourself fucking scarce.'

304

'The constable at the Dock will hear something, for sure,' Stevens says.

'True enough, and no doubt he will come running and blowing hard on his whistle. When he gets to the yard, he'll find two dead men each holding the gun that killed the other one. There are no witnesses anywhere, no other signs or indications. The peelers will scratch their heads a while, then take the bodies to the morgue and wait for them to be claimed, but no one will claim them. And what will happen next?'

He stares at Stevens, and Stevens shrugs.

'*Nothing* will happen next,' Baxter says. 'Nothing at all. That's beauty of the scheme. Two unknown men have killed each other. There are two murderers and two victims. The crime solves itself, and I am free of Henry Drax at last, free of his threats and his gouging, and free of his mad stench.'

'So after he shoots Sumner, I shoot *him*,' Stevens says.

'In the chest, not the back. In the back will only provoke questions. And put the gun in his right hand, not his left. Do you understand it now?'

Stevens nods.

'Good. Now take this bottle of brandy up to the attic for him. Empty his piss pot while you're there, and if he speaks to you, say nothing back.'

'That filthy bastard's time is coming, Mr Baxter,' Stevens says.

'Indeed it fucking is.'

24

Drax crouches alone in the corner of the shadowed timber yard. There is an open storage shed running along one side, and a sag-roofed, ramshackle cabin at the far end. The ground between is strewn with broken bottles, shattered crates and planking. Drax has the bottle of brandy in his pocket; every now and then, he takes it out, licks his lips, and drinks. At times like these, when the thirst is on him and he has money enough in his britches, he will drink for a week without pausing for breath. Two or three bottles each day. More. It is not a matter of need or pleasure, not a matter of wanting or not wanting. The thirst carries him forward, blindly, easily. Tonight he will kill, but the killing is not topmost in his mind. The thirst is much deeper than the rage. The rage is fast and sharp, but the thirst is lengthy. The rage always has an ending, a blood-soaked finale, but the thirst is bottomless and without limit.

He places the bottle carefully on the ground by his feet and checks his revolver. When he breaks open the cylinder, the bullets drop out onto the ground and, cursing, he reaches down to find them. He loses his balance, staggers sideways and then rights himself. When he stands again, the timber yard sways in front of him, and the moon tips and wobbles across the sky. He blinks and spits. His mouth fills up with vomit, but he swallows it down, picks up the bottle from the ground and drinks again. He has lost a bullet, but that makes no odds. He has four more left, and it will only need one to kill the Paddy surgeon. He will tarry here by the gate, and when they walk in, he will plug him in the head. That will be that. No warning or chatter. If that queer cunt Baxter or his idiot slavey had anything about them, they could do the job themselves, but, as it is, Henry Drax must do it for them. Oh, the others will talk and plan, and make oaths and promises, but there are precious few fuckers who will *do*.

The moon is smothered by clouds, and the shadows in the yard have thickened and merged. He sits on a barrel and peers out into the vague, uneven blackness. He can still make out the edges of the gate and the top of the wall running next to it. When he hears men's voices, he stands up and takes one slow step forward, then another one. The voices become louder and more distinct. He cocks the revolver and steadies himself to shoot. The gate creaks and begins to open inwards. He watches as they enter the yard side-by-side: two dark shapes, blank and featureless as shadows. One head, two heads. He hears the squeak and scurry of a rat, and feels the great thirst agitate inside him. He breathes in once, aims, then fires. The darkness splits open for an instant, swallows him, then spits him out again. The man on the left crumples and drops onto the cinders with a muted thud. Drax lowers the revolver, takes a snort of brandy and steps forward to check if he is fully dead or if some knife-work is required to finish the job. He crouches over the body and lights a lucifer. He peers down as the yellow flame lengthens in his hand, then rocks back on his heels and curses.

It is Stevens the slavey lying dead. He has shot the wrong fucking man, that's all. He stands up and looks about. Sumner didn't run back through the gate—he knows that—and the walls all around are high and topped with broken glass. He must still be in the yard somewhere.

'Are you in here, Mr Surgeon?' he shouts out. 'Why don't you show yourself? If you plan to capture me, now's your best chance. You won't ever get a finer one. Lookee here, I'll even lay down my gun.' He places the gun on the ground in front of him and holds up his hands. 'I'm offering you a fair fight now. No weapons, and I've got a drink or two inside me to help even things up.'

He pauses and peers around again, but there is no answer from the darkness and no sign of any movement.

'Come on now,' he shouts, 'I know you're in here. Don't be bashful. Baxter says you plan to hunt me down, to hire a man to look for me out in Canada, but here I am right in front of you. Alive and in the fucking flesh. So why not take your chances when they're offered?'

He waits a few seconds more, then picks up the gun and walks towards the cabin at the far end of the yard. When he gets close enough to look inside, he stops. The door is half open. There is one window at the front and another, smaller one at the side. Both are smashed and shutterless. He knows for certain someone will have heard the first gunshot; if he doesn't kill the surgeon soon, it will be too late and that will be the end of all his good fortune. But where has the sly fucker got to? Where is he lurking?

Inside the cabin, Sumner grips a rusted saw blade in both hands. He holds it poised, shoulder high, and waits. When Drax steps across the threshold, he swings it forward in a hard flat arc. The jagged edge strikes just above the collarbone. There is a hot squirt of arterial blood, a long repellent gurgle. Drax stands poised and upright for a moment as if waiting for something else—something better—to happen to him, then he topples back against the lintel. His head is askew. The ragged wound gapes like a second mouth. Sumner, without thought or qualm, as if moving in a dream, tugs the saw blade back, then drives it deeper in. Drax, half decapitated, pitches face first onto the black dirt outside; his gun clatters onto the cabin floor. Sumner stares a moment, horrified by the shape of his accomplishment, then grabs the gun and rushes back across the cindered yard.

In the silent darkness of the narrow street, he feels suddenly enormous, distended, as if his shaking body has swollen to twice its normal size. He walks back towards the town, maintaining a steady pace, not rushing and never looking rearwards. He ignores the first two pubs he sees, but enters the third. Inside, a man is playing the piano and a moon-faced woman is singing. All the tables and benches are filled, so he finds a stool by the bar. He orders a fourpenny ale, waits for his hands to stop trembling, then drinks it down and orders another. When he tries to light his pipe, he fumbles the match and when he tries again, the same thing happens. He gives up, and puts the pipe back into his pocket next to Drax's revolver. The barman watches on but says nothing.

'I need the railway timetable,' Sumner tells him. 'Do you have it there?'

The barman shakes his head.

'Which train is it you're wanting?'

'The soonest one to leave.'

The barman checks his pocket watch.

'The mail train is likely gone by now,' he says. 'It'll be the morning.'

Sumner nods. The woman begins singing 'The Flying Dutchman', and the men playing dominoes in the corner join in with the chorus. The barman smiles and shakes his head at their raucousness.

'Do you know a man named Jacob Baxter?' Sumner asks him.

'Everyone knows Baxter. Rich bastard, lives over on Charlotte Street, number 27. Used to be in the whaling business, but now it's to be coal oil and paraffin, they say.'

'Since when?'

'Since his two ships went down in Baffin Bay last season and he got paid off by the underwriters. The whaling trade is

dying anyway, and he got out just in time. You won't find no
flies on Jacob Baxter, I'll tell you that. You can look him over
all you want to, but you won't find nary a single one.'

'How much did he get paid for the sinking?'

The barman shrugs.

'A good deal, they say. He gave out some to the wives and
bairns of them that drowned, but he still kept plenty back for
hisself, you can be sure of that.'

'And now it's to be paraffin and coal oil?'

'The paraffin is cheap, and it burns a good deal cleaner
than the whale oil does. I'd use it myself.'

Sumner looks down at his hands, pale grey and blood-
spotted against the dark wood of the bar. He would like to
leave now, escape all this, but he feels a hot animal pressure
building in his face and chest like a creature grown large
inside him, scratching to get out.

'How far is Charlotte Street from here?'

'Charlotte Street? Not so far. You go up to the corner and
turn left by the Methodist Hall, then keep on going. You an
acquaintance of Mr Baxter, are you?'

Sumner shakes his head. He finds a shilling in his pocket,
pushes it across the bar and waves away the change. The
woman is singing 'Scarboro' Sands' as he leaves, and the men
have gone back to their games.

Baxter's house has a row of spear-top railings in front and
five stone steps leading up to the door. The windows are
shuttered, but he sees a light above the transom. He pulls the
bell and when the maid answers, he tells her his name and
that he is here to see Mr Baxter on an urgent matter. She

looks him up and down, pauses for thought, then opens the door wider and instructs him to wait in the hallway. The hallway smells of tar soap and wood polish; there is a whalebone hat stand, a rococo mirror, and a pair of matching Chinese vases. Sumner takes off his hat and checks that Drax's gun is still in his pocket. A clock chimes the quarter-hour in another room. He hears the clicking of boot heels across the tiled floor.

'Mr Baxter will see you in his study,' the maid says.

'Was he expecting me?'

'I couldn't say if he was or he wasn't.'

'But the name didn't alarm him at all?'

The maid frowns and shrugs.

'I told him what you asked me to, and he said to bring you right to his study. That's all I know about it.'

Sumner nods and thanks her. The maid leads him past the broad mahogany staircase to a room at the back of the house. She offers to knock for him but Sumner shakes his head and gestures her away. He waits until she has gone back upstairs, then he takes the revolver from his pocket and checks there is a bullet in the chamber. He turns the brass doorknob and pushes open the door. Baxter is sitting in a chair by the fire, he is wearing a black velvet smoking jacket and a pair of embroidered house shoes. His expression is alert but untroubled. When he begins to get up, Sumner shows him the revolver and tells him to stay just where he is.

'You don't need the gun now, Patrick,' Baxter scolds. 'There's no need for that.'

Sumner closes the door and steps into the centre of the

313

room. There are bookcases on two sides, a bearskin rug on the floor, and a seascape and a pair of crossed harpoons over the fireplace.

'I'd say that's for me to decide, not you,' he says.

'Perhaps so. Just a friendly suggestion, that's all. Whatever exactly has happened tonight, we can resolve it without the need for firearms, I'm quite sure of that.'

'What was your plan? What did you mean to happen in that timber yard?'

'Which timber yard would that be?'

'Your man Stevens is dead. Don't play the fucking fool.'

Baxter's mouth hangs open for a moment. He glances into the fire, coughs twice, then takes a sip of port. His lips are thin and damp, and his face is colourless aside from the faint blue bruise of his nose and the scribbles of broken vein across both cheeks.

'Let me explain something to you, Patrick,' he says, 'before you jump to any quick conclusions. Stevens was a good man, willing, loyal, biddable, but there are some men who can't be controlled. That's the simple truth of it. They're too vicious and too stupid. They won't take orders and they won't be led. A man like Henry Drax, for example, is a grave danger to everyone around him; he has no understanding of the greater good; he obeys no master but himself and his own vile urgings. When a man like myself, an honest man, a man of business and good sense, discovers that he has such a dangerous and unruly fucker in his employ the only question is: how best may I rid myself of him before he destroys me and everything I've worked for?'

'So why pull me into it?'

'That was wrong of me, Patrick, I confess, but I was in a tight corner. When Drax came back here a month ago, I thought to make him part of my plans. I knew he was a dangerous bastard, but I believed I could use him anyway. That was my mistake, of course. I had some doubts from the start, but when I got your letter from Lerwick, I understood for sure that I had bound myself to a monster. I knew I had to part from him before he sank his teeth even deeper into my flesh. But how could I work it? He's an ignorant fucker, but he's no fool. He's wary and he's guileful, and he'll kill a man just for the joy of it. A brute like that can't be reasoned with or talked to. You know that as well as I do. Force must be employed, violence if necessary. I realised I needed to set a trap for him, to lure him away and catch him unawares, and I thought I might use you as the bait. That was my design. It was reckless and ill-considered, I see that now. I should not have used you as I did, and if Stevens is dead now, as you say he is . . .'

He raises his eyebrows and waits.

'Stevens was shot in the back of the head.'

'By Drax?'

Sumner nods.

'And what's become of the evil bastard now?'

'I killed him.'

Baxter nods slowly and purses his lips. He closes his eyes, then opens them again.

'Shows some boldness,' he says. 'For a surgeon, I mean.'

'It was one of us or the other.'

'Will you have a glass of wine with me now?' Baxter asks. 'Or sit yourself down at least?'

'I'll stay as I am.'

'You did well to come here, Patrick. I can help you.'

'I didn't come here for your fucking help.'

'Then what? Not to kill me too, I hope? What would be the good of that?'

'I don't believe I was there as a lure. You wanted me dead.'

Baxter shakes his head.

'Why would I want such a thing?'

'You had Cavendish sink the *Volunteer*, and Drax and I are the only ones who might have known or guessed it. Drax shoots me, and then Stevens shoots Drax, and everything is neat and tidy. Except it didn't work like that. It misfired.'

Baxter tilts his head to one side and gives his nose a scratch.

'That's sharp thinking on your part,' he says, 'but it isn't right, not right at all. Take heed now, Patrick, listen carefully to what I'm saying. The plain fact is there are two men lying dead in that timber yard, one of them murdered by your hand. I'd say that puts you in fair need of my assistance.'

'If I tell the truth, I have little enough to fear from the law.'

Baxter snorts at the idea.

'Come, Patrick,' he says. 'You're not so innocent and child-like as to believe such a far-fetched notion. I know you're not. You're a man of the world, just as I am. You can tell the magistrate your theories, of course you can, but I've known the magistrate for some years, and I wouldn't be so sure he'll believe them.'

'I'm the only one left alive from the crew, the only one who knows.'

'Aye, but who *are* you exactly? An Irishman of uncertain provenance. There would have to be investigations, Patrick, probings into your past, your time in India. Oh, you could make things uncomfortable for me, I'm sure, but I could do the same for you and much worse if I wished to. Do you want to waste your time and energies like that? And for what end? Drax is dead now and the ships are both sunk. No bugger's coming back to life again, I promise you that.'

'I could shoot you dead right here and now.'

'You certainly could, but then you would have two murders on your hands and what good would that do you? You need to use your head now, Patrick. This is your chance to put everything behind you, to start afresh. How often in life does a man get such a rare opportunity? You've done me a great service by killing Henry Drax, however it came about, and I'll happily pay you for the work. I'll give you fifty guineas in your hand tonight, and you can put that gun down and walk out of this house and never look backwards.'

Sumner doesn't move.

'There's no train until morning,' he says.

'Then take a horse from my stable. I can saddle it for you myself.'

Baxter smiles, then stands up slowly and walks across to the large iron safe standing in one corner of the study. He unlocks it, takes out a brown canvas wallet, and passes the wallet to Sumner.

'There's fifty guineas in gold for you,' he says. 'Get yourself down to London. Forget the fucking *Volunteer*, forget Henry Drax. None of that is real any more. It's the future that matters now, not the past. And don't worry about the timber yard either. I'll make up some story about that to throw them off the trail.'

Sumner looks at the wallet, weighs it in his hand for a while, but doesn't answer. He thought he knew his limits, but everything is changed now—the world is unhinged, free-floating. He knows that he must act quickly, he must do *something* before it changes back again, before it hardens round and fixes him. But what?

'Are we agreed then?' Baxter says.

Sumner puts the wallet on the desk, and looks towards the open safe.

'Give me the rest of it,' he says, 'and I'll leave you be.'

Baxter frowns.

'The rest of what?'

'All that's in the safe there. Every fucking penny.'

Baxter smiles easily, as though taking it for a joke.

'Fifty guineas is a good amount, Patrick. But I'll happily give you twenty more on top if you truly feel the need of it.'

'I want all of it. However much is in there. Everything.'

Baxter stops smiling and stares.

'So you came here to *rob* me? Is that it?'

'I'm using my head as you advised me to. You're right, the truth won't help me now, but that pile of money surely will.'

Baxter scowls. His nostrils flare, but he makes no move towards the safe.

'I don't believe you'll murder me in my own house,' he says calmly. 'I don't believe you have the balls to do such a thing.'

Sumner points the gun at Baxter's head and cocks the hammer. Some men weaken at the death, he tells himself, some men start out strong then soften, but that can't be me. Not now.

'I just killed Henry Drax with a broken saw blade,' he says. 'Do you really think putting a bullet in your skull is going to strain my nerves?'

Baxter's jaw tightens, and his eager eyes jerk sideways.

'A saw blade, was it?' he says.

'Get that leather satchel,' Sumner tells him, pointing with the gun. 'Fill it up.'

After a minute's pause, Baxter does as he is told. Sumner checks the safe is empty, then tells him to turn about and face the wall. He cuts the satin cordage off the curtain swag with his pocketknife, binds Baxter's hands behind his back, then pushes a napkin into his mouth and gags him with his cravat.

'Now take me to the stables,' Sumner says. 'You lead the way.'

They pass along the rear hallway and then through the kitchen. Sumner unbolts the back door and they step down into the ornamental garden. There are gravel pathways and raised flowerbeds, a fish pond and a cast-iron fountain. He prods Baxter forward. They pass a potting shed and a fret-worked gazebo rimmed with box. When they reach the stable block, Sumner opens the side door and peers inside. There are three wooden stalls and a tack room with awls, hammers and a workbench. There is an oil lamp on a shelf near the door. He pushes Baxter into a corner, lights the lamp, then takes a length of rope from the tack room and forms a noose with one end of it. He puts the noose around Baxter's neck, tightens it until his eyes bulge and loops the other end of the rope over a joist. He tugs down hard until the chamois soles of Baxter's embroidered slippers are barely touching the grimy floorboards, then makes it fast to a peg on the wall. Baxter groans.

'You stay calm and quiet, and they'll find you alive in the morning,' Sumner says. 'If you fret or struggle, it may not end so well.'

There are three horses in the stable—two are black, young and lively-looking, and the other is an older grey. He takes the grey out from its stall and saddles it. When it snorts and shuffles about, he rubs its neck and hums a tune, until it quiets enough to take the bit. He turns down the oil lamp, then opens the main doors and waits a minute, listening and watching carefully. He hears the whine and burble of wind in the trees, the hissing of a cat, but nothing worse. The mews is empty: light seeps upwards from the sentried gas lamps into an umbrous sky. He swings the satchel onto the horse's withers and pushes his boot into the stirrup iron.

Dawn finds him twenty miles to the north. He passes through Driffield without pausing. At Gorton, he stops to let the horse drink from the mere, then continues in the semi-darkness north-west through the beech and sycamore woods and along the dry valley floors. As the sky lightens, ploughed fields appear stretched out on either side, their deep furrows specked with brighter lumps of chalk. The hedgerows are tangled and cross-hatched with dead nettle, knapweed and bramble. Close to noon he reaches the brow of the Wolds' northern scarp and descends to the patchwork plain below. When he enters the town of Pickering, it is night again, the blue-black sky is dense with stars, and he is dazed and queasy from hunger and lack of sleep. He finds a livery stable for the horse and takes a room at the inn beside it. When they ask, he tells them his name is Peter Batchelor and he is on his way from York to Whitby to see his uncle who has taken ill and may be dying.

He sleeps that night with Drax's gun gripped tight in his right hand and the leather satchel shoved beneath the iron bedstead. In the early morning, he eats porridge and kidneys for breakfast, and takes a heel of bread with dripping wrapped in butcher's paper for his tea. After six or seven miles, the road north begins to rise steadily past stands of pine and roughened sheep fields. Hedgerows stutter then disappear, grass gives way to gorse and bracken; the landscape hardens and reduces. Soon he is up on the moor. All around him, continents of dark-edged cloud dangle above a treeless undulance of purple, brown and green. He feels a sharp new chill in the heightened air. If Baxter sends men to look for him, he is almost sure they will not look for him here, not straight away at least—to the west perhaps or to the south in Lincolnshire, but not here, not yet. He has another day or so, he expects, before the reports from Hull reach Pickering, enough time for him to arrive at the coast and find a ship that will carry him east to Holland or Germany. When he gets to Europe, he will use Baxter's money to disappear, become someone else. He will take a new name and find a new profession. Everything erstwhile will be forgotten, he tells himself, everything that has lingered on will be wiped clean.

The clouds close together and darken, a steady rain begins to fall. He meets a carter travelling south with ewes for market, and they stop to talk. Sumner asks him how far to Whitby, and the carter scratches his grizzled chin and frowns as if the question is a puzzling one, then tells him he will be lucky to get there afore dark. A few miles further on, Sumner turns off the Whitby road and cuts north-west towards Goathland and Beck Hole. The rain ceases and the sky turns a pale, summery blue. The purple heather is patchy and burnt over on the slopes near the road, and further off there are clumps of trees and bushes gathered in the wet hollows. Sumner eats his bread and beef dripping, and scoops brown, peatish water from a stream. He passes through Goathland and moves on towards Glaisdale. The moor turns briefly back to grassland edged with bracken, stitchwort and low elder, then rises again and reverts to its tight shorn barrenness. That night, Sumner sleeps, shivering, in a half-collapsed barn, and in the morning, remounts and continues northward.

When he gets to the edge of Guisborough, he stops at a stables, sells the horse and saddle for half their value, then picks up his bag and walks on into the town. At a newsagent's near the railway station, he buys a copy of the Newcastle *Courant* and reads it on the platform. The report of the murder and robbery in Hull occupies a half-column on the second page. Patrick Sumner, an Irishman and former soldier, is named as the culprit, and there is a description of the stolen horse, and mention of a large reward offered by Baxter for anyone who comes forward with useful information. He leaves the newspaper folded on the bench and boards the next train to

Middlesbrough. The compartment smells of soot and hair oil; there are two women talking together and a man asleep in the far corner. He tips his hat at the women and smiles, but doesn't offer to speak. He lifts the leather satchel onto his knees and feels its reassuring pressure.

That night he seeks out foreign voices. He goes along the dockside from one tavern to the next listening for them: Russian, German, Danish, Portuguese. He needs someone who is clever, he thinks, but not too clever; greedy, but not too greedy. In the Baltic Tavern on Commercial Street, he finds a Swede, a captain whose brig is leaving for Hamburg in the morning with a cargo of coal and iron. He has a broad face and red eyes and hair so blond it is almost white. When Sumner tells him he needs a berth and will pay whatever is required for the privilege, the Swede looks him over sceptically, smiles and asks how many men he has murdered.

'Only the one,' Sumner says.

'Just one? And did he deserve it?'

'I'd say he deserved it sure enough.'

The Swede laughs, then shakes his head.

'Mine is a merchant ship. I'm sorry. We have no space for passengers.'

'Then set me to work. I can pull a rope if need be.'

He shakes his head again and takes a sip of his whisky.

'Not possible,' he says.

Sumner lights his pipe and smiles. He assumes this firmness is just a show, a way of driving up the price of his passage. He wonders for a moment if the Swede might read the Newcastle *Courant*, but decides that's hardly likely.

'Who are you anyway?' the Swede asks him. 'Where do you come from?'

'That doesn't matter.'

'You have a passport though, papers? They'll ask for them in Hamburg.'

Sumner takes a single sovereign from his pocket and pushes it across the tabletop.

'That's what I have,' he says.

The Swede raises his pale eyebrows and nods. The roar of drunken voices swells around them, then deflates. A door swings open, and the smoke-filled air shudders above their heads.

'So the man you killed was rich?'

'I didn't kill anyone,' Sumner says. 'I was only making a joke.'

The Swede looks down at the gold coin, but doesn't reach for it. Sumner leans back in his chair and waits. He knows the future is close by: he can feel its tug and sprawl, its shimmering blankness. He is standing on the very lip, poised and ready to step off.

'I think you will find someone to take you,' the Swede says eventually. 'If you pay them well enough.'

Sumner takes another sovereign from his pocket and places it down next to the first. The twin coins wink yellow in the flickering gaslight; on the wet, black tabletop, they shine like eyes. He looks back at the Swede and smiles.

'I do believe I found him,' he says.

25

One bright morning, a month later, he visits the *Zoologischer Garten* in Berlin. He is clean-shaven now, and he has a new suit of clothes and a new name. He strolls about the gravel paths, smoking his pipe and pausing every now and then to watch the animals as they yawn and shit and scratch themselves. The sky is cloudless, and the low autumn sun is broad and warming. He sees lions, camels and monkeys; he observes a small boy in a sailor suit feeding buns to a solitary zebra. It is close to noon, and he is beginning to lose interest, when he notices the bear. The cage it is standing in is no wider than the deck of a ship. There is a lead-lined pit at one end, filled up with water, and a low brick archway in the rear wall leading to a den with straw for bedding. The bear is standing at the back gazing indifferently forward. Its fur is shabby, lank and yellowish, its snout is mottled and threadbare. While

Sumner watches, a family arrives and stands beside him at the rail. One of the children asks in German if this is the lion or the tiger, and the other child laughs at him. They argue briefly and the mother scolds and quiets them. When the family leaves, the bear waits a while, then slouches slowly forward, its head twitching like a dowsing rod and its heavy feet scuffing gently against the cement floor. It reaches the front of the cage and pushes its nose through the black bars as far as it can manage, until its narrow wolfish face is only three feet from Sumner's. It sniffs the air and stares at him, its gimlet eyes like strait gates to a larger darkness. Sumner would like to look away, but can't. The bear's gaze holds him tight. It snorts, and its raw breath brushes against his face and lips. He feels a moment of fear and then, in its wake, as the fear fades and loses its force, an unexpected stab of loneliness and need.

Acknowledgements

Thanks to my great friend and colleague John McAuliffe for reading and commenting on the manuscript. Thanks also to my excellent agents, Judith Murray and Denise Shannon, and my terrific editors, Rowan Cope at Scribner and Michael Signorelli at Henry Holt, for their invaluable support and advice.

Ian McGuire grew up near Hull and studied at the universities of Manchester and Virginia, USA. He is the founder and co-director of the University of Manchester's Centre for New Writing. He writes criticism and fiction, and his stories have been published in the *Chicago Review*, *Paris Review* and elsewhere. *The North Water* is his second novel.